JULIAN TURN...
OPENED AND BLANCHE...

She was bedraggled, weary and beautiful.
"Come." He beckoned to her.

"You should not have waited up," she scolded
as she slumped tiredly against him and he
wrapped an arm about her.

"Look," he urged, pointing at the window.

They said nothing for a long time. Words were
unnecessary. The Christmas star beamed down
at them, the symbol of hope, a sign for all who
sought wisdom and meaning in their lives.
Julian was not sure what either of them had
learned about Christmas this year, but there
was something. It was beyond words at the
moment, and even beyond coherent thought.
But something had been learned. Something
had been gained....

–from "A Handful of Gold" by Mary Balogh

The Gifts of Christmas

MARY BALOGH

MERLINE LOVELACE

SUZANNE BARCLAY

HARLEQUIN®

TORONTO • NEW YORK • LONDON
AMSTERDAM • PARIS • SYDNEY • HAMBURG
STOCKHOLM • ATHENS • TOKYO • MILAN • MADRID
PRAGUE • WARSAW • BUDAPEST • AUCKLAND

ISBN 0-373-83372-5

THE GIFTS OF CHRISTMAS

Copyright © 1998 by Harlequin Books S.A.

The publisher acknowledges the copyright holders of the individual
works as follows:

A HANDFUL OF GOLD Copyright © 1998 by Mary Balogh

A DROP OF FRANKINCENSE Copyright © 1998 by Merline Lovelace

A TOUCH OF MYRRH Copyright © 1998 by Carol Suzanne Backus

This edition published by arrangement with Harlequin Books S.A.

® and ™ are trademarks of the publisher. Trademarks indicated with
® are registered in the United States Patent and Trademark Office, the
Canadian Trade Marks Office and in other countries.

Printed in U.S.A.

CONTENTS

A HANDFUL OF GOLD

Mary Balogh

For Robert,
with whom Christmas is always golden

Chapter One

The gentleman sprawled before the dying fire in the sitting room of his London lodgings was looking somewhat the worse for a night's wear. His gray knee breeches and white stockings were of the finest silk, but the latter were wrinkled and he had long before kicked off his shoes. His long-tailed evening coat, which had molded his frame like a second skin when he had donned it earlier in the evening, had now been discarded and tossed carelessly onto another chair.

His finely embroidered waistcoat was unbuttoned. His neckcloth, on the arrangement of which his valet had spent longer than half an hour of loving artistry, had been pulled open and hung unsymmetrically against his left shoulder. His dark hair, expertly cut to look fashionably disheveled, now looked unfashionably untidy from having had his fingers pass through it one too many times. His eyes were half closed—and somewhat bloodshot. An empty glass dangled from one hand over the arm of the chair.

Julian Dare, Viscount Folingsby, was indisputably foxed.

He was also scowling. Drinking to excess was not among his usual vices. Gaming was. So was womanizing. And so was reckless living. But not drinking. He had always been careful to exclude from habit anything that might prove to be also addictive. He had every intention of one day "settling down," as his father phrased it, of being done with his "wild oats," another of the Earl of Grantham's clichés. It would be just too inconvenient to have to deal with an addiction when the time came. Gambling was not an addiction with him. Neither were women. Though he was exceedingly fond of both.

He yawned and wondered what time it was. Daylight had not yet dawned, a small comfort when this was December and daylight did not deign to show itself until well on into the morning. Certainly it was well past midnight. *Well* past. He had left his sister's soirée before midnight, but since then he had been to White's club and to one or two—was it one or two?—card parties at which the play had been deep and the drinking deeper.

He should get himself up from his chair and go to bed, but he did not have the energy. He should ring for his valet, then, and have the man drag him off to bed. But he did not have even the energy to get up and ring the bell. Doubtless he would not sleep anyway. He knew from experience that when he was three sheets to the wind, an approximately vertical position was preferable to a horizontal one.

Why the devil had he drunk so deep?

But drunkenness had not brought oblivion. He remembered very well why. That heiress. Miss Plunkett. No, *Lady* Sarah Plunkett. What a name! And unfortunately the chit had the face and disposition to match it. She was going to be at Conway for Christmas with her mama and papa. Emma, his youngest sister, had mentioned the fact in the letter that had reached him this morning—no, yesterday morning. He had put two and two together without further ado and had come up with the inevitable total of four. But he had not needed to use any arithmetical or deductive skills.

His father's letter, which he had read next, had been far more explicit. Not only were the Plunkett chit and the Plunkett parents to join their family gathering for Christmas, but also Julian would oblige his father by paying court to the girl and fixing his interest with her. He was nine-and-twenty years old, after all, and had shown no sign of choosing anyone for himself. His father had been extremely patient with him. But it was high time he was finished with his wild oats and settled down. As the only son among five sisters, three of them still unmarried and therefore still unsettled, it was his duty…

Viscount Folingsby passed the fingers of his free hand through his hair again, unconsciously restoring it almost to simple dishevelment, and eyed the brandy decanter a short distance away. An impossible distance away.

He was not going to do it—marry the girl, that

was. It was as simple as that. No one could make him, not even his stern but annoyingly affectionate father. Not even his fond mama and doting sisters. He grimaced. Why had he been blessed with a singularly close and loving family? And why had his mother produced nothing but daughters after the initial triumph of his birth as heir to an earldom and vast properties and fortune—almost every last halfpenny of which was entailed and would pass to a rather distant cousin if he failed to produce at least one heir of his own?

His lordship eyed the brandy decanter again with some determination, but he could not somehow force resolution downward far enough to set his legs in motion.

There had been another letter in the morning's post. From Bertie. Bertrand Hollander had been his close friend and co-conspirator all through school and university. They were still close even though Bertie spent most of his time now overseeing his estates in the north of England. But Bertie had a hunting box in Norfolkshire and a mistress in Yorkshire and intended to introduce the two to each other over Christmas. He was avoiding his own family with the excuse that he was going to go shooting with friends over the holiday. He intended instead to spend a week with his Debbie away from prying eyes and the need for propriety. He wanted Julian to join him there with his own mistress.

Julian did not currently have a resident mistress. He had dismissed the last one several months before on the grounds that evenings spent in her company had become even more predictable and every bit as tedious as evenings spent at the insipid weekly balls at Almack's. Since then he had had a mutually satisfactory arrangement with a widow of his acquaintance. But she was a respectable woman of good ton, hardly the sort he might invite to spend a cozy week of sin in Norfolkshire with Bertie and his Debbie.

Damn! He was more foxed than he knew, Julian thought suddenly. He had gone somewhere tonight even before attending Elinor's soirée. He had gone to the opera. Not that he was particularly fond of music—not opera at least. He had gone to see the subject of the newest male gossip at White's. There was a new dancer of considerable charms, so it was said. But in the few weeks since she had made her first appearance onstage, she had not also made her first appearance in any of the beds of those who had attempted to entice her there. She was either waiting for the highest bidder or she was waiting for someone she fancied or she was a virtuous woman.

Julian, his father's summons and Bertie's invitation fresh in his mind, had gone to the opera to see what the fuss was all about.

The fuss was all about long, shapely legs, a slender, lithe body, and long titian hair. Not red, nothing so vulgar. Titian. And emerald eyes. Not that he had been able to see their color from the box he had occupied during the performance. But he had seen it through his quizzing glass as he had stood in the doorway of the greenroom afterward.

Miss Blanche Heyward had been surrounded by a court of appropriately languishing admirers. His lordship had looked her over unhurriedly through his glass and inclined his head to her when her eyes had met his across the room. And then he had joined the even larger crowd of gentlemen gathered about Hannah Dove, the singer who sang like her name, or so one of her court had assured her. For which piece of gross flattery he had been rewarded with a gracious smile and a hand to kiss.

Julian had left the greenroom after a few minutes and taken himself off to his married sister's drawing room.

It might be interesting to try his own hand at assaulting the citadel of dubious virtue that was Blanche Heyward. It might be even more interesting to carry her off to Bertie's for Christmas and a weeklong hot affair. If he went to Conway, all he would have was the usual crowded, noisy, enjoyable Christmas, and the Plunkett chit. If he went to Norfolkshire...

Well, the mind boggled.

What he *could* do, he decided, was make her decision his, too. He would ask her. If she said yes, then he would go to Norfolkshire. For a final fling. As a swan song to freedom and wild oats and all the rest of it. In the spring, when the season brought the fashionable world to town, the Plunkett girl among them, he would do his duty. He would have her big with child by *next* Christmas. The very thought had him holding his aching head with the hand that had been holding his glass a minute before. What the devil had he done with it? Dropped it? Had there been any brandy left in it? Couldn't have been or he would have drunk it instead of sitting here conspiring how he might reach the decanter, on legs that refused to obey his brain.

If she said no—Blanche, that was, not the heiress—then he would go down to Conway and embrace his fate. That way he would probably have a child *in the nursery* by next Christmas.

Julian lowered his hand from his head to his throat with the intention of loosening his neckcloth. But someone had already done it for him.

Dammit, but she was gorgeous. Not the heiress. Who the devil was gorgeous, then? Someone he had met at Elinor's?

There was a quiet scratching at the sitting room door, and it opened to reveal the cautious, respectful face of his lordship's valet.

"About time," Julian told him. "Someone took all the bones out of my legs when I was not looking. Deuced inconvenient."

"Yes, my lord," his man said, coming purposefully toward him. "You will be wishing someone took them from your head before many more hours have passed. Come along then, sir. Put your arm about my neck."

"Deuced impertinence," his lordship muttered. "Remind me to dismiss you when I am sober."

"Yes, my lord," the valet said cheerfully.

Several hours before Viscount Folingsby found himself sprawled before the fire in his sitting room with boneless legs and aching head, Miss Verity Ewing let herself into a darkened house on an unfashionable street in London, using her latchkey and a considerable amount of stealth. She had no wish to waken anyone. She would tiptoe upstairs without lighting a candle, she decided, careful to avoid the eighth stair, which creaked. She would undress in the darkness and hope not to disturb Chastity. Her sister was, unfortunately, a light sleeper.

But luck was against her. Before she could so much as set foot on the bottom stair, the door to the downstairs living room opened and a shaft of candlelight beamed out into the hall.

"Verity?"

"Yes, Mama." Verity sighed inwardly even as she put a cheerful smile on her face. "You ought not to have waited up."

"I could not sleep," her mother told her as Verity followed her into the sitting room. She set down the candle and pulled her shawl more closely about her shoulders. There was no fire burning in the hearth. "You know I worry until you come home."

"Lady Coleman was invited to a late supper after the opera," Verity explained, "and wanted me to accompany her."

"It was very inconsiderate of her, I am sure," Mrs. Ewing said rather plaintively. "It is thoughtless to keep a gentleman's daughter out late almost every night of the week and send her home in a hackney cab instead of in her ladyship's own carriage.''

"It is kind of her even to hire the hackney," Verity said. "But it is chilly and you are cold." She did not need to ask why there was no fire. A fire after ten o'clock at night was an impossible extravagance in their household. "Let us go up to bed. How was Chastity this evening?"

"She did not cough above three or four times all evening," Mrs. Ewing said. "And not once did she have a prolonged bout. The new medicine seems really to be working."

"I hoped it would." Verity smiled and picked up the candle. "Come, Mama."

But she could not entirely avoid the usual questions about the opera, what Lady Coleman had worn, who else had made up their party, who had invited them for supper, what they had eaten, what topics of conversation had been pursued. Verity answered as briefly as she could though she did, for her mother's sake, give a detailed description of the costly and fashionable gown her employer had worn.

"All I can say," Mrs. Ewing said in a hushed voice as they stood outside the door of her bedchamber, "is that Lady Coleman is a strange sort of lady, Verity. Most ladies hire companions to live in and run and fetch for them during the day when time hangs heavy on their hands. They do not allow them to live at home, and they do not require their services mostly during the evenings when they go out into society."

"How fortunate I am to have discovered such a lady, then," Verity said, "and to have won her approval. I could not bear to have to live in and see you and Chastity only on half days off. Lady Coleman is a widow, Mama, and needs company for respectability when she goes out. I could scarcely ask for more pleasant employment. It pays reasonably well, too, and will get better. Only this evening Lady Coleman declared that she is pleased with me and is considering raising my salary quite substantially."

But her mother did not look as pleased as Verity had hoped. She shook her head as she took the candle. "Ah, my love," she said, "I never thought to see the day when a daughter of mine would have to seek employment. The Reverend Ewing, your papa, left us little, it is true, but we might have scraped by quite comfortably if it had not been for Chastity's illness. And if General Sir Hector Ewing were not unfortunately in Vienna for the peace talks, he would have helped us, I am certain. You and Chastity are his own brother's children after all."

"Pray do not vex yourself, Mama." Verity kissed her mother's cheek. "We are together, the three of us, and Chastity is recovering her health after seeing a reputable physician and being prescribed the right medicine. Really, those are the only things that matter. Good night."

A minute later she had reached her own room and had entered it and closed the door. She stood for a moment against it, her eyes closed, her hands gripping the knob behind her back. But there was no sound apart from quiet, even breathing from her sister's bed. Verity undressed quickly and quietly, shivering in the frigid cold. After she had climbed into bed, she lay on her side, her knees drawn up, and pulled the covers up over her ears. Her teeth were chattering, though not just with the cold.

It was a dangerous game she played.

Except that it was no game.

How soon would it be, she wondered, before Mama discovered that there was no Lady Coleman, that there was no genteel and easy employment? Fortunately they had moved to London from the country so recently and under such straitened circumstances that they had few friends and none at all who moved in fashionable circles. They had moved because Chastity's chill, contracted last winter not long after their father's death, had stubbornly refused to go away. It had become painfully clear to them that they might well lose her if they did not consult a physician more knowledgeable than the local doctor. They had feared she had consumption, but the London physician had said no, that she merely had a weak chest and might hope to recover her full health with the correct medicines and diet.

But his fees and the medicines had been exorbitantly expensive and the need for his services was not yet at an end. The rent of even so unfashionable a house as theirs was high. And the bills for coal, candles, food and other sundries seemed always to be piling in.

Verity had searched and searched for genteel employment, assuring her mother that it would be only temporary, until her uncle returned to England and was apprised of their plight. Verity placed little faith in the wealthy uncle who had had nothing to do with them during her father's life. Her grandfather had held aloof from his youngest son after the latter had refused an advantageous match and had married instead Verity's mother, the daughter of a gentleman of no particular fortune or consequence.

In Verity's opinion, the care of her mother and sister fell squarely on her own shoulders and always would. And so when she had been unable to find employment as a governess or companion or even as a shop assistant or seamstress or housemaid, she had taken up the unlikely offer of an audition as an opera dancer. She was quite fit, after all, and she had always adored dancing, both in a ballroom and in the privacy of a shrubbery or empty room at the rectory. To her intense surprise she had been offered the job.

Performing on a public stage in any capacity—as an actress, singer or dancer—was not genteel employment for a lady. Indeed, Verity had been well aware even before accepting the employment that, in the popular mind, dancers and actresses were synonymous with whores.

But what choice had she had?

And so had begun her double life, her secret life. By day, except when she was at rehearsals, she was Verity Ewing, impoverished daughter of a gently born clergyman, niece of the influential General Sir Hector Ewing. By night she was Blanche Heyward, opera dancer, someone who was ogled by half the fashionable gentlemen in town, many of whom attended the opera for no other purpose.

But it was a dangerous game. At any time she might be recognized by someone she knew, though no one from her neighborhood in the country was in the habit of staying in London and sampling its entertainments. More important, perhaps, she was making it impossible to mingle with polite society in the future if the general should ever decide to help them. But she did not anticipate that particular problem.

There were more immediate problems to deal with.

But what she earned as a dancer was just not enough.

Verity huddled deeper beneath the bedcovers and set her hands between her thighs for greater warmth.

"Verity?" a sleepy voice asked.

Verity pushed back the covers from her face again. "Yes, love," she said softly, "I am home."

"I must have fallen asleep," Chastity said. "I always worry so until you are home. I *wish* you did not have to go out alone at night."

"But if I did not," Verity said, "I would not be able to tell you about all the splendid parties and theater performances I attend. I shall describe the opera to you in the morning or, more to the point, the people who were in the audience. Go back to sleep now." She kept her voice warm and cheerful.

"Verity," Chastity said, "you must not think that I am not grateful, that I do not know the sacrifice you are making for my sake. One day I will make it all up to you. I *promise*.''

Verity blinked back tears from her eyes. "Oh yes, you will, love," she said. "In the springtime you are going to dance among the primroses and daffodils, unseasonable roses in your cheeks. Then you will have repaid me double—no, ten times over—for the little I am able to do now. Go to sleep, you goose.''

"Good night." Chastity yawned hugely and only a minute or two later was breathing deeply and evenly again.

There was one way in which a dancer might augment her income. Indeed she was almost expected to do so. Verity hid her head beneath the covers once more and tried not to develop the thought. But it had been nagging at her for a week or more. And she had said those words to Mama earlier, almost as if she were preparing the way. *Lady Coleman declared that she is pleased with me and is considering raising my salary quite substantially.*

She had acquired quite a regular court of admirers in the greenroom following each performance. Two of the gentlemen had already made blatant offers to her. One had mentioned a sum that she had found quite dizzying. She had told herself repeatedly that she was not even tempted. Nor was she. But it was not a matter of temptation. It was a matter for cold decision.

The only possible reason she would do such a thing was her mother's and Chastity's security. A great deal more money was going to have to be found if Chass was to continue to have the treatment she needed. It was a matter of her virtue in exchange for Chastity's life, then.

Phrased that way, there was really no decision to make.

And then she thought of the advent of temptation that had presented itself to her just that evening in the form of the gentleman who had stood in the doorway of the greenroom, looking at her insolently through his quizzing glass for a minute or so before joining the crowd of gentlemen gathered about Hannah Dove. His actions had suggested that he was not after all interested in her, Verity—or rather in Blanche—and yet she had been left with the strange notion that he had watched her all the time he was in the greenroom.

He was Viscount Folingsby, a notorious rake, another dancer had told her later. Verity would likely have guessed it anyway. Apart from being almost incredibly handsome—tall, well formed, very dark, with eyes that were both penetrating and slumberous—there was an air of self-assurance and arrogance about him that proclaimed him to be a man accustomed to having his own way. There was also something almost unbearably sensual about him. A rake, yes. Without a doubt.

Yet she had been horribly tempted for that minute. If he had approached her, if he had made her an offer...

Thank heaven he had not done either.

But soon, *very* soon, she was going to have to

consider and accept someone's offer. There! Finally she was calling a spade a spade. She was going to have to become someone's mistress. No, that was calling a spade a utensil. She was going to have to become someone's *whore*.

For a dizzying minute the room spun about her, closed eyes notwithstanding.

For Chastity, she told herself determinedly. For Chastity's life.

Chapter Two

Julian visited the greenroom at the opera house two evenings after his previous appearance there. There were a few men talking with Blanche Heyward. Hannah Dove was invisible amidst her court of admirers. His lordship joined them and chatted amiably for a while. It was not part of his plan to appear overeager. Several minutes passed before he strolled over to make his bow to the titian-haired dancer.

"Miss Heyward," he said languidly, holding her eyes with his own, "your servant. May I commend you on your performance this evening?"

"Thank you, my lord." Her voice was low, melodic. Seductive, and deliberately schooled to sound that way, he guessed. Her eyes looked candidly—and shrewdly? back into his. He did not for a moment believe she was a virtuous woman. Or that what little virtue she had was not for hire.

"I have just been commending Miss Heyward on her talent and grace, Folingsby," Netherford said. "Damme, but if she were in a ballroom, she would put every other lady to shame. No gentleman would wish to dance with anyone but her, eh? Eh?'' He dug one elbow into his lordship's ribs.

There were appreciative titters from the other gentlemen gathered about her.

"Dear me,'' his lordship murmured. "I wonder if Miss Heyward would wish to court such—ah, fame.''

"Or such notoriety,'' she said with a fleeting smile.

"Damme,'' Netherford continued, "but one would love to watch you waltz, Miss Heyward. Trouble is, every other man present would want to stand and watch, too, and there would be no one to dance with all the other chits.'' There was a general gust of laughter at his words.

Julian raised his quizzing glass to his eye and caught a suggestion of scorn in the dancer's smile.

"Thank you, sir,'' she said. "You are flatteringly kind. But I am weary, gentlemen. It has been a long evening.''

And thus bluntly she dismissed her court. They went meekly, after making their bows and bidding her good-night—three of them out the door, one to join the crowd still clustered about Hannah Dove. Julian remained.

Blanche Heyward looked up at him inquiringly. "My lord?'' she said, a suggestion of a challenge in her voice.

"Sometimes I find,'' he said, dropping his glass and clasping his hands at his back, "that weariness

can be treated as effectively with a quiet and leisurely meal as with sleep. Would you care to join
me for supper?''

She opened her mouth to refuse—he read the intent in her expression—hesitated, and closed her
mouth again.

''For supper, my lord?'' She raised her eyebrows.

''I have reserved a private parlor in a tavern not
far from here,'' he told her. ''I would as soon have
company as eat alone.'' And yet, he told her with his
nonchalant expression and the language of his body,
he would almost as soon eat alone. It mattered little
to him whether she accepted or not.

She broke eye contact with him and looked down
at her hands. She was clearly working up a refusal
again. Equally clearly she was tempted. Or—and he
rather suspected that this was the true interpretation
of her behavior—she was as practiced as he in sending the message she wished to send. A reluctance
and a certain indifference, in this case. But a fixed
intention, nevertheless, of accepting in the end. He
made it easier for her, or rather he took the game
back into his own hands.

''Miss Heyward.'' He leaned slightly toward her
and lowered his voice. ''I am inviting you to supper,
not to bed.''

Her eyes snapped back to his and he read in them
the startled knowledge that she had been bested. She
half smiled.

''Thank you, my lord,'' she said. ''I *am* rather
hungry. Will you wait while I fetch my cloak?''

He gave a slight inclination of his head, and she stood up. He was surprised by her height now that he was standing close to her. He was a tall man and dwarfed most women. She was scarcely more than half a head shorter than he.

Well, he thought with satisfaction, the first move had been made and he had emerged the winner. She had agreed only to supper, it was true, but if he could not turn that minor triumph into a week of pleasure in Norfolkshire, then he deserved the fate awaiting him at Conway in the form of the ferret-faced Lady Sarah Plunkett.

He did not expect to lose the game.

And he did not believe, moreover, that she intended he should.

It was a square, spacious room with timbered ceiling and large fireplace, in which a cheerful fire crackled. In the center of the room was one table set for two, with fine china and crystal laid out on a crisply starched white cloth. Two long candles burned in pewter holders.

Viscount Folingsby must have been confident, Verity concluded, that she would say yes. He took her cloak in silence. Without looking at him, she crossed the room to the fire and held out her hands to the blaze. She felt more nervous than she had ever felt before, she believed, even counting her audition and her first performance onstage. Or perhaps it was a different kind of nervousness.

"It is a cold night," he said.

"Yes." Not that there had been much chance to notice the chill. A sumptuous private carriage had brought them the short distance from the theater. They had not spoken during the journey.

She did not believe it was an invitation just to supper. But she still did not know what her answer would be to the inevitable question. Perhaps it was understood in the demimonde that when one accepted such an invitation as this, one was committing oneself to giving thanks in the obvious way.

Could it possibly be that before this night was over she would have taken the irrevocable step? What would it *feel* like? she wondered suddenly. And how would she feel in the morning?

"Green suits you," Lord Folingsby said, and Verity despised the way she jerked with alarm to find that he was close behind her. "Not all women have the wisdom and taste to choose clothes that suit their coloring."

She was wearing her dark green silk, which she had always liked though it was woefully outmoded and almost shabby. But its simple high-waisted, straight-sleeved design gave it a sort of timeless elegance that did not date itself as quickly as more fussy, more modish styles.

"Thank you," she said.

"I fancy," he said, "that some artist must once have mixed his paints with care and used a fine brush in order to produce the particular color of your eyes. It is unusual, if not unique."

She smiled into the dancing flames. Men were always lavish in their compliments on her eyes, though no one had ever said it quite like this before.

"I have some Irish blood in me, my lord," she said.

"Ah. The Emerald Isle," he said softly. "Land of red-haired, fiery-tempered beauties. Do you have a fiery temper, Miss Heyward?"

"I also have a great deal of English blood," she told him.

"Ah, we mundane and phlegmatic English." He sighed. "You disappoint me. Come to the table."

"You like hot-tempered women, then, my lord?" she asked him as he seated her and took his place opposite.

"That depends entirely on the woman," he said. "If I believe there is pleasure to be derived from the taming of her, yes, indeed." He picked up the bottle of wine that stood on the table, uncorked it and proceeded to fill her glass and then his own.

While he was so occupied, Verity looked fully at him for the first time since they had left the theater. He was almost frighteningly handsome, though why there should be anything fearsome about good looks she would have found difficult to explain. Perhaps it was his confidence, his arrogance more than his looks that had her wishing she could go back to the greenroom and change her answer. They seemed very much alone together, though two waiters were bringing food and setting it silently on the table. Or perhaps it was his sensual appeal and the certain knowledge that he wanted her.

He held his glass aloft and extended his hand half-across the table. "To new acquaintances," he said, looking very directly into her eyes in the flickering light of the candles. "May they prosper."

She smiled, touched the rim of her glass to his and drank. Her hand was steady, she was relieved to find, but she felt almost as if a decision had been made, a pact sealed.

"Shall we eat?" he suggested after the waiters had withdrawn and closed the door behind them. He indicated the plates of cold meats and steaming vegetables, the basket of fresh breads, the bowl of fruit.

She was hungry, she realized suddenly, but she was not at all sure she would be able to eat. She helped herself to a modest portion.

"Tell me, Miss Heyward," the viscount said, watching her butter a bread roll, "are you always this talkative?"

She paused and looked unwillingly up at him again. She was adept at making social conversation, as were most ladies of her class. But she had no idea what topics were suited to an occasion of this nature. She had never before dined tête-à-tête with a man, or been alone with one under any circumstances for longer than half an hour at a time or beyond a place where she could be easily observed by a chaperon.

"What do you wish me to talk about, my lord?" she asked him.

He regarded her for a few moments, a look of amusement on his face. "Bonnets?" he said. "Jewels? The latest shopping expedition?"

He did not, then, have a high regard for women's intelligence. Or perhaps it was just her type of woman. *Her type.*

"But what do *you* wish to talk about, my lord?" she asked him, taking a bite out of her roll.

He looked even more amused. "You," he said without hesitation. "Tell me about yourself, Miss Heyward. Begin with your accent. I cannot quite place its origin. Where are you from?"

She had not done at all well with the accent she had assumed during her working hours, except perhaps to disguise the fact that she had been gently born and raised.

"I pick up accents very easily," she lied. "And I have lived in many different places. I suppose there is a trace of all those places in my speech."

"And someone," he said, "to complicate the issue, has given you elocution lessons."

"Of course." She smiled. "Even as a dancer one must learn not to murder the English language with every word one speaks, my lord. If one expects to advance in one's career, that is."

He gazed silently at her for a few moments, his fork suspended halfway to his mouth. Verity felt herself flushing. What career was he imagining she wished to advance?

"Quite so," he said softly, his voice like velvet. He carried his fork the rest of the way to his mouth. "But what are some of these places? Tell me where you have lived. Tell me about your family. Come, we cannot munch on our food in silence, you know.

There is nothing better designed to shake a person's composure.''

Her life seemed to have become nothing but lies. In each of her worlds she had to withhold the truth about the other. And withholding the truth sometimes became more than a passive thing. It involved the invention of lie upon lie. She had some knowledge of two places—the village in Somersetshire where she had lived for two-and-twenty years, and London, where she had lived for two months. But she spoke of Ireland, drawing on the stories she could remember her maternal grandmother telling her when she was a child, and more riskily, of the city of York, where a neighborhood friend had lived with his uncle for a while, and about a few other places of which she had read.

She hoped fervently that the viscount had no intimate knowledge of any of the places she chose to describe. She invented a mythical family—a father who was a blacksmith, a warmhearted mother who had died five years before, three brothers and three sisters, all considerably younger than herself.

''You came to London to seek your fortune?'' he asked. ''You have not danced anywhere else?''

She hesitated. But she did not want him to think her inexperienced, easy to manipulate. ''Oh, of course,'' she said. ''For several years, my lord.'' She smiled into his eyes as she reached for a pear from the dish of fruit. ''But all roads lead eventually to London, you know.''

She was startled by the look of naked desire that

flared in his eyes for a moment as he followed the movement of her hand. But it was soon veiled behind his lazy eyelids and slightly mocking smile.

"Of course," he said softly. "And those of us who spend most of our time here are only too delighted to benefit from the experience in the various arts such persons as yourself have acquired elsewhere."

Verity kept her eyes on the pear she was peeling. It was unusually juicy, she was dismayed to find. Her hands were soon wet with juice. And her heart was thumping. Suddenly, and quite inexplicably, she felt as if she had waded into deep waters, indeed. The air fairly bristled between them. She licked her lips and could think of no reply to make.

His voice sounded amused when he spoke again. "Having peeled it, Miss Heyward," he said, "you are now obliged to eat it, you know. It would be a crime to waste good food."

She lifted one half of the pear to her mouth and bit into it. Juice cascaded to her plate below, and some of it trickled down her chin. She reached for her napkin in some embarrassment, knowing that he was watching her. But before she could pick it up, he had reached across the table and one long finger had scooped up the droplet of juice that was about to drip onto her gown. She raised her eyes, startled, to watch him carry the finger to his mouth and touch it to his tongue. His eyes remained on her all the while.

Verity felt a sharp stabbing of sensation down through her abdomen and between her thighs. She felt a rush of color to her cheeks. She felt as if she had been running for a mile uphill.

"Sweet," he murmured.

She jumped to her feet, pushing at her chair with the backs of her knees. Then she wished she had not done so. Her legs felt decidedly unsteady. She crossed to the fireplace again and reached out her hands as if to warm them, though she felt as if the fire might better be able to take warmth from her.

She drew a few steadying breaths in the silence that followed. And then she could see from the corner of one eye that he had come to stand at the other side of the hearth. He rested one arm along the high mantel. He was watching her. The time had come, she thought. She had precipitated it herself. Within moments the question would be asked and must be answered. She still did not know what that answer would be, or perhaps she did. Perhaps she was just fooling herself to believe that there was still a choice. She had made her decision back in the greenroom—no, even before that. This was a tavern, part of an inn. No doubt he had bespoken a bedchamber here, as well as a private dining room. Within minutes, then...

How would it feel? She did not even know exactly what she was to expect. The basic facts, of course...

"Miss Heyward," he asked her, making her jump again, "what are your plans for Christmas?"

She turned her head to look at him. Christmas? It was a week and a half away. She would spend it with her family, of course. It would be their first

Christmas away from home, their first without the
friends and neighbors they had known all their lives.
But at least they still had one another and were still
together. They had decided that they would indulge
in the extravagance of a goose and make something
special of the day with inexpensive gifts that they
would make for one another. Christmas had always
been Verity's favorite time of the year. Somehow it
restored hope and reminded her of the truly important
things in life—family and love and selfless giving.

Selfless giving.

"Do you have any plans?" he asked.

She could hardly claim to be going home to that
large family at the smithy in Somersetshire. She
shook her head.

"I will be spending a quiet week in Norfolkshire
with a friend and his, ah, lady," he said. "Will you
come with me?"

A quiet week. A friend and his lady. She understood, of course, exactly what he meant, exactly to
what she was being invited. If she agreed now, Verity thought, the die would be cast. She would have
stepped irrevocably into that world from which it
would be impossible to return. Once a fallen woman,
she would never be able to retrieve either her virtue
or her honor.

If she agreed?

She would be away from home at Christmas of all
times. Away from Mama and Chastity. For a whole
week. Could anything be worth such a sacrifice, not
to mention the sacrifice of her very self?

It was as if he read her mind. "Five hundred pounds, Miss Heyward," he said softly. "For one week."

Five hundred pounds? Her mouth went dry. It was a colossal sum. Did he know what five hundred pounds meant to someone like her? But of course he knew. It meant irresistible temptation.

In exchange for one week of service. Seven nights. Seven, when even the thought of one was insupportable. But once the first had been endured, the other six would hardly matter.

Chastity needed to see the physician again. She needed more medicine. If she were to die merely because they could not afford the proper treatment for her illness, how would she feel, Verity asked herself, when it had been within her power to see to it that they *could* afford the treatment? What had she just been telling herself about Christmas?

Selfless giving

She smiled into the fire. "That would be very pleasant, my lord," she said, and then listened in some astonishment to the other words that came unplanned from her mouth, "provided you pay me in advance."

She turned her head to look at him when he did not immediately reply. His elbow was still on the mantel, his closed fist resting against his mouth. Above it his eyes showed amusement.

"We will, of course, agree to a compromise," he told her. "Half before we leave and half after we return?"

She nodded. Two hundred and fifty pounds before she even left London. Once she had accepted the payment, she would have backed herself into a corner. She could not then refuse to carry out her part of the agreement. She tried to swallow, but the dryness of her mouth made it well nigh impossible to do.

"Splendid," he said briskly. "Come, it is late. I will escort you home."

She was to escape for tonight, then? Part of her felt a knee-weakening relief. Part of her was strangely disappointed. The worst of it might have been over within the hour if, as she had expected, he had reserved a room and had invited her there. She felt a deep dread of the first time. She imagined, perhaps naively, that after that, once it was an accomplished fact, once she was a fallen woman, once she knew how it felt, it would be easier to repeat. But now it seemed that she would have to wait until they left for Norfolkshire before the deed was done.

He had fetched her cloak and was setting it about her shoulders. She came to attention suddenly, realizing what he had just said.

"Thank you, no, my lord," she said. "I shall see myself home. Perhaps you would be so kind as to call a hackney cab?"

He turned her and his hands brushed her own aside and did up her cloak buttons for her. He looked up into her eyes, the task completed. "Playing the elusive game until the end, Miss Heyward?" he asked.

"Or is there someone at home you would rather did not see me?"

His implication was obvious. But he was, of course, right though not in quite the way he meant. She smiled back at him.

"I have promised you a week, my lord," she said. "That week does not begin with tonight, as I understand it?"

"Quite right," he said. "You shall have your hackney, then, and keep your secrets. I do believe Christmas is going to be more...interesting than usual."

"I trust you may be right, my lord," she said with all the coolness she could muster, preceding him to the door.

Chapter Three

Julian was feeling weary, cold and irritable by the time Bertrand Hollander's hunting box hove into sight at dusk on a particularly gray and cheerless afternoon, two days before Christmas. He would feel far more cheerful, he told himself, once he was indoors, basking before a blazing fire, imbibing some of Bertie's brandy and contemplating the delights of the night ahead. But at the moment he could not quite convince himself that this Christmas was going to be one of unalloyed pleasure.

He had ridden all the way from London despite the fact that his comfortable, well-sprung traveling carriage held only one passenger. During the morning, he had thought it a clever idea—she would be intrigued to watch him ride just within sight beyond the carriage windows; he would comfort himself with the anticipation of joining her within during the afternoon. But during the noon stop for dinner and a change of horses, Miss Blanche Heyward had upset him quite considerably. No, that was refining too much on a trifle. She had *annoyed* him quite considerably.

And all over a mere bauble, a paltry handful of gold.

He had been planning to give it to her for Christmas. A gift was perhaps unnecessary since she was being paid handsomely enough for her services. But Christmas had always been a time of gift giving with him, and he knew he was going to miss Conway and all its usual warm celebrations. And so he had bought her a gift, spending far more time in the choosing of it than he usually did for his mistresses and instinctively avoiding the gaudy flash of precious stones.

On impulse he had decided to give it to her in the rather charming setting of the inn parlor in which they dined on their journey, rather than wait for Christmas Day. But she had merely looked at the box in his outstretched hand and had made no move to grab it.

"What is it?" she had asked with the quiet dignity he was beginning to recognize as characteristic of her.

"Why do you not look and see?" he had suggested. "It is an early Christmas gift."

"There is no need of it." She had looked into his eyes. "You are paying me well, my lord, for what I will give in return."

Her words had sent an uncomfortable rush of tightness to his groin, though he was not at all sure she had intended them so. He had also felt the first stirring of annoyance. Was she going to keep him with his hand outstretched, feeling foolish, until his dinner grew cold? But she had reached out a hand slowly, taken the box and opened it. He had watched her almost anxiously. Had he made a mistake in not choosing diamonds or rubies, or emeralds, perhaps?

She had looked down for a long time, saying nothing, making no move to touch the contents of the box.

"It is the Star of Bethlehem," she had said finally.

It was a star, yes, a gold star on a gold chain. He had not thought of it as the Christmas star. But the description seemed apt enough.

"Yes," he had agreed. He had despised himself for his next words, but they had been out before he could stop them. "Do you like it?"

"It belongs in the heavens," she had said after a lengthy pause during which she had gazed at the pendant and appeared as if she had forgotten about both him and her surroundings. "As a symbol of hope. As a sign to all who are in search of the meaning of their lives. As a goal in the pursuit of wisdom."

Good Lord! He had been rendered speechless.

She had looked up then and regarded him very directly with those magnificent emerald eyes. "Money ought not to be able to buy it, my lord," she had said. "It is not appropriate as a gift from such as you to such as I."

He had gazed back, one eyebrow raised, containing his fury. *Such as he?* What the devil was she implying?

"Do I understand, Miss Heyward," he had asked,

injecting as much boredom into his voice as he could summon, "that you do not like the gift? Dear me, I ought to have had my man pick up a diamond bracelet instead. I shall inform him that you agree with my opinion that he has execrable taste."

She had looked into his eyes for several moments longer, no discernible anger there at his insult.

"I am sorry," she had surprised him by saying then. "I have hurt you. It is very beautiful, my lord, and shows that you have impeccable taste. Thank you." She had closed the box and placed it in her reticule.

They had continued with their meal in silence, and suddenly, he had discovered, he was eating straw, not food.

He had mounted his horse when they resumed their journey and left her to her righteous solitude in his carriage. And for the rest of the journey he had nursed his irritation with her. What the devil did she mean *it is not appropriate as a gift from such as you?* How dared she! And why was it inappropriate, even assuming that the gold star was intended to be the Star of Bethlehem? The star was a symbol of hope, she had said, a sign to those who pursued wisdom and the meaning of their own lives.

What utter balderdash!

Those three wise men of the Christmas story—*if* they had existed, and *if* they had been wise, and *if* there had really been three of them—had they gone lurching off across the desert on their camels, clutching their offerings, in hopeful pursuit of wisdom and meaning? More likely they had been escaping overly affectionate relatives who were attempting to marry them off to the biblical era equivalent of the Plunkett chit. Or hoping to find something that would gratify their jaded senses.

They must all have been despicably rich, after all, to be able to head off on a mad journey without fear of running out of money. It was purely by chance that they had discovered something worth more than gold, or those other two commodities they had had with them. What the deuce were frankincense and myrrh anyway?

Well, he was no wise man even though he had set out on his journey with his pathetic handful of gold. And even though he was hoping to find gratification of his senses at the end of the journey. That was all he *did* want—a few congenial days with Bertie, and a few energetic nights in bed with Blanche. To hell with hope and wisdom and meaning. He knew where his life was headed after this week. He was going to marry Lady Sarah Plunkett and have babies with her until his nursery was furnished with an heir and a spare, to use the old cliché. And he was going to live respectably ever after.

It was going to snow, he thought, glancing up at the heavy clouds. They were going to have a white Christmas. The prospect brought with it none of the elation he would normally feel. At Conway there would be children of all ages from two to eighty gazing at the sky and making their plans for toboggan rides and snowball fights and snowman-building contests and skating parties. He felt an unwelcome wave of nostalgia.

But they had arrived at Bertie's hunting box, which looked more like a small manor than the modest lodge Julian had been expecting. There were the welcome signs of candlelight from within and of smoke curling up from the chimneys. He swung down from his horse, wincing at the stiffness in his limbs, and waved aside the footman who would have opened the carriage door and set down the steps. His lordship did it himself and reached up a hand to help down his mistress.

And that was another thing, he thought as she placed a gloved hand in his and stepped out of the carriage. She was not looking at all like the bird of paradise he had pictured himself bringing into the country. She was dressed demurely in a gray wool dress with a long gray cloak, black gloves and black half boots. Her hair—all those glorious titian tresses—had been swept back ruthlessly from her face and was almost invisible beneath a plain and serviceable bonnet. There was not a trace of cosmetics on her face, which admittedly was quite lovely enough without. But she looked more like a lady than a whore.

"Thank you, my lord," she said, glancing up at the house.

"I trust," he said, "you were warm enough under the lap robes?"

"Indeed." She smiled at him.

One thing at least was clear to him as he turned

with her toward Bertie, who was standing in the open doorway, rubbing his hands together, a welcoming grin on his face. He was still anticipating the night ahead with a great deal of pleasure, perhaps more so than ever. There was something unusually intriguing about Miss Blanche Heyward, opera dancer and authority on the Star of Bethlehem.

Verity felt embarrassment more than any other emotion for the first hour or so of her stay at Bertrand Hollander's hunting box, and what a misnomer *that* was, she thought, looking about at the well-sized, cozy, expensively furnished house that a gentleman used only during the shooting season. And, of course, for clandestine holidays with his mistress.

It was that idea that caused the embarrassment. Mr. Hollander appeared to be a pleasant gentleman. He had a good-looking, amiable face and was dressed with neat elegance. He greeted them with a hearty welcome and assured them that they must make themselves at home for the coming week and not even think of standing on ceremony.

He greeted her, Verity, with gallantry, taking her hand and raising it to his lips before tucking it beneath his arm and leading her into the house while begging her to call upon him at any time if he might be of service in increasing her comfort.

And yet there was something in his manner—a certain familiarity—that showed he was a gentleman talking, not with a lady, but with a woman of another class entirely. There was the frank way, for example, that he looked her over from head to toe before grinning at Viscount Folingsby. It was not quite an insolent look. Indeed, there was a good deal of appreciation in it. But he would not have looked at a lady so, not at least while she was observing him doing it. Nor would he have called a lady by her first name. But Mr. Hollander used hers.

"Come into the parlor where there is a fire, Blanche," he said. "We will soon have you warmed up. Come and meet Debbie."

Debbie was the other woman, Mr. Hollander's mistress. She was blond and pretty and plump and placid. She spoke with a decided Yorkshire accent. She did not rise from the chair in which she lounged beside the fire, but smiled genially and lazily at the new arrivals.

"Sit down there, Blanche," she said, pointing to the chair at the other side of the fire. "Bertie will send for tea, won't you, love? Ee, you look frozen, Jule. You'd better pull a chair closer to the fire unless you want to sit with Blanche on your lap."

She was addressing Viscount Folingsby, Verity realized in some shock as she took the offered chair and removed her gloves and bonnet, since no servant had offered to take them in the hall. She directed a very straight look at her new protector, but he was bowing over Debbie's outstretched hand and taking it to his lips.

"Charmed," he said. "I do hope you are not planning to order tea for me, too, Bertie?"

His friend barked with laughter and crossed the

room to a sideboard on which there was an array of
decanters and glasses. The viscount pulled up a chair
for himself, Verity was relieved to find, but Mr. Hollander, when he returned with glasses of liquor for
his friend and himself, raised his eyebrows at Debbie.
She sighed, hoisted herself out of the chair, and then
settled herself on his lap after he had sat down.

Verity refused to feel outrage. She refused to show
disapproval by even the smallest gesture. These were
two gentlemen with their mistresses. She was one of
the latter, by her own choice. There was already
more than two hundred pounds safely stowed away
in a drawer at home. The rest of the advance payment
had been spent on another visit to the physician for
Chastity and more medicine. A small sum was in her
purse inside her reticule. It was too late to go back
even if she wanted to. The money was not intact to
be returned.

And so she resigned herself to what must be. But
she had made one decision during the days since she
had accepted Viscount Folingsby's proposition. She
was not going to act a part besides what she had
already committed herself to. She spoke with some
sort of accent to disguise the refinement of her lady's
voice. She had invented a family at a smithy in
Somersetshire. But beyond those things she was not
going to go. She was not going to try to be deliberately vulgar or stupid or anything else she imagined
a mistress would be.

She had brought with her the clothes she usually
wore at home. She had dressed her hair as she usu-

ally wore it there. She had kept her end of the bargain by coming here. She would keep it by staying over Christmas and allowing Viscount Folingsby to do *that* to her. Her mind still shied away from the details and from the alarming fact that she was ignorant of many of them. She had hardly been in a position to ask her mother, as she would have done had she been getting married and was facing a wedding night.

She had told Mama and Chastity that Lady Coleman was going into the country for Christmas and required her presence. She had told them that she was being paid a very generous bonus for going, though she had not mentioned the incredible sum of five hundred pounds. They had both been upset at the prospect of her absence over Christmas, and she had shed a few tears with them, but they had consoled themselves with the belief that as a member of a house party she would have a wonderful time.

"Are you warmer now?" Viscount Folingsby asked suddenly, bringing Verity's mind back to Mr. Hollander's sitting room, into which a servant was just carrying a tea tray. He leaned forward and took one of her hands in both of his. His were warm; hers was not. "Perhaps I should have cuddled you on my lap after all."

"I believe the fire and the tea between them will do the trick nicely for now, my lord," she said before turning her attention to Mr. Hollander, who was smiling genially at them. "I have never before been into this part of the world, sir. Do tell me about it. What beauties of nature characterize it? And what history and buildings of note are there here?''

She would no longer be mute, wondering what topics of conversation were appropriate for an opera dancer and a gentleman's mistress.

''Ee, Bertie, love,'' Debbie said, ''there is a right pretty garden out back. Tell Blanche about it. Tell her about the tree swing.''

It was not tree swings exactly that Verity had had in mind, but she settled back in her chair with a smile as the servant handed her her tea. Viscount Folingsby relinquished her hand.

''For now,'' he murmured. ''But later, Blanche, I beg leave to do service in place of the fire and the tea.''

It took her a moment to realize he was referring to her earlier words. When she did so, she wished she were sitting a little farther back from the fire. Her face felt as if it were being scorched.

It did not seem, she thought suddenly, as if Christmas was close. Tomorrow would be Christmas Eve. For a few moments there was the ache of tears in her throat.

There must have been a goodly number of bed-chambers in the house, Julian guessed later that night as he ascended the staircase with Blanche on his arm. But Bertie, of course, had assigned them only one. It was a large room overlooking the small wooded park at the back of the house. It was warmed by a log fire in a large hearth and lit by a single branch of candles. Heavy velvet curtains had been drawn back from the large canopied bed and the covers had been turned down.

He was glad he had not had her before, he decided as he closed the door behind them and extinguished the single candle that had lit their way upstairs. Pleasurable anticipation had been building in him for over a week. It had reached a crescendo of desire this evening. She had been looking almost demure in the green silk dress she had worn the evening they first supped together, her hair dressed severely but not unattractively.

And she had been acting the part of a lady, keeping the conversation going during dinner and in the sitting room afterward with observations about their journey, about the Christmas decorations and carol singers in London, and about—of all things—the peace talks that were proceeding in Vienna now that Napoleon Bonaparte had been defeated and was imprisoned on the island of Elba. She had asked Bertie what plans had been made for their own celebration of Christmas. Bertie had looked surprised and then blank. He obviously had no plans at all beyond enjoying himself with his pretty, buxom Debbie.

Paradoxically Julian had found Blanche's demure appearance and ladylike behavior arousing. He considered both erotic. She had too many charms to hide effectively.

"Come here," he said now.

She had gone to stand in front of the fire. She was holding out her hands to the blaze. But she turned her head, smiled at him and came to stand in front of him. She was clever, he thought. She must know that an overeagerness on her part would somehow dampen his own. Though there was just a chance she was not quite as eager as he. This was a job to her, after all. He would soon change that. He set his hands on either side of her waist and drew her against him, fitting her body against his own from the waist down. He could feel the slimness of her long legs, the flatness of her abdomen. His breath quickened. She looked back into his eyes, a half smile on her lips.

"At last," he said.

"Yes." Her smile did not waver. Neither did her eyes.

He bent his head and kissed her. She kept her lips closed. He teased them with his own and touched his tongue lightly to the seam, moving it slowly across in order to part her lips and gain entrance. Her head jerked back.

"What are you doing?" She sounded breathless.

He stared blankly at her. But before he could frame an answer to such a nonsensical question, her look of shock disappeared, she smiled again, and her hands came up to rest on his shoulders.

"Pardon me," she said. "You moved just a little too fast for me. I am ready now." She brought her mouth back to his, her lips softly parted this time, and trembling against his own.

What the devil?

His mind turned cold with suspicion. He closed his arms about her and thrust his tongue deep into her mouth without any attempt at subtlety. She made no move to pull away, but she went rigid in every limb for a few moments before relaxing almost to limpness. He moved his hands forward quite deliberately and cupped her breasts with them, his thumbs seeking and pressing against her nipples. Again there was the momentary tensing followed by relaxation.

He was looking down at her a moment later, his eyes half-closed, his hands again on either side of her waist.

"Well, Miss Heyward," he asked softly, "how have you enjoyed your first kiss?"

"My first..." She gazed blankly at him.

"I suppose it would be strange indeed," he said, "if I were to discover in a few minutes' time on that bed that you are not also a virgin?"

She had nothing to say this time.

"Well?" he asked her. "Shall I put the matter to the test?" He watched her swallow.

"Even the most hardened of whores," she said at last, "was a virgin once, my lord. For each there is a first time. I will not flinch or weep or deny you your will, if that is what you fear. You are paying me well. I will do all that is required of me."

"Will you, indeed?" he said, releasing her and crossing the room to the hearth to push a log farther into the blaze with his foot. He watched the resulting shower of sparks. "I am not paying for the pleasure of observing martyrdom."

"I was not acting the martyr," she protested. "You took me by surprise. I did not know... I am perfectly willing to do whatever you wish me to do. I am sorry that I will be awkward at first. But I will learn tonight, and tomorrow night I will know better what it is you expect of me. I hope I...perhaps under the circumstances you will decide that you have already paid me handsomely enough. I believe you have. I will try to earn it.''

Did she realize, he wondered in some amazement, that she was throwing a pail of cold water over his desire with every sentence she uttered? Anger was replacing it—no, fury. Not so much against her. She had told him no lies about her experience, had she? His fury was all against himself and his own cleverness. He would keep her for Bertie's, would he? He would savor his anticipation, would he, until it was too late to change his mind, to go to Conway as he ought to have done? He would have one last fling, would he, before he did his duty by his family and name? Well, he had been justly served.

In the middle of the desert, far from home, had the wise men ever called themselves all kinds of fool?

''I do not deal in virgins, Miss Heyward,'' he said curtly.

''Ah,'' she said, ''you do not like to face what it is you are purchasing, then, my lord?''

He raised his eyebrows in surprise and regarded her over his shoulder in silence for a few moments. This woman had sharp weapons and did not scruple to wield them. ''Is your need for the money a personal one?'' he asked her, turning from the fire. ''Or is it your family that is in need?" He did not want to know, he realized after the questions were out. He had no wish to know Blanche Heyward as a person. All he had wanted was one last sensual fling with a beautiful and experienced and willing partner.

"I do not have to answer that," she said. "I will pay back all I can when we have returned to London. But I am still willing to earn my salary."

"As I remember," he said, "our agreement was for a week of your company in exchange for a certain sum, Blanche. There was no mention of your warming my bed during that week, was there? We will spend the week here. It is too late now for either of us to make other arrangements for Christmas. Besides, those were snow clouds this afternoon if ever I have seen any. We will salvage what we can of the holiday, then. It might be the dreariest Christmas either of us has ever spent, but who knows? Maybe not. Maybe I will decide to give you lessons in kissing so that your next, ah, employer will make his discovery rather later in the process than I did. Undress and go to bed. There is a dressing room for your modesty."

"Where will you sleep?" she asked him.

He looked down at the floor, which was fortunately carpeted. "Here," he said. "Perhaps you will understand that I have no wish for Bertie to know that we are not spending the night in sensual bliss together."

"You have the bed," she said. "I will sleep on the floor."

He felt an unexpected stirring of amusement. "But I have already told you, Blanche," he said, "that I have no wish to gaze on martyrdom. Go to bed before I change my mind."

By the time she came back from the dressing room a few minutes later, dressed in a virginal white flannel nightgown, her head held high, her cheeks flushed and her titian hair all down her back, he had made up some sort of bed for himself on the floor close to the fire with blankets he had found in a drawer and a pillow he had taken from the bed. He did not look at her beyond one cursory glance. He waited for her to climb into the bed and pull the covers up over her ears, and then extinguished the candles.

"Good night," he said, finding his way back to his bed by the light of the fire.

"Good night," she said.

What a marvelously just punishment for his sins, he thought as he lay down and his body registered the hardness of the floor. But why the devil was he doing this? She had been willing and he was paying her handsomely. Heaven knows, he had wanted her badly enough, and still did.

It was not any real reluctance to violate innocence, he decided, or any unwillingness to deal with awkwardness or the inevitable blood. It was exactly what he had said it was. He had no desire to watch martyrdom or to inflict it.

I will not flinch or weep or deny you your will.

If there were less erotic words in the English language, he could not imagine what they might be. Sheer martyrdom! If only she had wanted it, wanted *him* just a little bit, even if she had been nervous…

Miss Blanche Heyward, he was discovering to his cost, was not the average, typical opera dancer. In fact she was turning out to be a royal pain.

A fine Christmas this was going to be. He thought glumly of Conway and of what he would be missing there tomorrow and the day after. Even the Plunkett chit was looking mildly appealing at this particular moment.

"What would you have done for Christmas," a soft voice asked him as if she had read his thoughts, "if you had not come here with me?"

He breathed deeply and evenly and audibly.

Perhaps tomorrow he would teach her to see a night spent in bed with him as fitting a different category of experience from Christians being prodded into the arena with slavering lions. But unlike his usual confident self, he did not hold out a great deal of hope of succeeding.

Surprisingly he slept.

Chapter Four

Verity did not sleep well during the night. But as she lay staring at the window and the suggestion of daylight beyond the curtains, she was surprised that she had slept at all.

There were sounds of deep, even breathing coming from the direction of the fireplace. She listened carefully. There were no sounds from beyond the door. Did that mean no one was up yet? Of course, Mr. Hollander and Debbie had probably been busy all night and perhaps intended to be busy for part of the morning, too.

It should have been all over by this morning, she thought. She should be a fallen woman beyond all dispute by now. And he had been wrong. It would not have felt like martyrdom. Even in the privacy of her own mind she was a little embarrassed to remember how exciting his hard man's body had felt against her own and how shockingly pleasurable his open mouth had felt against her lips. All her insides had performed some sort of vigorous dance when he had put his tongue into her mouth. What an alarmingly intimate thing to do. It should have been disgusting but had not been.

Well, she thought with determined honesty, she had actually wanted to experience the whole of it. And deny it as she would, she had to confess to herself that there had been some disappointment in his refusal to continue once he had realized the truth about her.

And so here they were in this ridiculous predicament with all of Christmas ahead of them. How could she possibly earn five hundred pounds when one night was already past and he had slept on the floor?

All of Christmas was ahead of them. What a depressing thought!

And then something in the quality of the light beyond the window drew her attention. She threw back the bedcovers, ignored her shivering reaction to the frigid air beyond their shelter and padded across the room on bare feet. She drew aside the curtain.

Oh!

"Oh!" she exclaimed aloud. She turned her head and looked eagerly at the sleeping man. "Oh, do come and look."

His head reared up from his pillow. He looked deliciously tousled and unshaven. He was also scowling.

"What?" he barked. "What the devil *time* is it?"

"Look," she said, turning back to the window. "Oh, look."

He was beside her then, clad only in his shirt and

last night's knee breeches and stockings. "For this you have dragged me from my bed?" he asked her. "I told you last night that it would snow today."

"But look!" she begged him. "It is sheer magic."

When she turned her head, she found him looking at her instead of at the snow beyond the window, blanketing the ground and decking out the bare branches of the trees.

"Do you always glow like this in the morning?" he asked her. "How disgusting!"

She laughed. "Only when Christmas is coming and there is a fresh fall of snow," she said. "Can you imagine two more wonderful events happening simultaneously?"

"Finding a soft warm bed when I am more than half asleep and stiff in every limb," he said.

"Then have my bed," she said, laughing again. "I am getting up."

"A fine impression Bertie is going to have of my power to keep you amused and confined to your room," he said.

"Mr. Hollander," she told him, "will doubtless keep to his room until noon and will be none the wiser. Go to bed and go to sleep."

He did both. By the time she emerged from the dressing room, clad in the warmest of her wool dresses, her hair brushed and decently confined, he was lying in the place on the bed where she had lain all night, fast asleep. She stood gazing down at him for a few moments, imagining that if she had not been so gauche last night…

She shook her head and straightened her shoulders. Mr. Hollander had made no preparations for Christmas. Doubtless he thought that spending a few days in bed with the placid Debbie would constitute enough merrymaking. Well, they would see about that. She was not being allowed to earn her salary in the expected way. The least she could do, then, was make herself useful in other ways.

Two coachmen, one footman, one groom, a cook, Mr. Hollander's valet, and four others who might in a more orderly establishment have been dubbed a butler, a housekeeper and two maids were in the middle of their breakfast below stairs. A few of them scrambled awkwardly to their feet when Verity appeared in their midst. A few did not. Clearly it was not established in any of their minds whether they should treat her as a lady or not. The cook looked as if she might be the leader of the latter faction.

Verity smiled. "Please do not get up," she said. "Do carry on with your breakfast. Doubtless you all have a busy day ahead."

If they did, their expressions told Verity, this was the first they had heard of it.

"Preparing for Christmas," she added.

They might have been devout Hindus for all the interest they showed in preparing for Christmas.

"Mr. Hollander don't want no fuss," the woman who might have been the housekeeper said.

"He said we might do as we please provided he has his victuals when he is ready for them and provided the fires are kept burning." The possible-butler was the speaker this time.

"Oh, splendid," Verity said cheerfully. "May I have some breakfast with you, by the way? No, please do not get up." No one had made any particular move to do so. "I shall just help myself, shall I?" She did so. "If you have been given permission to please yourselves, then, you may be pleased to celebrate Christmas. In the traditional way, with Christmas foods and wassail, with carol singing and gift giving and with decorating the house with holly and pine boughs and whatever else we can devise with only a day's warning. Everyone can have a wonderful time."

"When I cook a goose," the cook announced, "nobody needs a knife to cut it. Even the edge of a fork is too sharp. It melts apart."

"Ooh, I do love a goose," one of the maids said wistfully. "My ma used to cook one a treat for Christmas whenever we could catch one. But it weren't never cooked tender enough to cut with a fork, Mrs. Lyons," she added hastily.

"And when I make mince pies," the cook continued as if she had not been interrupted, "no one can stop eating after just one of them. *No one*."

"Mmm." Verity sighed. "You make my mouth water, Mrs. Lyons. How I would love to taste just one of those pies."

"Well, I can't make them," Mrs. Lyons said, a note of finality in her voice. "Because I don't have the stuff."

"Could the supplies be bought in the village?" Verity suggested. "I noticed a village as I passed through it yesterday. There appeared to be a few shops there."

"There is nobody to go for them," Mrs. Lyons said. "Not in all this snow."

Verity smiled at the groom and the two coachmen, all of whom were trying unsuccessfully to blend into the furniture. "Nobody?" she said. "Not for the sake of goose tomorrow and mince pies and probably a dozen other Christmas specialties, too? Not for Mrs. Lyons's sake when it sounds to me as if she is the most skilled cook in all of Norfolkshire?"

"Well, I am quite skilled," the cook said modestly.

"There are pine trees and holly bushes in the park, are there not?" Verity asked of no one in particular. "Is there mistletoe anywhere?" She turned her eyes on the younger of the two maids. "What is Christmas without a few sprigs of mistletoe appearing in the most unlikely places and just over the heads of the most elusive people?"

The maid turned pink and the valet looked interested.

"There used to be some on the old oaks," the butler said. "But I don't know about this year, mind."

"The archway leading from the kitchen to the back stairs looks a likely place to me for one sprig," Verity said, looking critically at the spot as she bit into a piece of toast.

Both maids giggled and the valet cleared his throat.

After that the hard work seemed to be behind her, Verity found. The idea had caught hold. Mr. Hollander had given his staff carte blanche even if he had not done so consciously. And the staff had awakened to the realization that it was Christmas and that they might celebrate it in as grand a manner as they chose. All lethargy magically disappeared, and Verity was able to eat her eggs and toast and drink down two cups of coffee while warming herself at the kitchen fire and listening to the servants make their animated plans. There were even two volunteers to go into the village.

"You cannot all be everywhere at once, though," Verity said, speaking up again at last, "much as I can see you would like to be. You may leave the gathering of the greenery and just come to help drag it all indoors. Mr. Hollander, Lord Folingsby, Miss, er, Debbie, and I will do the gathering."

Silence and blank stares met this announcement until someone sniggered—the groom.

"I don't think so, miss," he said. "You won't drag them gents out of doors to spoil the shine on their boots nor 'er to spoil 'er complexion. You can forget that one right enough."

The valet cleared his throat again, with considerably more dignity than before. "You will speak with greater respect of Mr. Hollander, Bloggs," he told the groom, who looked quite uncowed by the reprimand.

Verity smiled. "You may safely leave Mr. Hollander and the others to me," she said. "We are *all* going to enjoy Christmas. It would be unfair to exclude them, would it not?"

Her words caused a burst of merriment about the table, and Verity tried to imagine Julian pricking his aristocratic fingers in the cause of gathering holly. He would probably sleep until noon. But she had done him an injustice. He appeared in the archway that was not yet adorned with mistletoe only a moment later, as if her thoughts had summoned him. He was dressed immaculately despite the fact that he had not brought his valet with him.

"Ah," Julian said languidly, fingering the handle of his quizzing glass, "here you are, Blanche. I began to think you had sprouted wings and flown since there are no footprints in the snow leading from the door."

"We have been planning the Christmas festivities," she told him with a bright smile. "Everything is organized. Later you and I will be going out into the park with Mr. Hollander and Debbie to gather greenery with which to decorate the house."

Suddenly that part of the plan seemed quite preposterous. His lordship raised his quizzing glass all the way to his eye and moved it about the table, the better to observe all the conspirators seated there. It came to rest finally on her.

"Indeed?" he said faintly. "What a delightful treat for us."

Julian was sitting awkwardly on the branch of an ancient oak tree, not quite sure how he had got up there and even less sure how he was to get down again without breaking a leg or two or even his neck. Blanche was standing below, her face upturned, her arms spread as if to catch him should he fall. Just a short distance beyond his grasp was a promising clump of mistletoe. Several yards away from the oak, Bertie was standing almost knee-deep in snow, one glove on, the other discarded on the ground beside him, complaining about a holly prick on one finger with all the loud woe of a man who had just been run through with a sword. Debbie was kissing it better.

A little closer to the house, in a spot sheltered by trees and therefore not as deeply covered with snow, lay a pathetically small pile of pine boughs and holly branches. Pathetic, at least, considering the fact that they had been outdoors and hard at work for longer than an hour, subjected to frigid temperatures, buffeting winds and swirling flakes of thick snow. The heavy clouds had still not finished emptying their load.

"Oh, do be careful," Blanche implored as Julian leaned out gingerly to reach the mistletoe. "Don't fall."

He paused and looked down at her. Her cheeks were charmingly rosy. So was her nose. "Did I imagine it, Blanche," he asked, using his best bored voice, "or did the drill sergeant who marched us out here and ordered me up here really wear your face?"

She laughed. No, she did not—she giggled. "If you kill yourself," she said, "I shall have them write on your epitaph—He Died In The Execution Of A Noble Deed."

By dint of shifting his position on the branch until he hung even more precariously over space and scraping his boot beyond redemption to get something of a toehold against the gnarled trunk, he finally succeeded in his mission. He had dislodged a handful of mistletoe. There was no easy way down to the ground. Indeed, there was no possible way down. He did what he had always done as a boy in a similar situation. He jumped.

He landed on all fours and got a faceful of soft snow for his pains.

"Oh, dear," Blanche said. "Did you hurt yourself?" He looked up at her and she giggled again. "You look like a snowman, a snowman whose dignity has been bruised. Do you have the mistletoe?"

He got to his feet and brushed himself off with one hand as best he could. His valet, when he got back to London, was going to take one look at his boot and resign.

"Voilà!" He held up his snow-bedraggled prize. "Oh, no, you don't," he said when she reached for it. He swept it up out of her reach. "Certain acts have certain consequences, you know. I risked my life for this at your instigation. I deserve my reward, you deserve your punishment."

She grinned at him as he backed her against the

tree and held her there with the weight of his body. He was still holding the mistletoe aloft.

''Yes, my lord,'' she said meekly.

His mind was not really on the night before, but if it had been, he might have reflected with some satisfaction that she had learned well her first lesson in kissing. Her lips were softly parted when he touched them with his own, and when he teased them wider and licked them and the soft flesh behind them with his tongue, she made quiet sounds of enjoyment. The contrast between chilled flesh and hot mouths was heady stuff, he decided as he slid his tongue deep. She sucked gently on it. Through all the layers of their clothing he could feel the tautly muscled slenderness of her dancer's body. Total femininity.

Someone was whistling. Bertie. And someone was telling him to be quiet and not be silly, love, and come away to look at *this* holly.

''Well,'' Julian said, lifting his head and feeling a little dazed and more than a little aroused. He had not anticipated just such a kiss. ''The mistletoe *was* your idea, Blanche.''

''Yes.'' Her nose was shining like a beacon. She looked healthy and girlish and slightly disheveled and utterly beautiful. ''And so it was.''

And he was cold and wet from the snow that had slipped down inside his collar and was melting in trickles down his back, and utterly happy. Or for the moment anyway, he thought more cautiously when he remembered the situation.

Someone was clearing his throat from behind Julian's back—Bertie's groom, Julian saw when he looked. The man was looking for Bertie, who stuck his head out from behind the holly bushes at the mention of his name.

"What is it, Bloggs?" he asked.

Bloggs told his tale of a carriage half turned over into the ditch just beyond the front gates with no hope of its being hauled out again until the snow stopped falling and the air warmed up enough to melt some of it. And the snow was so deep everywhere, he added gloomily, that there was no going anywhere on foot either any longer, even as far as the village. He should know. He and Harkiss had had the devil's own time of it wading home from there all of two hours since, and the snowfall had not abated for a single second since that time.

"A carriage?" Bertie frowned. "Any occupants, Bloggs?" A foolish question if ever Julian had heard one.

"A gentleman and his wife, sir," Bloggs reported. "And two nippers. Inside the house now, sir."

"Oh, good Lord," Bertie said, grimacing in Julian's direction. "It looks as if we have unexpected guests for Christmas."

"The devil!" Julian muttered.

"Oh, the poor things!" Blanche exclaimed, pushing away from the tree and striding houseward through the snow. "What has been done for their comfort, Mr. Bloggs? Two children, did you say? Are they very young? Was anyone hurt? Have you…"

Her voice faded into the distance. Strange, Julian thought before following her with Bertie and Debbie. Most women who had had elocution lessons spoke well except when they were not concentrating. Then they tended to lapse into regionalism and worse. Why did the opposite seem to happen with Blanche? Bloggs was trotting after her like a well-trained henchman, just as if she were some grand duchess ruling over her undisputed domain.

Funnily enough, she had just *sounded* rather like a duchess.

Chapter Five

The Reverend Henry Moffatt had been given un-expected leave from the parish at which he was a curate in order to spend Christmas at the home of his wife's family thirty miles distant. Rashly—by his own admission—he had made the decision to begin the journey that morning despite the fact that the snow had already begun to fall and he had the safety of two young children to concern himself with—not to mention that of his wife, who was in imminent expectation of another interesting event.

He was contrite over his own foolishness. He was distressed over the near disaster to which he had brought his family when his carriage had almost overturned into the ditch. He was apologetic about foisting himself and his family upon strangers on Christmas Eve of all days. Perhaps there was an inn close by?

"In the village three miles away," Verity told him. "But you would not get there in this weather, sir. You must, of course, stay here. Mr. Hollander will insist upon it, you may be sure.''

''Mr. Hollander is your husband, ma'am?'' the Reverend Moffatt asked.

''No.'' She smiled. ''I am a guest here too, sir. Mrs. Moffatt, do come into the sitting room so that you may warm yourself by the fire and take the weight off your feet. Mr. Bloggs, would you be so kind as to go down to the kitchen and request that a tea tray be sent up? Oh, and something for the children, as well. And something to eat.'' She smiled at the two little boys, who were gazing about with open curiosity. The younger one, a mere infant of three or four years, was unwinding a long scarf from his neck. She reached out a hand to each of them. ''Are you hungry? But that is a foolish question, I know. In my experience little boys are always hungry. Come into the sitting room with your mama and we will see what Cook sends up.''

It was at that moment that Mr. Hollander came inside the house with Debbie and Viscount Folingsby close behind him. The Reverend Moffatt introduced himself again and made his explanations and his apologies once more.

''Bertrand Hollander,'' that young gentleman said, extending his right hand to his unexpected guest. ''And, er, my wife, Mrs. Hollander. And Viscount Folingsby.''

Verity was leading Mrs. Moffatt and the children in the direction of the sitting room, but she stopped so that the curate could introduce them to his host.

"You have met my wife, the viscountess?" Julian asked, his eyes locking with Verity's.

"Yes, indeed." The Reverend Moffatt made her a bow. "Her ladyship has been most kind."

One more lie to add to all the others, Verity thought. Her new husband, having divested himself of his outdoor garments, followed her into the sitting room, where she directed the very pregnant Mrs. Moffatt and the little boys to chairs close to the fire. The viscount stood beside Verity, one hand against the back of her waist. But during the bustle of the next few minutes, she felt her left hand being taken in a firm grasp and bent up behind her back. While Julian smiled genially about him as the tea tray arrived and cups and plates were passed around and everyone made small talk, he slid something onto Verity's ring finger.

It was the signet ring he normally wore on the little finger of his right hand, she saw when she withdrew the hand from her back and looked down at it. The ring was a little loose on her, but with some care she would be able to see that it did not fall off. It was a very tolerable substitute for a wedding ring. A glance across the room at Debbie assured her that that young woman's left hand was similarly adorned.

One could only conclude that Viscount Folingsby and Mr. Hollander were born conspirators and had had a great deal of practice at being devious.

"I will hear no more protests, sir, if you please," Mr. Hollander was saying with all his customary good humor and one raised hand. "Mrs. Hollander and I will be delighted to have your company over Christmas. Much as we have been enjoying that of our two friends, we have been regretting, have we not, my love, that we did not invite more guests for the holiday. Especially those with children. Christmas does not seem quite Christmas without them."

"How kind of you to say so, sir," Mrs. Moffatt said, one hand resting over the mound of her pregnancy.

"Ee," Debbie said, "it is going to be right good fun to hear the patter of little feet about the house and the chatter of little voices. You sit down too, Rev, and make yourself at home. Set your cup and saucer down on that table there. It must have been a right nasty fright to land in the ditch like that."

"We tipped up like *this*," the older of the little boys said, listing over sharply to one side, his arms outspread. "I thought we were going to turn over and over in a tumble-toss. It was ever so exciting."

"I was not scared," the younger boy said, gazing up at Verity before depositing his thumb in his mouth and then snatching it determinedly out again. "I am not scared of anything."

"That will do, Rupert," their father said. "And David. You will speak when spoken to, if you please."

But Rupert was pulling at his father's sleeve. "May we go out to play?" he whispered.

"Children!" Mrs. Moffatt laughed. "One would think they would be glad enough to be safe indoors after that narrow escape, would you not? And on such a cold, stormy day. But they love the outdoors.''

''Then I have just the answer for them,'' Julian said, raising his eyebrows and fingering the handle of his quizzing glass. ''There is a pile of Christmas greenery out behind the house in dire need of hands and arms to carry it inside. We will never be able to celebrate Christmas with it if it remains out there, will we?'' He leveled his glass at each of the boys in turn, a frown on his face. ''I wonder if those hands and arms are strong enough, though. What do you think, Bertie?''

Two pairs of eyes turned anxiously Mr. Hollander's way. *Please yes, please yes,* those eyes begged while both children sat with buttoned lips in obedience to their father's command.

''What do I think, Jule?'' Mr. Hollander pursed his lips. ''I think—but wait a minute. Is that a muscle I spy bulging out your coat sleeve, lad?''

The elder boy looked down with desperate hope at his arm.

''It is a muscle,'' Mr. Hollander decided.

''And have you ever seen more capable fingers than this other lad's, Bertie?'' Julian asked, magnifying them with the aid of his glass. ''I believe these brothers have been sent us for a purpose. You will need to put your scarves and hats and gloves back on, of course, and secure your mama's permission. But once that has been accomplished, you may follow me.''

Verity watched in wonder as two rather bored and

jaded rakes were transformed into kindly, indulgent uncles before her eyes. The two boys were jumping up and down before their mother's chair in an agony of suspense lest she withhold her permission.

"You are too kind, my lord," she said with a weary smile. "They will wear you out."

"Not at all, ma'am," he assured her. "It is a sizable pile."

"Oh," Verity said, beaming down at the children, "and after you have it all inside and dried off, you may help decorate the house with it. There are mistletoe and holly and pine boughs. And Mrs. Simpkins has found ribbons and bows and bells in the attic. Deb—Mrs. Hollander and I will sort through them and decide what can be used. Before Christmas comes tomorrow, this house is going to be bursting at the seams with good cheer. I daresay we will have one of the best Christmases anyone ever had."

Her eyes met Viscount Folingsby's as she spoke. He regarded her with one raised eyebrow and a slightly mocking smile. But she was no longer fooled by such an expression. She had seen him without his mask of bored cynicism. Not just here with the two little boys. She had seen him climb a tree like a schoolboy, not just because she had asked him to do so, but because the tree was there and therefore to be climbed. She had seen him with a twinkle in his eye and a laugh on his lips.

And she had—oh dear, yes—she had felt his kiss. It was not one she could censure even if it had occurred to her to do so. He had earned it, not with five hundred pounds, but with the acquisition of mistletoe. The mistletoe had sanctified the kiss, deep and carnal as it had been.

"It seems," the Reverend Moffatt said as the other two gentlemen left the room with the exuberant children, "that we are to be guests here at least until tomorrow. It warms my heart to have been stranded at a place where we have already been made to feel welcome. Sometimes it seems almost as if a divine hand is at play in guiding our movements, taking us where we had no intention of going to meet people we had no thought of meeting. How wonderful that you are all preparing with such enthusiasm to celebrate the birth of our Lord."

"I am going to make a kissing bough," Debbie announced, looking almost animated. "We had kissing boughs to half fill the kitchen ceiling when I was a girl. Nobody escaped a few good bussings in our house. I had almost forgotten. Christmas was always a right grand time."

"Yes, Mrs. Hollander," Mrs. Moffatt said with a smile. "It is always a grand time, even when we are forced to spend it away from part of our families as I assume we are all doing this year. Your husband is being very kind to our boys. And yours, too, my lady." She turned her smile on Verity. "They have been in the carriage all day and have a great deal of excess energy."

"There will be no going into the village tonight or tomorrow morning if what you said is true, Lady Folingsby," the Reverend Moffatt said. "You will be unable to attend church as I daresay you intended to do. I shall repay a small part of my debt to you, then. I shall conduct the Christmas service here. We will all take communion here together. With Mr. Hollander's permission, of course.''

''What a splendid idea, Henry,'' his wife said.

''Ee,'' Debbie said, awed into near-silence.

Verity clasped her hands to her bosom and closed her eyes. She had a sudden image of the church at home on the evening before Christmas, the bells pealing out the news of the Christ child's birth, the candles all ablaze, the carved Nativity scene carefully arranged before the altar, her father in his best vestments smiling down at the congregation. Christmas had always been his favorite time of the liturgical year.

''Oh, sir,'' she said, opening her eyes again, ''it is we who will be in your debt. Deeply in your debt.'' She blinked away tears. ''I would like it of all things. I am sure Mr. Hollander and Vi—and my husband will agree.''

''It is going to be a grand Christmas, Blanche,'' Debbie said. ''I did not expect it, lass. Not in this way, any road.''

''Sometimes we come to grace by unexpected paths,'' the Reverend Moffatt commented.

''Do you ever have the impression that events have galloped along somewhat out of your control, Jule?'' Bertie asked his friend just before dinner was served and they stood together in the sitting room waiting for everyone else to join them. They were surrounded by the sights and smells of Christmas. There was greenery everywhere, artfully draped and colorfully decorated with red bows and streamers and silver bells. There was a huge and elaborate kissing bough suspended over the alcove to one side of the fireplace. There was a strong smell of pine, more powerful for the moment than the tantalizing aromas wafting up from the kitchen.

"And do you ever have the impression," Julian asked without answering the question, which was doubtless rhetorical anyway, "that you ought not to simply label a woman as a certain type and expect her to behave accordingly?" Blanche, changing for dinner a few minutes before in the dressing room while he made do with the bedchamber, had informed him with bright enthusiasm that the Reverend Moffatt was planning to conduct a Christmas service in this very room sometime after dinner. And that the servants had asked to attend. And that they were going to have to see to it on the morrow that the little boys had a wonderful Christmas. If there was still plenty of snow, they could...

He had not listened to all the details. But Miss Blanche Heyward, opera dancer, would have made a superlative drill sergeant if she had just been a man, he had thought. Consider as a point in fact the way she had organized them all—*all* of them—over the decorations. They had rushed about and climbed and teetered and adjusted angles at her every bidding. She had been flushed and bright eyed and beautiful.

On the whole, he concluded as an afterthought, he was glad she was not a man.

"And have you ever had a cook for all of three or four years, Jule," Bertie continued, "and suddenly discovered that she could *cook?* Not that I have tasted any of the things that go with those smells yet, but if smell is anything to judge by...well, I *ask* you."

The staff, it seemed, had been as busy below stairs as all of them had been above. But their busyness had had the same instigator—Miss Blanche Heyward. Julian even wondered if somehow she had conjured up the clergyman and his family out of the blizzard. What a ghastly turn of events that had been.

"Do you suppose," he asked, "anyone noticed the sudden appearance of rings on our women's fingers, Bertie?"

But the door opened at that moment to admit their mistresses, who had come down together. Debbie clucked her tongue.

"Now did I do all that work on the kissing bough just to see it hang over there and you men stand here?" she asked. "Go and get yourself under it, Bertie, love, and be bussed."

"Again?" he said, grinning and waggling his eyebrows and instantly obeying.

They had all sampled the pleasures of the kissing bough after it had been hung. Even the Reverend Moffatt had kissed his wife with hearty good humor and had pecked Debbie and Blanche respectfully on the cheek.

"Well, Blanche." Julian looked her up and down. She was dressed in the dark green silk again. Her hair was neatly confined at the back of her head. She should have looked drably dreary but did not. "Are you enjoying yourself?"

Some of the sparkle that had been in her eyes faded as she looked back at him. "Only when I forget my purpose in being here," she said. "I have already taken a great deal of money from you and have done nothing yet to earn it."

"Perhaps I should be the judge of that," he said.

"Perhaps tonight I can make some amends," she said. "I have had a day in which to grow more accustomed to you. I may still be awkward—I daresay I will be because I am very ignorant of what happens, you know—but I will not be afraid and I will not act the *martyr*. Indeed, I believe I might even enjoy it. And it will be a relief to know that at last I have done something to earn my salary."

If Bertie and Debbie, now laughing like a pair of children and making merry beneath the kissing bough, had been the only other occupants of the house apart from the servants, Julian thought he might have excused Blanche and himself from dinner and taken her up to bed without further ado. Despite the reference to earning salaries, he found her words arousing. He found *her* arousing. But there were other guests. Besides, he was not sure he would have done it anyway.

If this stay in Norfolkshire had proceeded according to plan, he would have enjoyed a largely sleepless night with Blanche last night. They would have stayed in bed until noon or later this morning. They would have returned to bed for much of the afternoon. By now he would have been wondering how long into the coming night his energies would sustain him. But there would have been all day tomorrow to look forward to—in bed.

The prospect had seemed appealing to him all last week and up until just last night. Longer than that. He had felt disgruntled and cheated all through the night and when he had woken this morning. Or when she had awoken him, rather, with her excited discovery that it had snowed during the night.

But surprisingly he had enjoyed the day just as it had turned out. And the kiss against the oak tree had seemed in some strange way as satisfying as a bedding might have been. There had been laughter as well as desire involved in that kiss. He had never before thought of laughter as a desirable component of a sexual experience.

"You are disappointed in me," Blanche said now. "I am so sorry."

"Not at all," he told her, clasping his hands at his back. "How could I possibly be disappointed? Let me see. A night spent on the floor, an early wake-up call in the frigid dawn to watch snow falling, an expedition out into the storm in order to climb trees, murder my boots and risk my neck. The arrival of a clergyman as a house guest, an hour spent finding occupation for two energetic infants, another hour of climbing on furniture and pinning up boughs only to move them again when it was discovered that they were half an inch out of place, a church service in the sitting room to look forward to. My dear Miss Heyward, what more could I have asked of Christmas?''

She was laughing. "I have the strangest feeling," she said, "that you *have* enjoyed today."

He raised his quizzing glass to his eye and regarded her through it. "And you believe that you might enjoy tonight," he said. "We will see, Blanche, when tonight comes. But first of all, Bertie's guests. I believe I hear the patter of little feet and the chatter of little voices approaching, as Debbie so poetically phrased it. I suppose we are to be subjected to their company as well as that of their mama and papa since there is no nursery and no nurse."

"For all your expression and tone of voice," Blanche said, "I do believe, my lord, you have an affection for those little boys. You do not deceive me."

"Dear me," Julian said faintly as the sitting room door opened again.

There was a spinet in one corner of the sitting room. Verity had eyed it a few times during the day with some longing, but its lid was locked, she had discovered. While the Reverend Moffatt was setting up the room after dinner for the Christmas service, his wife asked about the instrument. Mr. Hollander looked at it in some surprise, as if he were noticing it for the first time. He had no idea where the key was. It hardly mattered anyway unless someone was able to play it.

There was a short silence.

"I can play," Verity said.

"Splendid!" The Reverend Moffatt beamed at her. "Then we may have music with the service, Lady Folingsby. I would lead the singing if I had to, but I have a lamentably poor ear for pitch, do I not, Edie? We would be likely to end a hymn several tones lower than we started it." He laughed heartily.

Mr. Hollander went in search of the key. Or rather, he went in search of a servant who might know where it was.

"Where did you learn to play, Blanche?" Debbie asked.

"At the rectory." Verity smiled and then wished she could bite out her tongue. "The rector's wife taught me," she added hastily. That was the truth, at least.

Mr. Hollander came back in triumph, a key held aloft. The spinet was sadly out of tune, Verity discovered, but not impossibly so. There was no music, but she did not need any. All her favorite hymns, as well as some other favorite pieces, had been committed to memory when she was still a girl.

A table had been converted into an altar with the aid of a crisp white cloth one of the maids had ironed carefully, candles in silver holders, and a fancy cup and plate the housekeeper had found somewhere in the nether regions of the house and the other maid had polished to serve as a paten and chalice. The butler had dusted off a bottle of Mr. Hollander's best wine. The cook had found time and space in her oven to bake a round loaf of unleavened bread. The Reverend Moffatt had clad himself in vestments he had brought with him and suddenly looked very young and dignified and holy.

The sitting room, Verity thought, gazing about her, had become a holy place, a church. Everyone, even the children, sat hushed as they would in a church, waiting for the service to begin. Verity did not wait. She began to play quietly some of her favorite Christmas hymns.

It was Christmas, she thought, swallowing and blinking her eyes. She had not thought it would come for her this year except in the form of an ugly self-sacrifice. But for all the lies and deceptions—with every glance down at her hands she saw the false wedding ring Christmas had come. Christmas, she reminded herself, and the reminder had never been more apt, was for sinners, and they were all sinners: Mr. Hollander, Debbie, Viscount Folingsby and she. But Christmas had found them out, despite themselves, in the form of the clergyman and his family, stranded by a snowstorm. And Christmas was offering all its boundless love and forgiveness to them in the form of the bread and the wine, which were still at this moment just those two commodities.

A child had been born on this night more than eighteen hundred years ago, and he was about to be born again as he had been each year since then and would be each year in the future. Constant birth. Constant hope. Constant love.

"My dear friends." The clergyman's voice was quiet, serene, imposing, unlike the voice of the Reverend Moffatt who had conversed with them over tea and dinner. He smiled about at each one of them in turn, bathing them—or so it seemed—in the warmth and peace and wonder of the season.

And so the service began.

It ended more than an hour later with the joyful singing of one last hymn. They all sang lustily, Verity noticed, herself included. Even one of the coachmen, who was noticeably tone-deaf, and the housekeeper, who sang with pronounced vibrato. Mr. Hollander had a strong tenor voice. Debbie sang with a Yorkshire accent. David Moffatt sang his heart out to a tune of his own devising. They would not have made a reputable choir. But it did not matter. They made a joyful noise. They were celebrating Christmas.

And then Mrs. Moffatt spoke up, a mere few seconds after her husband had said the final words of the service and wished them all the compliments of the season.

"I do apologize, Mr. and Mrs. Hollander," she said, "for all the inconvenience I am about to cause you. Henry, my dear, I do believe we are going to have a Christmas child."

Chapter Six

Henry Moffatt was pacing as he had been doing almost constantly for the past several hours.

"One would expect to become accustomed to it," he said, pausing for only a moment to stare, pale faced and anxious eyed, at Julian and Bertie, who were sitting at either side of the hearth, hardly any less pale themselves, "after two previous confinements. But one does not. One thinks of a new child—one's own—making the perilous passage into this world. And one thinks of one's mate, flesh of one's own flesh, heart of one's heart, enduring the pain, facing all the danger alone. One feels helpless and humble and dreadfully responsible. And guilty that one does not have more trust in the plans of the Almighty. It seems trivial to recall that we have hoped for a daughter this time."

He resumed his journey to nowhere, back and forth from one corner of the room to the other. "Will it never end?"

Julian had never before shared a house with a

woman in labor. When he thought about it, about what was going on above stairs—and how could he *not* think about it?—he felt a buzzing in his ears and a coldness in his nostrils and imagined in some horror the ignominy of fainting when he was not even the prospective father. He remembered how glibly just a few days before he had planned to have a child of his own in the nursery by next Christmas or very soon after.

It must hurt like hell, he thought, and that was probably the understatement of the decade.

There was no doctor in the village. There was a midwife, but she lived, according to the housekeeper, a mile or so on the other side of the village. It would have been impossible to reach her, not to mention persuading her to make the return journey, in time to deliver the child who was definitely on its way.

Fortunately, Mrs. Moffatt had announced with a calm smile—surely it had been merely a brave facade—she had already given birth to two children, as well as attending the births of a few others. She could manage very well alone, provided the housekeeper would prepare a few items for her. It was getting late. She invited everyone else to retire to bed and promised not to disturb them with any loud noises.

Julian had immediately formed mental images of someone screaming in agony.

Debbie had looked at Bertie with eyes almost as big as her face.

"If you are quite sure, ma'am," Bertie had said, as white as his shirt points.

"Come, Henry," Mrs. Moffatt had said, "we will put the children to bed first. Perhaps I can see you in here for a few minutes afterward, Mrs. Simpkins."

Mrs. Simpkins had been looking a delicate shade of green.

That was when Blanche had spoken up.

"You certainly will *not* manage alone," she had assured the guest. "It will be quite enough for you to endure the pain of labor. You will leave the rest to us, Mrs. Moffatt. Sir," she said, addressing the clergyman, "perhaps you can put the children to bed yourself tonight? Boys, give your mama a kiss. Doubtless there will be more than one wonderful surprise awaiting you in the morning. The sooner you fall asleep, the sooner you will find out what. Mrs. Lyons, will you see that a large pot of water is heated and kept ready? Mrs. Simpkins, will you gather together as many clean cloths as you can find? Debbie—"

"Ee, Blanche," Debbie had protested, "no, love."

"I am going to need you," Blanche had said with a smile. "Merely to wield a cool, damp cloth to wipe Mrs. Moffatt's face when she gets very hot, as she will. You can do that, can you not? I will be there to do everything else."

Everything else. Like delivering the baby. Julian had stared, fascinated, at his opera dancer.

"Have you done this before, Blanche?" he had asked.

"Of course," she had said briskly. "At the rectory—ah. I used to accompany the rector's wife on occasion. I know exactly what to do. No one need fear."

They had all been gazing at her, Julian remembered now. They had all hung on her every word, her every command. They had leaned on her strength and her confidence in a collective body.

Who the hell *was* she? What had a blacksmith's daughter been doing hanging around a rectory so much? Apart from learning to play the spinet without music, that was. And apart from delivering babies.

Everyone had run to do her bidding. Soon only the three men—the three useless ones—had been left in the sitting room to fight terror and nausea and fits of the vapors.

The door opened. Three pale, terrified faces turned toward it.

Debbie was flushed and untidy and swathed in an apron made for a giant. One hank of blond hair hung to her shoulder and looked damp with perspiration. She was beaming and looking very pretty, indeed.

"It is all over, sir," she announced, addressing herself to the Reverend Moffatt. "You have a new…baby. I am not to say what. Your wife is ready and waiting for you."

The new father stood very still for a few moments and then strode from the room without a word.

"Bertie." Debbie turned tear-filled eyes toward him. "You should have been there, love. It came out all of a rush into Blanche's hands, the dearest little slippery thing, all cross and crying and—and human. Ee, Bertie, love.'' She cast herself into his arms and bawled noisily.

Bertie made soothing noises and raised his eyebrows at Julian. ''I was never more relieved in my life,'' he said. ''But I am quite thankful I was not there, Deb. We had better get you to bed. You are not needed any longer?''

''Blanche told me I could go to bed,'' Debbie said. ''She will finish off all that needs doing. No midwife could have done better. She talked quietly the whole time to calm my jitters and Mrs. Simpkins's. Mrs. Moffatt didn't have the jitters. She just kept saying she was sorry to keep us up, the daft woman. I have never felt so—so honored, Bertie, love. Me, Debbie Markle, just a simple, honest whore to be allowed to see *that*.''

''Come on, Deb.'' Bertie tucked her into the crook of his arm and bore her off to bed.

Julian followed them up a few minutes later. He had no idea what time it was. Some unholy hour of the morning, he supposed. He did not carry a candle up with him and no one had lit the branch in his room. Someone from below stairs had been kept working late, though. There was a freshly made up fire burning in the hearth. He went to stand at the window and looked out.

The snow had stopped falling, he saw, and the sky had cleared off. He looked upward and saw in that single glance that he had been wrong. It was not an *unholy* hour of the morning at all.

He was still standing there several minutes later when the door of the bedchamber opened. He turned his head to look over his shoulder.

She looked as Debbie had looked but worse. She was bedraggled, weary and beautiful.

"You should not have waited up," she said.

"Come." He beckoned to her.

She came and slumped tiredly against him when he wrapped an arm about her. She sighed deeply.

"Look." He pointed.

She did not say anything for a long while. Neither did he. Words were unnecessary. The Christmas star beamed down at them, symbol of hope, a sign for all who sought wisdom and the meaning of their lives. He was not sure what either of them had learned about Christmas this year, but there was something. It was beyond words at the moment and even beyond coherent thought. But something had been learned. Something had been gained.

"It is Christmas," she said softly at last. Her words held a wealth of meaning beyond themselves.

"Yes," he said, turning his face and kissing the untidy titian hair on top of her head. "Yes, it is Christmas. Did they have their daughter?"

"Oh yes," she said. "I have never seen two people so happy, my lord. On Christmas morning. Could there be a more precious gift?"

"I doubt it," he said, closing his eyes briefly.

"I held her," she said softly. "What a gift that was."

"Blanche," he asked after a short while, "where was this rectory you speak of? Close to the smithy?"

"Yes," she said.

"And you went to school there," he said, "and were given lessons in playing the spinet and delivering babies."

"Y-yes." She had the grace to sound hesitant.

"Blanche," he said, "I have the strange suspicion that you may be the biggest liar of my acquaintance."

She had nothing to say to that.

"Go and get ready for bed," he told her. "I am not sure whether it would be more accurate to say it is late or early."

She lifted her head then and looked at him. "Yes, my lord," she said—the martyr being brave.

He was in bed when she came from the dressing room, wearing the virginal nightgown again with her hair down her back. She was still looking brave, he saw in the dying light of the fire. She approached the bed without hesitation.

"Get in," he told her, holding back the bedcovers and stretching out his other arm beneath her pillow.

"Yes, my lord."

He turned her as she lay down, and drew her snugly against him in order to warm her. He tucked the bedcovers neatly behind her. He found her mouth with his own and kissed her with lingering thoroughness.

"Go to sleep now," he told her when he was done.

That brought her eyes snapping open. "But—" she began.

"But nothing," he said. "You are at the point of total exhaustion, Blanche, and would be quite unable either to enjoy or to be enjoyed. Go to sleep."

"But—" she began again, a protest he silenced with another kiss.

"I have no desire to hear about five hundred pounds and the necessity of earning it," he said. "You promised to be mine for a week, obedient to my will. This is my command for tonight, then. Go to sleep."

He waited for her protest. All he had instead was a quiet, almost soundless sigh, deepened breathing and total relaxation. She was asleep.

And the funny thing was, he thought, feeling her slim, shapely woman's body pressed to his from toes to forehead, he did not feel either frustrated or deprived. Quite the contrary. He felt warm and relaxed and sleepy, more like a man who had just had good sex than one who had had none at all.

He followed her into sleep.

Verity awoke a little later than usual in the morning. She snuggled sleepily into the warmth of the bed and then came fully awake when she realized that she was alone. She opened her eyes. He was gone. He was not in the room, either, she saw when she looked about.

It was Christmas morning.

He had slept with her last night. Just that. He had

slept with her. He had had her in bed with him, he had held her close, and he had told her to go to sleep. It had not taken her long to obey. But had there been tenderness in his arms and his kiss? Had she imagined it? Certainly there had been no anger.

He was a likable man, she thought suddenly, throwing back the covers and making for the dressing room. It was a surprising realization. She had thought him impossibly attractive from the start, of course. But she had not expected to find him a pleasant person. Certainly not a *kind* one.

She washed in the tepid water that stood on the washstand and dressed in the white wool dress she had made herself back in the autumn to wear after she left off her mourning. It was very simply styled, with a high neckline, straight long sleeves, and an unadorned skirt flaring from beneath her bosom. She liked its simplicity. She brushed her hair and dressed it in its usual knot at the back of her head. She took one last look at herself in the looking glass and hesitated.

Should she? She looked at the plain neckline of her dress.

She opened the drawer in which she had placed most of her belongings and stared at the box before drawing it out and opening it. It really was beautiful. It must have cost a fortune. Not that its charm lay in its monetary value. It was well crafted, tasteful. The chain was fine and delicate. It was easily the most lovely possession she had ever owned. She touched a finger to the star, withdrew, and then, after hesitating a moment longer, lifted the chain from its silken nesting place. She undid the catch, lowered her head and lifted her arms.

"Allow me," a voice said from behind her, and hands covered her own and took the chain from her.

She kept her head bent until he had secured the chain.

"Thank you," she said, and looked up into the glass.

His hands were on her shoulders. He was dressed with his usual immaculate elegance, she could see.

"It is beautiful," she told him. It really was the perfect ornament for the dress.

"Yes." He turned her to face him. "Is that sadness I see in your eyes, Blanche? It is where it belongs, you know. You have earned the right to wear the Christmas star on your bosom."

She smiled and touched a hand to it. "It is a lovely gift," she said. "I have something for you, too."

She had spoken entirely on impulse. When she left London, she had given no thought to a Christmas gift. She had expected him to be merely an employer, who would pay her for the unlimited use of her body. She had not expected him to become...yes, in some strange way he had become her friend. Someone she cared about. Someone who had shown her care.

She turned to the drawer and reached to the back of it. She could not believe she was about to give away such a treasure and to *him* of all people. And yet she knew that she wanted to do it, that it was the right thing to do. Not that it was either an elaborate or a costly gift. But it had been Papa's.

"Here," she said, holding it out to him on her palm. It was not even wrapped. "It is precious to me. It was my father's. He gave it to me when I left home. I want you to have it." All it was was a handkerchief, folded into a square. It was of the finest linen, it was true. But still only a handkerchief.

He transferred it to his own palm and then looked into her eyes. "I believe," he said, "your gift might be more valuable than mine, Blanche. Mine only cost money. You have given away part of yourself. Thank you. I will treasure it."

"Happy Christmas, my lord," she said.

"And to you." He leaned toward her and set his lips against hers in what was a gentle and achingly sweet kiss. "Happy Christmas, Blanche."

And she felt happy, she thought, even though her thoughts had gone to her mother and Chastity, celebrating the day without her. But they had each other, and she had…

"I wonder how the baby is this morning," she said eagerly. "I can scarcely wait to see her again. Did she sleep? I wonder. Did Mrs. Moffatt sleep? And have the little boys met their new sister yet? I wonder if their papa will have time to spend with them today. It is Christmas Day, such an important day for children. Perhaps—"

"Perhaps, Blanche," Viscount Folingsby said, looking and sounding his bored, cynical self again suddenly, "you will conceive ideas again, as you did yesterday, for everyone's delectation. I do not doubt that the boys and the rest of us will be worn to a thread by the time you have finished with us.''

"But did you not enjoy yesterday?" she asked him. Surely he had. "It is *Christmas,* my lord, and Mr. Hollander had made no plans to celebrate it. What choice did I have? Poor man, I daresay he has always had a mother or some other relatives to plan the holiday for him.''

"Precisely." He sighed. "It was our idea to escape such plans this year, Blanche. To spend a quiet week instead with the women of our choice. Not gathering greenery in the teeth of a blizzard, but making love in a warm bed. Not loading down the house with Christmas cheer and making merry noise with Christmas carols and entertaining energetic little boys and delivering babies, but—well, making love in a warm bed.''

"You did *not* enjoy yesterday," she said, dismayed. "And you *are* disappointed. I *have* failed you. And I have ruined the holiday for Mr. Hollander, too. And—'' He had set two fingers firmly against her lips.

"The baby slept through the night," he said, "and has only just begun to fuss. Mrs. Moffatt had a few hours of sleep and declares herself to be refreshed and in the best of health this morning. The Reverend Moffatt is in transports of delight and proclaims himself to be the most fortunate man alive—as well as the cleverest, I do believe—to have begotten a daughter.

"The little boys have been given their gifts and have met their sister, with whom they seem far less impressed than their papa. They are roaring around the sitting room, obeying the paternal command to confine their energies to it until they hear otherwise. Cook is banging around the kitchen with great zeal and has every other servant moving at a brisk trot. Bertie and Debbie have not yet put in an appearance. I daresay they are making love in a warm bed. And you are looking more beautiful than any woman has any right to look. Virginal white becomes you."

"I am sorry it is not the Christmas you intended," she said.

"Are you?" He smiled lazily. "I am not sure I am, Blanche. Sorry, I mean. It is an interesting Christmas, to say the very least. And it is not over yet. *Do* you have plans for us?"

She felt herself flush. "Well," she said, "I did think that since there are children here and their mother is indisposed and their father will wish to spend much of the day with her…and I thought that since there are still heaps of snow out there even though no more is falling…and I thought that since the rest of us have nothing particular to do all day except…" Her cheeks grew hotter.

"Make love in a warm bed?" he suggested.

"Yes," she said. "Except that. I thought that perhaps we could…that is, unless you wish to do the other. I am quite willing. It is what I came here to do, after all."

He was grinning at her. "Outdoor sports," he said.

"I wonder how Bertie and Debbie will greet the happy prospect?"

"Well," she said, "they cannot spend *all* day in bed, can they? It would not be at all polite to the Reverend and Mrs. Moffatt."

He merely chuckled. "Let the day begin," he said, offering her his arm. "I would not miss it for the world, you know, or even for all the warm beds in the world, for that matter."

Chapter Seven

Julian did not change his mind all through the day though he had hardly exaggerated when he had predicted that Blanche would have run them all ragged before they were done with Christmas.

As soon as breakfast was over, they took the children outside to play in the snow. *They* being he and Blanche until Bertie and Debbie came out to join them. They romped in the snow for what seemed only minutes but must have been hours until Bloggs appeared to inform them that their Christmas dinner was ready. His expression suggested also that Cook would have their heads if they did not come immediately to partake of it.

But long before that they had engaged in a vigorous snowball fight, which turned out to be grossly unfair in Julian's estimation—and he complained loudly about it—as he and Bertie were pitted against both boys as well as both the ladies, two against four. And if Debbie had ever been a member of a rifle regiment, there would surely not be a Frenchman left in France without a hole through his heart. She had a deadly accurate aim and was wildly cheered by her side, and herself, whenever she demonstrated it.

They built snowmen. Or at least Julian and Bertie did while the boys danced around "helping" and Debbie ran off to beg ashes and carrots and one ancient straw hat from the kitchen. Blanche, reclining on a snowbank, declared that as judge she had the hardest job of all. She awarded the prize of one leftover carrot to Bertie and David.

They made snow angels until Rupert declared with loud disgust that it was a girl's game. Blanche and Debbie continued with the sport notwithstanding while the men constructed a long slippery slide on a bit of a slope and risked their necks zooming along it. Somehow Julian ended up with David on his shoulders, clinging to his hair after his hat had proved to be an untrustworthy anchor. The child whooped with mingled fright and glee.

Debbie sought out the tree swing, brushed the snow off it and cleared a path beneath it before summoning everyone else. They all sampled its delights, singly and in pairs, all of them as noisy and exuberant as children. The adults continued even after the children had rushed away at the appearance of their father to bury him up to his neck in snow.

"The snow is starting to melt," Blanche said wistfully as they were going indoors for dinner. "How sad."

"It is in the nature of snow," Julian said, wrapping one arm about her waist. "Just as it is in the nature of time to pass. That is why we have memories.''

"The children have had a marvelous morning, have they not?'' she said, beaming happily at him.

"Now to which children are you referring?'' he asked, kissing her cold red nose. "To the very little ones? Or to the rest of us? For myself I would as soon have been sitting with my feet up before a roaring fire.''

She merely laughed.

Christmas dinner proved to be a culinary delight beyond compare. They all ate until they were close to bursting and then Bertie sent for the cook and made a rather pompous speech of congratulation.

But that was not enough for Blanche, of course. If Mr. Hollander would be so good, she suggested, perhaps all the staff could be invited to the sitting room for a drink of the excellent wassail. She for one would like to thank them all for the hard work they had put into giving everyone such a wonderful Christmas.

"I can only echo your sentiments, Lady Folingsby,'' the Reverend Moffatt remarked. "Though by my observations, the servants are not the only ones who have been hard at work. My wife and I will not soon forget the warm welcome we have received here and the efforts you have all put into entertaining our children. Not to mention last night for which we will never be able to repay you, my lady, and you, Mrs. Hollander. We will not try, of course, as we know that you acted out of the goodness of your hearts. We humbly accept the gift from two true ladies.''

Debbie sniffled and blew her nose in the handkerchief Bertie handed her. ''That is one of the nicest things anyone ever said to me,'' she said. ''But it was Blanche who did all the work.''

The servants spent the best part of an hour in the sitting room, eating cakes and mince pies and drinking wassail and accepting Christmas bonuses from their employer, as well as from both Julian and the Reverend Moffatt. Julian was never afterward sure who suggested singing Christmas carols again, though he did not doubt it was Blanche. They did so anyway to her accompaniment on the spinet and sang themselves into a thoroughly genial and sentimental mood.

And then after the servants had gone back below stairs, Mrs. Moffatt made a surprise appearance in the sitting room with the baby.

Julian had always been fond of children. He had had to be, for there had always been enough of them at family gatherings to make life miserable for anyone who was not. But he had never been much for infants or newborns. They were a woman's preserve, he had always thought, needing only to be fed and rocked and sung to and changed.

But he felt a certain proprietary interest in the little Moffatt girl, he discovered. Her birth had somehow brought Christmas alive for him more than ever before. And Blanche had delivered her. And now Blanche was holding her and gazing down at her with such a look of tenderness in her face that he felt dazzled. She looked so right thus, dressed with simple elegance, glowing with health and vitality and warmth, holding a newborn infant in her arms.

If it were her child, his...

He jerked his mind free of such an alarming daydream and found himself gazing deep into her eyes. She smiled at him.

Ah, Blanche. It was hard to believe that just a week ago he had looked on her only as a desirable candidate for his bed. He had seen her beauty—the long, shapely legs, the taut slender body, the glorious hair and lovely face—and not given even one moment's consideration to the fact that there must be a person behind the facade.

And what a person was there. Even more beautiful, perhaps, than the body in which she resided.

He was in love with her, he thought in some astonishment. He had never been in love before. He had been in lust more times than he could recall and had sometimes called it love, especially when he had been younger. But he had never before felt this ache of longing for a *person*. It was not just that he wished to bed her, though he did, of course. It was more than that. Much more. He wanted to be a part of her, a part of her life, not just a very temporary occupant of her body.

He smiled back at her a little uncertainly.

"I daresay," Mrs. Moffatt said, having noticed perhaps the exchange of smiles, "you and her ladyship have not been married long, my lord." Not long enough for the union to have been fruitful, her words implied.

"Not long, ma'am," he agreed.

He was glad, he thought some hours later, after tea, after the vigorous indoor games Blanche and the Reverend Moffatt had organized for the amusement of the children and everyone else that he had not gone to Conway for Christmas. He had been thinking about it on and off all day and had been missing his family. Had his Christmas gone according to plan, he realized now, he would be regretting his decision. The sort of activity he had planned would not have been any way to celebrate such an occasion. But as events had turned out, he had discovered everything one was surely meant to discover at Christmas— love, hospitality, merriment, kindness, sharing, decency... The list could go on and on.

Sometimes it seemed almost as if one were led blind by some guiding hand toward something for which one had not known one searched. By a star perhaps. To the stable at Bethlehem perhaps. Perhaps he had more in common with the wise men than he had realized until this moment.

The children, yawning and protesting, were finally led away by their father to bed after hugging their adopted "uncles" and "aunts" as if they had known them all their lives.

"I do not believe we will be far behind them, Deb," Bertie said, yawning hugely after they had left. "Have you enjoyed Christmas?"

"Ee, love," Debbie said, "it has been the grandest

Christmas since I left home. Maybe grander than then. The Rev is the kindest of gents and the boys are darlings. And the baby! I will never forget last night. I never will. It has been a Christmas to end Christmases.''

"I believe," Bertie said, pulling her down onto his lap, perhaps feeling free to do so since the clergyman had expressed his intention of joining his wife and the baby after he had put the boys to bed, "we have you to thank for much of the joy of the past two days, Blanche."

"Oh," she said, "how foolish. It is Christmas. Christmas has a way of happening without any assistance from anyone."

"Nonsense," Julian said. "It needed a whole host of angels to get the shepherds moving off their hillside. It has taken one angel to set us off on a similar pilgrimage."

"Do you mean me?" she asked, blushing. "A strange angel indeed. One with very tarnished wings."

He got to his feet and held out a hand for hers. "It has been a long day," he said, "and you had only a few hours of sleep last night. It is bedtime."

Her eyes met his as she took his hand. There was not even a hint of martyrdom in their expression.

"Good night, Mr. Hollander," she said as the two couples took their leave of one another. "Good night, Debbie. Thank you for helping make Christmas such a joy."

He was standing at the window when she came out of the dressing room. He was wearing a nightshirt. The room was warm from the fire that had been built high.

"Is the star still there?" she asked him, going to stand at his side and looking up.

"Gone," he said. "Or merely hidden by clouds. It is warming up out there. The snow will disappear rapidly tomorrow."

"Ah." She sighed. "Christmas is over."

"Not quite." He set an arm about her, and she rested her head on his shoulder. It felt perfectly right to do so. She felt strangely comfortable with him as if, perhaps, she had come to believe the myth that they belonged together. She had even found herself imagining downstairs during the afternoon that that newborn baby was hers, theirs.

"Blanche," he said softly.

And then they were in each other's arms, pressed together, kissing each other with such passion that it seemed indeed that they were one, that they were not meant to be two separate beings, that they would find wholeness and happiness and peace only together like this.

"Blanche." He was kissing her temples, her jaw, her throat, her mouth again. "Ah, my dear one."

It was not enough to touch him with her mouth, her tongue, her arms, her hands. She touched him with her breasts, her hips, her abdomen, her thighs. She wanted...ah, she wanted and wanted. He was warm and hard muscled. He smelled musky and male. And he felt safe, solid, dependable. He felt like a missing part of herself for which she craved. She wanted him. She wanted wholeness.

She did not know how her nightgown had become unbuttoned down the front. She did not care. She needed him closer. She needed his hands and then his mouth on her breasts. She needed...ah, yes.

"Ah, yes," she said from somewhere deep in her throat, and she twined her fingers in his hair and tipped her head back as he suckled first one nipple and then the other, sucking gently, laving the tips with his tongue, sending raw aches down between her thighs and up through her throat into her nostrils. "Ah, yes. Please." Her knees no longer quite belonged to her.

"Come, my love," he whispered against her mouth, lifting her into his arms. "Come to bed."

He slid her nightgown down over her feet after setting her down and pulled his nightshirt off over his head. She gazed at him in the flickering light of the fire, her eyes half-closed. He was beautiful, beautiful.

"Come." She lifted her arms to him. "Come."

His hands and his mouth moved over her, worshiping her, arousing her. She touched him, explored him, rejoiced in the feel of him, the heat of him. But she could not touch him *there* though she became increasingly aware of that part of him, thick and long and hard. He touched her where she had never thought to be touched with a hand, with fingers. She felt an ache so intense it was pain and pleasure all strangely mixed together. And she heard wetness and was curiously unembarrassed.

She could not wait—for she knew not what.

"Please," she begged him, her voice sounding not quite her own. "Please."

"Yes," he said, coming to her open arms, coming down into them, coming down between her thighs, pressing them apart with his own, coming heavy and warm and eager to her nakedness. "Yes, my love. Yes."

She would not believe at first that it could be possible. He pressed against her and she was almost surprised, although she knew her own body, when he found an opening there and pushed into it, stretching her wide, not stopping, coming and coming.

"Don't tense," he murmured against her ear. "Just relax. Ah, my dear one, my love. I don't want to hurt you."

But it did not hurt. Not really. It only surprised her and filled her with wonder and gave her a moment's panic when she thought he could come no farther but he pressed on. There was what she expected to be pain, and then he pressed past it until he was deep, deep inside. She lifted her legs from the bed and twined them about his. He moaned.

And then, just when she thought ecstasy had been arrived at and finally relaxed, he moved. He moved to leave her.

"No," she murmured in protest.

He lifted his head, looked down into her face and kissed her. "Yes," he said. "Like this, you see."

And from the brink of her he pressed deep again. And withdrew and pressed deep.

Final ecstasy came several minutes or hours later—time no longer had any meaning—after they had loved together with sweet, strong rhythm, with a sharing of bodies and pleasure, with a mingling of selves. It came with a building of almost unbearable need, with an involuntary tightening of every inner muscle, and with a final relinquishing of self, a final trust in the power of union. It came as shivering relaxation and quiet peace. It came with shared words.

"My sweet life," he whispered. "My dear angel."

"My love," she heard herself murmuring. "My love, my love."

She fell asleep moments later, after he had drawn out of her and rolled onto his side, taking her with him and keeping her against him. Just after he drew the bedcovers warmly about her.

Julian did not fall sleep for a long while, even though he lay in a pleasant lethargy. He was sexually sated. He was also deeply happy.

He had never set much store by happiness. It was strange, perhaps, when for all his adult years he had directed almost all his energies into activities that would bring him pleasure or gratification in varying degrees. But he had never really believed in *happiness*. He had never either expected or craved it for himself.

Happiness, he thought, was a feeling of rightness, of having arrived at a place one had always sought, however halfheartedly, but never quite believed existed. With a person of whose existence one had always dreamed, even if not always consciously, but had never thought to find. Happiness was a moment in time when one was at peace with life and the universe, when one felt one had found the meaning of one's existence. And it was more than a moment. It was a direction for the rest of life, an assurance that the future, though not, of course, a happily ever after, would nevertheless be well worth living.

He had never really believed in romantic love.

But he was in love with Blanche Heyward.

There was more to it than that, though. He would perhaps, even now, have laughed at himself if that had been all. But it was not. He *loved* her. She had become in the course of a few days—though he felt he had known her from the eternity before birth—as essential to his life as the air he breathed.

Fanciful thoughts. He would be writing a poem to her left eyebrow if he did not watch himself. He mocked himself as he smoothed the hair back from her sleeping face and settled her head more comfortably in the hollow between his neck and shoulder. He had been teased by her for a few days, that was all, and had finally had very good sex indeed with her. In a few weeks' time, when they were back in London and he had set her up properly as his mistress, he would already be tiring of her. He had quickly tired of every mistress he had ever kept.

He kissed her brow and then her lips. She made little protesting sounds but did not wake.

No, it was not so. He wished it were. She was a blacksmith's daughter and an opera dancer. He was a viscount, heir to an earldom. No other relationship was possible between them but that of protector and mistress. He could not...

But as he stared into the darkness, lit only by the dying embers of the fire, he knew that there was one thing he would never be able to do. He could never marry anyone else. Ever. Even though he owed it to his father to secure the succession for the next generation. Even though he owed it to his mother and his sisters to secure their future. Even though he owed it to his birth, his upbringing, his position.

If he could not marry Blanche—and he did not see how he ever could—then he would not marry anyone.

Perhaps he would see things differently tomorrow, next week, next year. He did not know. All he did know now was that he loved, that he was happy, that—he had been led to one of those earth-shattering experiences one sometimes read about that had changed the whole direction of his life.

He would wake her up later, he decided, and make slow, lazy love to her again. And if they stayed awake afterward, he would take the risk of telling her how he felt. It was no very great risk, he thought. She felt about him as he felt about her. That was a part of the miracle. Unworthy as he was of her, she felt as he did. *My love,* she had called him over and over again as he had spilled his seed into her. And her body had told him the same thing even if she had not spoken the words aloud, and their minds and their very souls had intertwined as their bodies had merged.

Later he would love her again. In the meantime he slept.

Not for one moment did Verity feel disoriented when she awoke. Neither did she entertain any illusions.

She had given in to naïveté and passion and the sentimentality that had surrounded Christmas. She had given in to a practiced seducer. Not that she would have resisted even if she had realized the truth at the time. She would not have done so. She would have given her body just as unprotestingly. She would have done so as part of the bargain she had made with him in London. But she would have guarded her heart. She would not so foolishly have imagined that it was a love encounter.

He had been a man claiming his mistress.

She had been a woman at work, earning her pay.

And now, beyond all argument, she was a fallen woman. A whore. She had done it for Chastity. Strange irony, that. But that fact notwithstanding, she was and always would be a whore.

She could not bear to face him in the morning. She could not bear to see the knowing look in his eyes, the triumph. She could not bear to play a part. She could not bear to become his regular mistress, to be used at his convenience until he tired of her and discarded her. She could not even bear to finish out this week, after which she would be free to withdraw from any future commitment.

Perhaps at the end of the week she would not have the strength to do so.

She could not bear to face him in the morning and see from his whole attitude how little their encounter had meant to him.

She had no choice but to live out the week. Even if there were a way of leaving now, she still had two hundred and fifty pounds to earn. And he had already paid her that same amount. Had she earned that advance? With what had happened here a few hours ago? With her willingness to allow it to happen on the two previous nights? *Two hundred and fifty pounds?* If she were a governess, she would be fortunate to earn that amount in four years.

There *was* a way of leaving. There was a village three miles away. A stagecoach stopped there early each morning. She had heard the servants mention it. But there was snow on the ground. And would the stage run on the day after Christmas? The snow had been melting since yesterday afternoon. It had been a cloudy night, perhaps a mild night. Why would the stage *not* run?

She would surely wake him if she tried to get out of bed, if she tried to dress and creep away.

But now that the mad, impossible idea had entered her mind, she could not leave it alone. She *could* not face him in the morning. If she felt nothing for him, she would do so with all the cheerful good sense she could muster. She had taken this employment quite deliberately, after all, knowing what was involved. She had been prepared to do what she had done with him earlier as many times as he chose. It was not from that she shrank.

In her naïveté she had not realized that her feelings might become involved. It had not occurred to her that spending a few days in close proximity with a man would reveal him to her as a person, or that she would find this particular man likable, charming, lovable. She had never for one moment expected to fall in love. She had done even worse than that. She had *loved* and still did and always would.

After removing herself from his arms while he grumbled sleepily, she edged her way across and then out of the bed. The room was cold, she realized, shivering, and she was naked and stiff. She silently gathered up her nightgown from the floor and tiptoed to the dressing room, the door of which was fortunately ajar. She slipped inside and shut the door slowly. Fortunately the hinges were well oiled and made no sound.

She lit a single candle, washed quickly in the ice-cold water, dressed in her warmest clothes, packed her belongings, and wondered if her luck would hold while she tried to leave the house undetected.

She had not packed everything. She had left his signet ring on the washstand. And one other thing. She wasted several precious moments gazing at it, spread across the top of the chest of drawers, where she had put it the night before. Should she take it? She wanted desperately to do so. It would be the one memento. But she would not need a memento. And it had been too extravagant a gift, especially under the circumstances.

She set one fingertip lightly to the gold star on its chain and then left it where it was. She did not go back into the bedchamber. There was a door leading directly from the dressing room to the corridor beyond.

It had always seemed rather silly, she thought as she made her way cautiously downstairs and let herself out of the front door, to talk about a heart aching. How could a heart *ache?* But this morning it no longer seemed silly. She hurried along the driveway to the road, past the still-stuck carriage, relieved to see that the snow had melted sufficiently that she should be able to walk to the village without any great difficulty.

Her heart ached for a little gold star and chain that would fit into the palm of her hand. And for the Christmas star that had brought such joy and such hope this year and had lured her into a great foolishness. And for the man who she hoped was still asleep where she had slept with him a mere half hour ago.

She would never see him again, if only she was in time for the stage. *Never* could sometimes be a terrifying word.

She would love him forever.

Chapter Eight

It took Julian three months to find her. Though even then he had the merest glimpse of her only to lose her again without a trace, it seemed. Just as he had lost her on Christmas night.

He had woken up by daylight and been half amused, half exasperated to find her gone from bed and from their room. He had washed and shaved and dressed in leisurely fashion, hoping she would return before he was ready, and had then gone in search of her. Even when he had not found her in any of the day rooms or in the kitchen he had not been alarmed, or even when he had peered out of doors and not seen her walking there. He had assumed she must be in the only possible place left, Mrs. Moffatt's room, admiring the baby.

The morning had been well advanced before he had discovered the truth. She was gone and so were all her possessions except the star and chain. He had picked up the necklace, squeezed it tight in his palm and tipped back his head in silent agony.

She had left him.

Why?

He had returned to London the same day, having concocted a whole arsenal of new lies for the edification of Bertie, Debbie and the Moffatts. And so had begun his search for her. She had left her job at the opera without a word to anyone there. She had not gone to any other theater—he had checked them all. And none of her former co-workers knew of her whereabouts. They had not seen or heard of her since before Christmas.

Eventually he bribed the manager of the opera house to give him her address, but it was a false one. There was no one by the name of Blanche Heyward living there, the landlady informed him, and no one of her description, either, except that Miss Ewing, who used to live there, had been tall. But Miss Ewing had been no opera dancer and nor had any other lady who had ever rented her house. The very idea! She had glared at him with indignation. He became almost desperate enough to travel down to Somersetshire in search of the smithy that had been her home. But how many smithies must there be in Somersetshire?

Blanche clearly did not want to be found.

He tried to put her from his mind. Christmas had been an unusually pleasurable interlude, largely thanks to Blanche, and sleeping with her had been the icing on an already scrumptious cake. But really there was no more to it than that. One could not carry Christmas about with one all year long, after all. One had to get back to the mundane business of everyday life.

But he did at the end of January make a three-day visit to Conway, where he was greeted with such affection by his parents and such a scold from his youngest sister that he almost lost his courage. He found it again when sitting alone with his father in the library one afternoon. He would not marry Lady Sarah Plunkett, he had announced quite firmly. And before his father could draw breath to ask him—as he was obviously about to do—whom he *would* marry then, he had added that there was only one woman in the world he would consider marrying, but she would not marry him and anyway she was ineligible.

"Ineligible?" his father had asked, eyebrows raised.

"Daughter of a blacksmith," his son had told him.

"Of a *blacksmith.*" His father had pursed his lips. "And *she* will not marry *you,* Julian? She has more sense than you."

"I love her," Julian had said.

"Hmm" was all the comment his father had made. Perhaps that was all the comment he had thought necessary since the marriage seemed in no danger of becoming a reality.

Back in London Julian had searched hopelessly, aimlessly, until the afternoon in March when he spotted her on a crowded Oxford Street. She was on the opposite side of the street, coming out of a milliner's shop. He came to an abrupt halt, unable to believe the evidence of his own eyes. But then her eyes locked on his and he knew he was not mistaken. He started forward as she turned abruptly and hurried away along the pavement.

At the same moment a gentleman's curricle and a tradesman's wagon decided to dispute the right-of-way along the street, whose width had been narrowed by the presence of a large carriage picking up two passengers loaded with parcels. They confronted each other head-on and refused to budge an inch for each other.

The tradesman swore foully and the gentleman only a little more elegantly; the horses protested in the way horses did best. A whole host of bystanders took sides or merely gathered to enjoy the spectacle, and Julian got caught up in the tangle for a few seconds too long. He was across the street in less than a minute, but during that minute Blanche Heyward had disappeared totally. He hurried along the street in the direction she had taken, peering into every shop and along every alley. But there was no sign of her. Or of the young girl who had been with her.

One thing was clear to him. If she had ever regretted running away from Bertie's hunting box, she regretted it no longer. She had no wish to be found. She had no wish even to claim the second half of her week's salary.

She had played the martyr after all, then, on that night and with such courage that he had not even known that she played a part. Fool that he was, he had thought her feelings matched his own. He had thought she enjoyed losing her virginity to a rake who had paid for her favors. What a fool!

He gave up looking for her. Let her live out her life in peace. He just hoped that the two hundred and fifty pounds had proved sufficient to cover whatever need at the smithy had impelled her to accept his proposition, and that there had been some left over for her.

But his resolve slipped when he attended a rout at his eldest sister's in April. Her drawing room and the two salons that had been opened up for the occasion were gratifyingly full, she told him, her arm drawn through his as she led him through. New families were arriving in town every day for the season. But he drew her to a sudden halt.

"Who is that?" he asked, indicating with a nod of the head a thin, pretty young girl who was standing with an older lady and with General Sir Hector Ewing and his wife.

"The general?" she asked. "You do not know him, Julian? He—"

"The young girl with him," he said.

She looked archly at him and smiled. "She *is* pretty, is she not?" she said. "She is the general's niece, Miss Chastity Ewing."

Ewing. *Ewing!* The name of the tall lady who had lived at the false address given to the opera house manager by Blanche Heyward. And Miss Chastity Ewing was the young lady who had been with Blanche on Oxford Street.

"I have an acquaintance with the general, Elinor,"

he said, "but not a close one. Present me to Miss Ewing, if you please."

"Smitten after one glance," his sister said with a laugh. "This is *very* interesting, Julian. Come along, then."

"Who?" Verity asked faintly. She had waited up for Chastity even though it was late and even though they no longer shared a room. She was sitting on her sister's bed.

"Viscount Folingsby," Chastity said. "At least I think I have the name correct. He is Lady Blanchford's brother. He is *very* handsome and *very* charming, Verity."

There was a slight buzzing in her head. It had been almost inevitable, of course. She knew that he was in London—she had *seen* him—and that therefore, he would attend ton events, especially now that the season was beginning. Since her uncle had returned from Vienna the week after Christmas, brought them all to live with him, and was now undertaking to introduce Chastity to society, then Chass would surely attend some of the same balls and parties as he. Verity had just hoped that pretty and healthy as Chastity was, she would be just too youthful to attract the notice of Viscount Folingsby.

"Is he?" she said in answer to her sister's words.

But Chastity was smiling at her with bright mischief and came to sit on the bed beside her, still clad in her evening gown. "Of course he is," she said. "You know him, Verity."

Her heart performed a somersault. "Oh?" she said. "Do I?"

Chastity laughed merrily and clapped her hands. "Of course you do," she said, "and I can tell from your guilty expression that you remember him very well. He *told* us. About Christmas."

Verity could feel the blood draining out of her head, leaving it cold and clammy and dizzy.

Chastity took one of her sister's cold, nerveless hands in her own. "Dear Verity," she said. "I daresay you have convinced yourself that he did not really notice you. But I knew it would happen sooner or later. I *told* you, did I not? How could any gentleman look at your beauty and not be struck by it and by *you*. No matter who you were."

"Does Mama know?" Verity was whispering.

"Of course," Chastity said, laughing gleefully. "She was there with me and our uncle."

"*Uncle* knows?" They would all be turned out on the street tomorrow, she thought. Was there any way of persuading him to dismiss her alone? She had already displeased him by refusing to participate in any of the social entertainments of the season. She had pleaded advanced age. Could Mama and Chastity be saved?

"The viscount knew that Lady Coleman went to Scotland the day after Christmas," Chastity said. "He assumed you had gone with her. Imagine his surprise and gratification to learn that you had not, that you were here in London."

"What?" There *was* no Lady Coleman, and he did not know her as Verity Ewing.

"Oh, Verity, you silly goose." Chastity raised her sister's hand to her cheek and held it there. "Did you think he would not notice you because you were merely a lady's companion? Did you think he would not wish to renew the acquaintance? He told Mama how you quietly set about making everyone's Christmas comfortable and joyful, not just Lady Coleman's. He told us about the clergyman's family being stranded and about you delivering the baby. Oh, Verity, why did you not tell us about that? And he confessed to Mama that he had kissed you beneath the kissing bough. He has the most roguish smile."

"Oh," Verity said.

"And you thought he would forget you?" Chastity said. "He has not forgotten. He asked Mama if he might call upon you. And he asked Uncle for a private word. They went walking off together. Verity, he is *wonderful*. Almost wonderful enough for you, I do believe. Viscountess Folingsby. Yes." She laughed again. "It will suit. I declare it will. And *now* I know why you have refused to go into society. You have been afraid of meeting him. You have been afraid he would not remember you. You goose!"

Verity could only cling to her sister's hand and stare wide-eyed. He knew who she was! Somehow Mama or Chastity must have mentioned Lady Coleman to him and he had played along with the game. And he wanted to see her. Why? To pay her the rest of her salary? But she had not earned it. To demand part of the other half back, then? The irony of that was that her sacrifice had been unnecessary. Her uncle had taken over their care and the payment of Chastity's medical bills within two days of her return to London.

Perhaps he wanted her to earn what he had already paid her. Perhaps he wanted her to be his mistress here, in town. But he knew she was General Sir Hector Ewing's niece.

She did not *want* to see him. The very thought of doing so was enough to throw her into a panic, as the reality had that afternoon on Oxford Street.

And yet in almost four months the pain had not diminished even one iota. It only seemed to grow worse. She had even found herself bitterly disappointed, as well as knee-weakeningly relieved, when she had discovered that their one encounter had not borne fruit.

"Verity." Her sister's eyes were softly glowing. "You *have* remembered him. You are in love with him. Do not think you can deceive me. How splendid this is. How very romantic. It is like a fairy tale."

Verity snatched her hand away and jumped to her feet. "Foolish girl," she said. "It is high time you were asleep. You have recovered your health even if you are still just a little too thin, but you must not tax your strength. Go to bed now. Turn around and let me undo your buttons."

But Chastity was not so easily distracted. She got to her feet, too, and flung her arms about her sister. Her eyes shone with tears. "I am healthy because of the sacrifice you made for me," she said. "I will never *ever* forget what I owe you, Verity. But you are going to be rewarded. You never would have met him if you had not taken employment with Lady Coleman and if you had not given up your Christmas with us to go away with her. So you see it is a just reward. And I am so happy I could *weep*."

"Go to bed and to sleep," Verity said firmly. "You are drawing far too many conclusions from Viscount Folingsby's courtesy this evening. Besides, I do not like him above half."

Chastity was laughing softly as she left the room.

Verity stood against the door of her own room after she had closed it behind her, her eyes tight shut.

He had found her. But did she want to be found? Perhaps, after all, she needed to be. There was a yawning emptiness in her life, a sense of something unresolved, unfinished. Perhaps it should be finished. She did not know quite why he wished to see her—certainly not for any of the reasons Chastity imagined—but perhaps she should find out. Perhaps if she saw him again, if she found out exactly what it was he wanted of her, she would finally be able to close the book on that episode from the past and move on into the future.

Perhaps she would be able to stop loving him.

He had spoken with her uncle the evening before. He had met him again during the morning in order to discuss and settle details. And now, this afternoon, he had spoken with her mother. Mrs. Ewing had gone to send her daughter down to the visitors' salon in which he waited, feeling more nervous than he had ever felt in his life before.

The door opened and closed quietly. She stood against it, her hands behind her, probably still gripping the knob. She was dressed in pale green muslin, a dress of simple design. Her hair was dressed plainly, too. She had lost some weight and some color. But even if she tried twice as hard she would never be able to disguise the fact that she was an extraordinarily beautiful woman. He made her his most elegant bow.

"Miss Ewing?" he said.

She stared at him for several moments before releasing her hold on the knob and curtsying. "My lord."

"Miss *Verity* Ewing," he said. "You were misnamed."

She had nothing to say to that.

"Verity," he said.

"I have two hundred pounds left," she told him then, her voice soft, her chin up, her shoulders back. "I have not needed it after all. I will return it to you. I hope you will agree to forget the fifty pounds. I did partly earn it, after all."

The younger girl had been ill. Verity Ewing had taken employment in order to pay the physician's bills and to buy medicines. She had worked as a companion to Lady Coleman. She had done it for her sister.

"I believe your virginity was worth fifty pounds," he said. "Where is the rest?"

"Here."

She carried a small reticule over her arm, he saw. She opened it and took a roll of banknotes from it. She held them out to him and then brought them to him when he did not move. He took the money with one hand and the reticule with the other and set them down on the chair beside him.

"You are satisfied now?" he asked her. "It is all finished now?"

She nodded, looking down at the money. "I should have returned it to you before," she said. "I did not know quite how. I am sorry."

"Verity," he said softly. "My love."

She closed her eyes and kept them closed. "No," she said. "It is finished. I will not be your mistress. I will always be a...a fallen woman, but I will not be your mistress. Please leave now. And thank you for not exposing me to my mother and sister. Or to my uncle."

"My love." He was not at all sure of himself. Verity Ewing, alias Blanche Heyward, was, as he knew from experience, a woman of strong will and firm character. "Must I go? Or may I stay—forever? Will you marry me?"

She opened her eyes then and raised them to his chin. She smiled. "Ah," she said, "of course. I am a gentleman's daughter and you are a gentleman. No, my lord, you do not have to do the decent thing. I will not expose you, either, you see."

"It was your first time," he told her. "I could not expect you to understand, you had not the experience. Usually when sex is purchased, it is simply for pleasure, on the man's part at least. It was pleasing, was it not? For both of us? But it was more. In a sense it was my first time too, you see. I had never made love before.

"What happened *was* love, Verity. I knew with my body while we loved, with my mind after it was over, that you had become the air I breathed, the life I lived, the soul I cherished. I thought you felt the same. It did not occur to me that perhaps you did not until I discovered that you had left me. Did you feel as much pain on that day, I wonder, as I did? I have never felt an agony more intense."

"I was a blacksmith's daughter," she said, "an opera dancer, and a whore. What you would have offered then would have been far less than marriage. I have not changed, my lord. I am the daughter of a clergyman, but I am still a whore. I will not be your mistress or your wife."

He possessed himself of both her hands. They were like ice. "You will scrape together the money," he said fiercely. "The fifty pounds. Every penny of it. I want it returned. And then I will hear you take back that ugly name you call yourself. Tell me something. And tell me the truth, *Verity*. Why did you allow me to bed you that night? Were you a working girl earning her pay? Or were you a woman making love, giving and receiving love without a thought to money? Which was it? *Look* at me."

She raised her eyes to his.

"Tell me." He was whispering, he realized. The whole of his future, the whole of his happiness depended upon her reply. He was far from sure of what it would be.

"How could I not love you?" she said. "They were magical days. And I was taken off guard. I went there with a cynical, arrogant rake. And I discovered there a warm, gentle, fun-loving, caring man. I have no experience with such situations, my lord. How could I not love you with my body and my heart and everything that is me? It did not once occur to me as *that* was happening that I was becoming a whore."

"You were not," he told her. "You were becoming mine as I was becoming yours. What we did was wrong. It should not have been done outside wedlock. But worse sins than that can be forgiven, I believe. Let me say one more thing before I plead with you again. I visited my father at Conway Hall after Christmas. He is the Earl of Grantham. Did you know that? I am his heir.

"He has been very eager for some time for me to marry and produce an heir since I have no brothers. I love my father, Verity. And I know my duty to him and to my position. But I told him that I could never marry anyone but you. That was when I still thought you the daughter of a blacksmith and an opera dancer. I *never* thought of you as a whore. What we did in bed together was love, not business."

"And how did your father reply?" she asked.

He smiled at her. "My father loves me, Verity. My happiness is important to him. In our family love has always been of more importance than duty. He would have given his blessing—a little reluctantly, it is true—to my marriage even to a blacksmith's daughter."

She dropped her glance again to stare down at their joined hands. He squeezed hers tightly and his heart hammered painfully against his chest.

"My love," he said. "Verity. Miss Ewing. Will you do me the great honor of marrying me?"

She kept her head down. "It was Christmas," she said. "Everything looks different at Christmas. More rosy, more possible, more unreal. This is a mistake. You should not have come. I do not know how you discovered who I am."

"I believe," he said, "the mistake is ours, Verity. We act as if Christmas is for one day of the year only, as if peace and hope and happiness can exist only then. It was not meant to be that way. Was all that business at Bethlehem intended to bring joy to the world for just one day of the year? What little trust we have in our religion. How little we demand of it and give to it. Why can it not be Christmas now, today, for you and me?"

"Because it is not," she said.

He released her hands then and reached into an inner pocket of his coat. "Yes, it is," he said. "It will be. How about this?" He held in his palm the linen handkerchief she had given him as a gift. He unfolded it carefully until she could see the gold star on its chain nestled within.

"Oh," she said softly.

"Do you remember what you said about it when I gave it to you?" he asked her.

She shook her head. "I hurt you."

"Yes," he said. "You did. You told me the Star of Bethlehem belonged in the heavens to bring hope, to guide its followers to wisdom and the meaning of their lives. Perhaps some power did not quite agree with you. Here it is, lying here between us. I believe we did follow it at Christmas, Verity, perhaps with as little understanding as the wise men themselves of where exactly it was leading us and to what. It led us to each other. To hope. To love. To a future that could hold companionship and love and happiness if we are willing to follow it to the end. Come with me. All the way. That one more irrevocable step. Please?"

Her eyes, when they looked up into his, were swimming with tears. "It can be Christmas today?" she said. "And every day?"

"But not in any magical sense," he said. "We can *make* every day Christmas. But only if we work hard at it. Only if we remember the miracle every day of our lives."

"Oh, my lord," she said.

"Julian."

"Julian." She gazed at him and he could feel his anxiety ease as she slowly smiled.

"Marry me," he whispered.

She lifted her hands then and framed his face with them. "I should have trusted my heart more than my head," she said. "My heart told me it was a shared love. My head told me how foolish I was. Julian." Her arms twined about his neck. "Oh, Julian, my love. Oh yes, if you are quite sure. But I know you are. And I am, too. I have loved you with so much pain, so much longing, so little trust. I *love* you."

He stopped her babbling with his mouth. He wrapped his arms about her and held her tightly to him. He held everything that was most dear in his life and vowed that he would never ever let her go, that he would never even for a single moment forget the strange, undeserved chance that had led him out into the desert to follow a star along an unknown route to an unknown destination. He would never cease marveling that he had been led, bored and cynical and arrogant, to peace and redemption and love.

In one palm, clasped tightly at her back as they kissed eagerly, joyfully, passionately, he held the linen handkerchief, which had been a treasured memento of her father, and the gold star, which he would hang about her neck in a few minutes' time.

The gifts of Christmas.

The gifts of love.

* * * * *

A DROP OF FRANKINCENSE

Merline Lovelace

To Al, my bright, shining star who's given me the greatest gift of all—a love to last a lifetime.

Chapter One

Plymouth, England
December, 1587

"I've no other choice in the matter, Violet. I shall have to seduce the wretched man!"

Twitching her black velvet skirts to free them of the clinging, sweet-scented rushes, Lady Margaret Walsh paced her oak-paneled bedchamber. The blaze in the great hearth chased away most of the winter chill seeping under the sills of the mullioned windows, but did little to chase away the coldness that gripped her heart.

"Seduce Sir Christopher?" The plump, berry-eyed matron seated in a wooden chair drawn up beside the fire screen stared at her charge in shocked disapproval. "Are you daft, child?"

"No." Meg's mouth tightened. "Merely desperate."

With good reason, she thought grimly. Here she was, a woman wed for nigh onto six years, yet still a virgin. And her husband, damn his soul, showed not the least inclination to end her sorry state!

Unless sooner consummated, their accursed union would dissolve at the stroke of midnight on Christmas Eve, less than a week hence. Meg had always thought it a cruel mischance that she'd been wed in what should have been the merriest of seasons. Instead, she'd made the least merry of brides. Sick with trepidation and still grieving for the father she'd lost but a month before, she'd sniffled and sobbed through the entire ceremony.

For most of the six years since that sorry day, Meg had wanted only to see the wretched matter of her marriage over and done with. Of late, however, she'd been forced to acknowledge that a union with Christopher Walsh, however detestable, far outweighed the frightening alternatives.

"He's at the Bird and Crown," she continued, taking another agitated turn about the room. "They all are, even Drake himself. I've decided go to the inn and bring my husband to his duty."

"Lady Margaret!" Her four chins quivering, Violet shook her coiffed head. "You speak like the innocent you are! Were you truly a wife, you'd know well enough that a woman cannot force a man to this particular duty, be he husband or no."

"Force? Ha!"

Hands on hips, Meg rounded on her companion. Scorn filled her moss green eyes, gifted to her by the mother she'd never known.

"From all I've heard of Kit Walsh these many

years, he requires little enough encouragement to bed with anyone *except* his wife. Even the queen calls him the most rascally of her sea dogs, and that is speaking some!''

''You cannot believe all the tales that come from the court,'' Violet protested. Her gaze flitted to the stout oak door. Instinctively she lowered her voice. ''Especially when it is your cousin who carries them. For all he professes to admire Sir Christopher's boldness on the seas, Sir Robert makes no secret of the fact that he would see you free of your marriage vow.''

''Yes, I know.''

Meg's chest tightened with a now-familiar dread. Robert Clive would see her free of one husband, all right, and married to another forthwith.

Himself.

He had already petitioned the queen for her hand upon the dissolution of her union with Kit Walsh. The convoluted ties of kinship that connected Meg to Robert didn't, to her unceasing regret, fall within the forbidden degree for marriage.

He wanted her. He'd made that plain enough these past weeks. He wanted her estates even more.

A shiver coursed down Meg's back. Resolutely she shook it off. Robert Clive would have neither her hand nor her lands, she swore fiercely. Not if she had aught to say in the matter.

In her youth and wretchedness over her father's illness and death, she had agreed to the husband he'd chosen for her. She would not agree to another out of fear. With Elizabeth on the throne of England, women could no longer be forced into marriages against their will as they had in previous times.

The alternative to marriage, however, appealed to Meg even less. Widows and unmarried heiresses could, and often did, find themselves made wards of the Crown. For all Elizabeth's kindness to her many subjects who loved her dearly in this, the twenty-ninth year of her reign, the queen did not hesitate to make use of such wardships as she saw fit.

At this moment, war with Spain loomed ever nearer with each passing day. The queen had armies to raise and ships to outfit. If the harried monarch assumed control of Meg's estates, her ministers would divert the revenues to the royal treasury. Moreover, they'd no doubt order Meg's lands enclosed to increase their yield, as was being done throughout England with disastrous results to the crofters who'd farmed the fields for centuries.

Meg wasn't about to see the people who depended on her displaced, nor watch her revenues flow into the royal coffers. Nor would she take Robert Clive to husband. The very thought of his thin, white hands on her body made her stomach clench.

No, her only course was to consummate her long-standing marriage to Kit Walsh. One night in his arms, one hour even, and they could both continue as they had these many years, with him off on his endless sea voyages and her snug and content in Devon, managing her estates as she always had.

But how was Meg to bring about this one hour in

her husband's arms? There was the rub! She'd not seen him nor spoken a single word to the man since the summer after their marriage.

Despite herself, she shivered at the memory of that awful, awful time. Half the residents of Plymouth, Meg included, had fallen prey to a scabrous disease brought in by one of the ships that plied the city's busy harbor. Scorning rampant rumors of the plague, Sir Christopher had appeared at his child bride's bedside.

Meg had shrunk away from him, terrified by both her illness and the towering stranger she'd wed. Ignoring her protests, the gruff, broad-shouldered captain had bid Violet wrap her charge all over in cold cloths, then he'd forced the most noxious drafts down Meg's throat. Between bouts of violent retching, she had protested both his brusque handling and assumption of command over her and the sickroom.

It didn't matter a whit that she'd repented her whimpering demand that he be gone from her life almost as soon as he'd walked out the door. Nor that she'd sent a stiff missive just last year, informing him she was ready to assume her wifely duties, should he wish her to do so.

He did not, he'd replied curtly.

He'd even ignored the urgent summons Meg sent yesterday, when she learned that his ship, the *Golden Gull,* had joined the fleet gathered at Plymouth, not three miles down the coast from Oak Manor. Instead, he'd sent a note that he was content to let time take its course.

Well, Meg was not. Not any longer, at any rate.

With a tinkle of the silver-tipped ribbons attaching her long, puffed sleeves to her gown, she tucked her arms across her chest. Her bosom swelled above the pearl-encrusted bodice that flattened her breasts and narrowed her waist to a fashionable, waspish point. One embroidered shoe tapped the rushes.

"Do you not see, Violet? It's my husband's very reputation which emboldens me to this course. If he had taken some other woman to his heart, or said that he wished to end our farcical marriage so he might wed more advantageously, I would concur most willingly. But he spends what little time he's not at sea dancing attendance on the queen. Such close attendance," she finished darkly, "that rumor has it he far prefers his virgin queen to his virgin bride...and she him."

Her companion had heard the troublesome rumors, as well, but Violet was ever loath to stoop to gossip.

"It's true men don't take to marriage," she murmured. "My own dear Huthburt always said that wedding is destiny, and hanging likewise."

Since Violet's own dear Huthburt had met his end not by hanging but by a drunken fall from his horse, leaving his widow destitute, Meg had little use for his sayings. Violet quoted him with every breath, however, and such was Meg's love for the woman who'd raised her that she kept her opinion to herself.

Crossing the room, she knelt beside her companion. "Say you'll aid me, my kindest, sweetest Violet. Please."

A sigh escaped the older woman. She gazed down into Meg's face.

"What would you have me do?"

"Help me slip out of the manor this night without my cousin's being the wiser. And tell me how best to entice Sir Christopher to bed with me."

Reaching out with her other hand, Violet stroked a mittened finger down her charge's cheek. "If your husband would but look upon your face since you've come to womanhood, he would need no enticing."

"The last time my husband looked upon my face, it was covered all over with disgusting pustules," Meg returned with a grimace. "He would not know me now if he passed me in the street."

"All right," the older woman agreed reluctantly. "I'll help you. But you'd best remember what Huthburt used to say."

Meg stifled a groan. "What?"

"Like will to like, girl. Like will to like."

Before Meg could protest that she was nothing like the brash, freebooting privateer her father had chosen for her, Violet heaved her well-padded figure out of the wooden chair.

"Do you still have that little casket Sir Christopher gave you as one of your wedding gifts? The one with the perfumed oil from Araby?"

Meg hesitated, reluctant to admit that she'd tucked the little sandalwood box away in her clothespress. She didn't know why she'd kept the silly thing. Certainly not because of any attachment to the man who'd given it to her.

"Come, child, you must needs cut your coat from your cloth, as Huthburt would say. You'll need this perfumed oil and more to snare your rowdy sea captain."

"I don't wish to snare him! Only to…" Her mouth firmed. "To bed with him."

"And once you've bedded him?" Violet demanded. "What then? How will you explain what you have done?"

Meg waved a dismissive hand. "He'll be off again on the next tide, for who knows how many years this time. I'll deal with explanations when he returns."

Shaking her head, Violet trailed the younger woman to the massive clothespress that stood against one wall. A moment later, she took the sandalwood box from her charge's hands and opened the lid. A blue Venetian glass vial sat nestled in crimson velvet. When Violet removed the stopper, it tinkled like a silvery bell and released a rich, exotic scent into the air.

Musk. Frankincense. A touch of jasmine. All blended in a most provocative manner. Firmly suppressing her doubts about this course of action, Violet set to work dousing every exposed inch of her charge's skin with the scented oil.

"Stop!" Gasping, Meg flapped a hand before her nose. "That's too much!"

"You'll learn soon enough, child, too much is never enough when it comes to seducing a husband."

The night had dwindled to the small hours when Kit took the dark, narrow stairs leading to the Bird and Crown's second story.

He turned a sharp corner and whacked his forehead on a low timber. Cursing roundly, he ducked and continued up the stairs with something less than his usual, surefooted grace. He was weary, bone weary, and his senses swam from the endless flagons of ale he had downed this night. He shook his head in a vain attempt to clear it.

God's teeth, preparing to sail with Sir Francis Drake was both a blessing and a curse! The man had the unerring navigational skills of a dolphin and the killing instincts of a shark, but there was not an ounce of patience to be found in his short, stocky frame. After months at court, Drake had finally gotten a charter from the queen to launch a preemptive strike against Spain. He'd summoned his most trusted captains to Plymouth and readied to sail, but had to delay his departure at the last moment waiting on a load of round shot.

As was his way, the admiral had taken out his ill humor at the delay on his captains. Luckily Kit had sailed with the crafty old sea dog often enough to separate the salt from the brine. By the time Drake had worked himself back into a good humor, the ale had been flowing freely for hours.

Truth be told, Kit was as impatient as Sir Francis to feel the wind in his face and the roll of a deck under his feet again. Like Drake, he'd spent too much time at court these past months. The petty intrigues and jealousies of those surrounding the queen would have amused Kit if the results weren't so often deadly. Although not as vengeful as her father and older sister, Elizabeth had sent her share of men and women to the block. They felt the ax's bite just as that foolish, most dangerous Mary, Queen of Scots.

No, Kit thought, lifting the latch to his chamber, he wouldn't miss the intrigues of the court, nor would he...

He took a single step into the darkened room and caught a strange, exotic scent. Abruptly he halted. His hand dropped to the basket hilt of his rapier. His narrowed eyes swept the low-ceilinged chamber, lit only by the banked fire smoldering in the hearth.

He traced the scent to the massive carved bed...and to the woman occupying it. Clutching the counterpane to her chest, she stared at him with eyes as round as cannon shots. Her face was a pale oval in the dimness. Her hair fell like a black silk curtain about her shoulders.

Her very tantalizing, very naked shoulders.

Fresh from court, where the game of love was played freely by countesses and serving maids alike, Kit felt only a passing twist of cynicism at finding a strange female in his bed. Anyone the queen smiled on more than once could expect to be gifted with late-night visits from women ambitious for themselves or their families. Sometimes it amused Kit to accept their gifts. Most times, it did not.

This time...

He gave the woman a slow perusal. From the shadows of the bed, she returned his stare, wetting her lips nervously. At the sight of that small, pink tongue, the blood grew heavy in his loins. By the stars, she was a toothsome little thing. Whatever her game might be, he decided to play it out.

He swept the room with another, quick glance. The small sea chest he'd brought ashore with him sat against the far wall, its lock still securely attached to the brass hasp. The shadows revealed no other concealed figures, nor did the thick curtains drawn across the window show any untoward bulges.

Kicking the door shut, he shot the bolt.

His visitor jumped at the clunk and clutched the coverlet tighter to her chest. Lazily Kit drew his dagger from the sheath attached to his belt. The woman's eyes widened at the sight of the wickedly sharp blade.

"I mean no harm by you," she gasped. "I swear it!"

Her speech removed her at once from the category of serving wench or street trollop. At the same time, it carried none of the simpering affectations of the women Kit had associated with at court. A rich merchant's wife, he thought derisively. Plymouth abounded with them, and with tales of how they amused themselves by diddling both their husbands and the sea captains they employed. Drake himself had kept one such goodwife as mistress for years, before he'd married for the second time.

"What do you mean by me, then?" Kit drawled.

"Only..." She swiped her tongue across her lips

once more. "Only the pleasure of your company abed."

"How do you know I'll bring you pleasure?" Idly he flipped the dagger end over end. The jeweled hilt smacked into his palm. "Mayhap I'm of the sort who enjoys pain."

She shrank back against the massive headboard of the four-poster. "Are you?" she whispered.

"Will you leave my bed if I say yes?"

A shudder rippled across the smooth skin of her shoulders. Her lids came down to mask her eyes for the space of a breath, then slowly lifted.

"No."

Odd's bodkin, the woman was desperate! Kit moved closer, studying her face. He saw fear in those wide, dark eyes, yes, but a fierce determination, as well. Despite himself, he felt a twist of pity for a woman forced, for whatever reasons, to whore for him.

He understood desperation. He'd tasted it often enough as a boy. A yeoman archer, his father had died fighting for King Harry in Flanders. Before Kit had seen his sixth summer, he'd buried his mother, brother and two sisters. Alone and near to starving, he'd stolen away aboard the next ship that pulled up to the docks.

He found out soon enough that life as a ship's boy was not for the weak of mind or body. He took the beatings and blows willingly, though, in exchange for learning to sail the winds and gauge the sluicing tides of the Thames estuary. Eventually he left that hellish ship for one captained by Sir Francis Drake. Since then, Kit had sailed with the audacious privateer on many a raid to plunder the Spanish Main.

He'd proved himself almost as bold as the great captain himself, and had earned both his own ship and the right to hang a "Sir" before his name. He'd also earned the queen's favor, which in turn brought strange women to his bed.

Strange, desperate women.

"You can rest easy," he said gruffly. "I take my pleasure as I find it."

With seeming casualness, he set the dagger within easy reach and unbuckled his rapier. Then his hands went to the points that tied his starched ruff. The gold-tipped strings gave easily.

Meg watched him remove his ruff, not sure whether she was more relieved or dismayed by his easy capitulation. Could she do this? Dear heaven, could she do this?

Gradually a niggling sense of pique broke through the welter of her emotions. Had the man no further questions of her? Did her husband bed so many women he did not even want to know their names? She had one ready, should he ask it of her.

He did not, the rogue! He simply tossed his ruff aside and unlaced his richly embroidered black velvet doublet. While he drew the garment over his head, she battled a growing sense of indignation. She hadn't expected him to recognize her. Nor to turn her away, given his reputation. Still, it pricked her pride

that he would lie with a stranger when his wife resided not three miles distant.

When he turned to face her again, she abandoned
her prickly pride, her indignation, almost her resolve.
Her stomach plunged like a bucket dropped down a
well.

Holy saints above! Had his doublet contained no
padding? No horsehair stiffening, no whalebone to
give it shape? Did her husband really possess such
width of shoulders and broad, muscled chest?

He was so big! Far bigger than she remembered,
and her girlish memories were of a veritable giant.
In white lawn shirt and the Venetian breeches that
had come of fashion in recent years, he loomed even
larger than her hazy memories painted him.

The gold ring in his left ear was as she remembered, though, and the sun-spun gilt of his hair, but
the slow, rakish grin he now sent her way was new.

"Let's hope the pleasure was worth the wait,
lass."

His fingers went to the drawstrings of his Venetians. Despite every admonition Meg had muttered
to herself, every fierce reminder of why she needed
to entice this man to his bed and her body, panic beat
like a trapped dove in her chest.

"I...I would have a taste of wine first."

A golden brow arched. "Would you?"

"Please." The tremor in her voice shamed her, but
not enough to release her death grip on the feather-
filled counterpane. "I gave the innkeeper extra coins
to leave a flagon of his best. He swore to me that

it's a rare fine Madeira, stolen from the Spanish by Drake himself.''

A chuckle drifted across the room. "I doubt it not. Sir Francis has stolen more than wine from under the noses of the Spanish."

"As have you," Meg murmured.

His grin widened. "Aye, that I have."

She could scarce believe it. Naked and trembling, she'd now exchanged more words with her husband than she had in all the years they'd been wed.

Mayhap she'd see this deed done, after all. Her nervousness lessened perceptibly...until her husband turned once more to the bed. Meg eyed the single pewter goblet in his hand with sudden alarm.

"Will you not drink?" she urged.

Something flashed in his eyes, quickly come and quickly gone.

"Aye, sweeting, I will." The casualness of his reply did not disguise the note of steel beneath. "After you take a taste of it."

He was no fool, this husband of hers. He could not be, Meg acknowledged, to have won riches and the favor of the queen.

Nor was she.

Holding his eyes, she reached for the goblet. He watched her, hawklike, as she tipped it to her lips and downed a goodly swallow. To her relief, the powder she'd stirred into the dark liquid earlier left no trace of bitterness on her tongue.

The potion would but relax her, Violet had promised. Loosen her limbs and ease the pain at the breaching of her maidenhead. It would relax her husband, as well, but not so much he could not raise his rod, the experienced matron had added with a droll twist of her lips.

But of a certainty he'd sink into a satisfied stupor after he'd found his release, Violet had predicted. Huthburt always did. Meg had but to wait until her husband had taken his pleasure of her and fallen asleep, then slip away.

The bold plan had seemed far simpler in the planning than in the doing! Still clutching the bolster with one hand, Meg held the goblet out with the other.

"The landlord spoke truly. This is a rare, fine Madeira. Will you not drink of it?"

"Since you find it so pleasing, I will."

The feather mattresses dipped as her husband sat on the edge of the bed and drank deeply. She fought the urge to shrink away, as his gaze traveled from her face to her shoulders to the slopes of her breasts, and back again. Mindful of Violet's instructions, Meg let the bolster slip an inch or two. Cool air prickled her bare skin, and heat stained her face at such wanton behavior.

She was wed to this man, she reminded herself fiercely. He was her husband.

"Take another sip, sweeting." His voice was lower, huskier, rasping on her nerves like rough, uncured leather. "And I'll drink from your lips."

Obediently Meg took another sip from the goblet he held to her mouth. Closing her eyes, she lifted her face to his. A moment later, his mouth closed on hers.

He had kissed her before, of course. At the ceremony that sealed their betrothal, and again a few months later during their marriage rites. Yet those perfunctory touches of lip to cheek could not come near to preparing Meg for the impact of his mouth on hers.

Then, he'd held back in consideration of her tender years. And she, timid, untutored girl that she'd been, had made a most reluctant bride. But now she was a woman grown. A woman who had suppressed her body's natural urges for too many years.

With her husband's mouth on hers and his big, rough-palmed hands curling on her bare shoulders, Meg felt those urges leap to life. Stunned, she understood for the first time why Violet still sighed over her own dear Huthburt, and why the younger housemaids so often crept out to the stables for a night.

Holy saints above! This heat, this sudden, streaking fire in her belly from a mere kiss! Instinctively Meg tipped her head farther back.

When his tongue found entrance to her mouth, she gasped and would have pulled away. The grip on her shoulders kept her in place. He held her still and slowly, deliberately, drank the residue of wine from her.

One taste, Kit thought fiercely. He would allow himself just one taste. 'Struth, she kissed like an untried maid, all hesitation and puckered lips. Yet her mouth branded his, and her tongue...sweet stars, her tongue played havoc with his already unsteady senses.

Bunching his muscles, he brought her up against him. Just one taste. He'd take but this one taste.

A moment later, he could not decide what had changed his mind. Mayhap it was the way she lifted her arms and curled them about his neck. Or the press of her lush breasts against his chest. Or the need that fired his loins at her soft, mewling moan. The ale he'd consumed no doubt contributed to his change of course, as well.

Whatever the cause, he acceded to it with the same, gut-sure instinct that led him to attack a heavily armed treasure ships against great odds.

He would have her.

Whatever this creature's game, he would have her.

One of his hands left her shoulder. Shoving down the counterpane, he kneaded the soft flesh of her breast. His thumb and forefinger found the nipple. The bud went tight and hard at his touch.

Dragging free of her clinging arms, Kit stood and rid himself of the rest of his clothes. She tumbled back onto the mounded pillows, her hands scrabbling for the bolster to cover her nakedness as he revealed his.

Kit's eyes narrowed. For an uncomfortable moment, her nervousness reminded him of the scrawny, sickly child he'd wed. He would have abandoned the game at that point had she not mastered her momentary qualms and lifted her gaze to his.

"Will you not take another sip of wine, sir? I

would..." She met his eyes with a steady resolve. "I would drink from your lips this time."

Kit's doubts vanished. This was no frightened child. This was a woman who knew what she wanted of a man. His body tightening with anticipation, he poured a full measure of wine into the goblet.

Chapter Two

The thump of a fist on the door brought Kit to instant, pounding wakefulness. He lifted his face from the down pillow, wincing at the pain that spiked through his temples.

"Aye?"

"Ye said to fetch yer hot water afore cock's crow, sor. Be ye wantin' it now?"

"Bring it in."

The clatter of the iron door latch added to the splintering in Kit's skull. Gritting his teeth, he rolled upright. He didn't need to examine the Bird and Crown's well-feathered bed to know his companion of the night had disappeared. Her scent lingered on the linens, fragrant and most damnably seductive. His fogged mind could scarce recall her face, but her perfume pulled at his senses like the call of a sea siren.

When he tried to stand, the room spun. Kit sank back on the bed, his jaw tight. Daggers of pain stabbed up the back of his skull. He'd drunk enough wine and ale over the years to know the little witch had drugged him. He had no idea why she'd not succumbed to her own brew, unless the ale Kit had consumed so freely with Drake and the others before he'd sought his bed had compounded the potion's effect.

"Be ye wishin' me to stir the coals and stoke the fire, sor?"

Thoroughly disgusted with himself for proving such an easy mark, Kit nodded to the broad-hipped chambermaid. Within moments, leaping flames chased the shadows to the corners of the room. Expecting the worst, he cast a glance about the room.

His sea chest still sat beside the window, he saw, its brass lock secure. The clothes and gold-tipped points he'd shed last night lay where he'd dropped them. To his surprise, his money pouch was still attached to his belt, as was his rapier, crafted for his hand by the queen's own armorer and crusted with sapphires.

He'd just concluded that the mysterious, black-haired wench had not traded her virginity for ill-gotten gain when he saw that his jeweled dagger no longer lay atop the shelf where he'd placed it.

His mouth twisted. He would have given her far more than the dagger's worth, had she asked it of him. As hazy as his memories were of their joining, Kit could not forget his stunned surprise when he'd met the barrier of her maiden's shield. By then, he could not pull back, even had he wished to. She drugged him with more than wine, he admitted with an involuntary tightening of his loins.

If he wasn't sailing with the morning tide, he'd track the wench down. Plymouth boasted a goodly number of citizens within its walls and among the outlying farms and manors, but Kit could afford to spread enough gold around to discover this particular female's whereabouts.

He'd seek her out when he returned, he decided with a tight smile, and take another taste of her damnably seductive sweetness. When he did, he'd make sure she dished up no potions. Nor would she slip away in the night, before he was done with her. He'd take his time and his pleasure of her, and hear again her surprised, breathless moans.

He'd have to put back into Plymouth after this voyage anyway, he told himself, as if in justification of the blood that heated his veins. He needed to insure his wife fully understood the settlements that would devolve on her with the dissolution of their marriage. He would have attended to the business before he sailed, had Drake not kept him jumping from corder to quartermaster from the moment the *Golden Gull* dropped anchor in Sutton Harbor.

Now he had an added incentive to return to Plymouth Towne. His gut tightening at the thought, Kit rose and gathered his clothes.

The chambermaid eyed his naked form appreciatively. A saucy smile lit her eyes. "Be ye wishin' me to stoke yer fire, too, sor?"

Grinning, Kit dug a coin from his purse and tossed

it to her. "Not this time, lass. I've a ship to ready for sail."

Dawn feathered the eastern sky when Kit left the Bird and Crown. After dispatching a bleary-eyed sailor to carry his sea chest to the *Gull*, he drew the chill, salty air into his lungs and strode the cobbled streets to the final gathering Drake had ordered when they broke last night. A surging sense of anticipation pushed the pounding out of Kit's head. He'd sailed with Drake on many a voyage, but this one looked to be the most bold...and the most dangerous.

Short minutes later, he climbed the stairs to the ornate gallery that ran the length of Drake's elegant town house. A steady stream of lackeys passed him, hauling trunks loaded with the captain's personal plate and clothing to the wheeled carts waiting outside. Like Kit, Sir Francis had spent his last night ashore for many weeks to come. Unlike Kit, he insisted on living in the same formal state aboard his ship as he did at home.

His cook, trumpeter and personal body servants had no doubt already boarded the 450-ton *Revenge* to prepare the admiral's quarters for his imminent occupancy. Soon Drake himself would board, and the galleons of the Plymouth squadron would once more sail to singe Philip of Spain's beard!

One glance at the glum faces of the captains gathered in the upper gallery sent Kit's eager anticipation plunging to his boots. The fiery red on Drake's countenance confirmed his sudden, hollowing suspicions.

He'd sailed with Sir Francis often enough to read the signs. Only one person had the power to engender that expression of frustrated fury and helplessness.

"Do not say it!" Kit exclaimed. "Her majesty has changed her mind yet again."

"Aye, she has," one of his fellow captains replied. "A courier brought a new commission not a half hour ago, marked with the queen's personal seal. She orders us not to strike at Spain."

"God's bones!" Kit exploded. "I thought we'd convinced her majesty that attack is our only defense against this fleet Philip is putting together. We must hit his ships while they lie at anchor, not wait until they sail!"

Drake spun to face Kit. "And did we both not so argue and plead all these months at court?" he thundered. "Damne me, the pettifogging cautionaries have prevailed upon the queen yet again!"

As if sensing how closely he skirted treason, the stocky admiral sucked in a steadying breath and took some of the volume from his voice.

"The queen advises that she yet desires to avoid open war with Spain...if it can be done."

It could not. Every man in the room understood that. War had become inevitable the day the Catholic queen of Scots walked to the executioner's block at Fotheringhay. Spain, backed by Catholic France and the immense wealth of the papacy, had been building its armada ever since. They were determined to remove the heretical Elizabeth from her throne and restore the true faith to England.

"Her majesty seeks to buy England more time,"
Drake said, still breathing heavily. "I'm to join the
Lord High Admiral in the Dover Strait. You, Fro-
bisher..." He nodded to the dour-faced captain
who'd gained fame for his raids on the Spanish Main.
"You'll patrol the North Sea. You, Walsh, will take
on additional stores and take up station in the Atlantic."

Kit spit out a colorful curse that only someone
who'd attempted to use a ship's head in a stormy,
contrary sea could appreciate.

"It makes even less sense to split our fleet now
than it does to sit on our arses and wait for the Spanish to attack!"

"Do you think I don't know that?" Drake fired
back.

He glared at his subordinate, as if the altered orders were his fault and not that of a monarch well-
known for the changeability of her mind.

"Send Martin to cruise the Atlantic," Kit argued.
"Or young Tom Nevers. Their ships are new built
and swift."

"But not as swift as the *Gull,* and so her majesty
knows." Drake blew out a long breath, forcing himself to calm. "I much dislike detaching you from my
squadron, Kit, but if the Spanish should defy all odds
and sail to attack Ireland or Scotland—"

"They won't," Kit interjected. "All intelligence
indicates they will come up the channel to rendez-
vous with Alva's army in the lowlands, then turn to
attack England's eastern shores!"

"And so I believe they will. But our spies could be wrong. If the Spanish fleet indeed heads for Ireland, I trust you to bring word with the swiftest dispatch." Drake forced a smile. "So, too, does the queen. You've made your mark on her, lad...and not just with your pretty face," he added with an attempt at levity. "She names you specifically to this task."

A flush mounted the aforesaid face. In recent weeks, Kit had taken a good number of digs from Drake and the other captains over the queen's partiality for the man she called the handsomest of sea rovers.

At first, the queen's attention had flattered Kit. How could it not? To be singled out by a monarch still slender and stunningly charismatic in this, her fifty-fourth year, could swell any man's head. God's teeth, she kept young Essex, some thirty years her junior, lapping at her heels like a lovesick pup! Robert Dudley, her much-loved favorite for two decades, almost lost his head when he secretly wed the Countess of Hereford a few years ago, yet still he clung to whatever crumbs of favor his queen would bestow upon him. Even Drake, who'd sailed the world over and amassed untold treasures, bowed to the whims and will of the queen.

Such was the power of the woman who ruled England.

Kit had felt that power the first time he'd been shown into her presence, flush with riches and gifts from a daring raid on the Spanish treasure fleet. He'd felt it even more during his recent months at court when Elizabeth had singled him out for intimate audiences and, some whispered behind their hands, for intimate affections.

Kit had shrugged off the whispers and kept his own counsel, but in his heart of hearts, he could not wait to get away from court. The petty jealousies and intrigues of those in the queen's orbit carried the stink of bilgewater to his mind. He was no courtier, nor did ambition for titles and political position spur him. All he wanted was a sound deck under his feet.

He couldn't imagine spending the rest of his days tied like a love knot to Elizabeth's skirts...any more than he desired to remain tied to the timid, sickly little female he'd wed so many years ago. He would be shed of his reluctant wife soon enough, but, as he now discovered, the queen had woven a far tighter net about him.

None of his arguments swayed Drake. Walsh would follow the queen's orders and be done with it.

Consigning all women to the devil, Kit stood on the raised poop deck of the *Gull* less than an hour later and watched the squadron warp out of Sutton Harbor. One after another, the brightly painted galleons made for the sound. First the *Revenge,* then the *Triumph,* followed by the huge, 800-ton *Mary Rose,* christened after another ship of the same name sunk some years before.

Colorful pennants fluttered and dipped almost to the waves in the light breeze. Trumpets rang out. Shouted commands carried across the waters. With a series of sharp cracks, the baggy flax sails caught the breeze. Cheers and cries of "Godspeed" broke out among the watchers ashore and on the high plateau above the harbor known as the Hoe. Moments later, the shore battery roared a farewell.

With the sound of the canons ringing in his ears, Kit turned his back on the brave parade and gave orders to take on the additional stores the queen had authorized. His second in command soon had the matter in hand. The wiry Greek had spent thirty of his thirty-eight years on the sea and knew the *Gull* as well as her master.

Leaving the task to Xanthos, Kit raked a hand through his hair and pondered how best to employ his remaining hours in Plymouth. Instantly an image of the black-haired witch he'd found in his bed last night leapt into his mind. The urge to hunt her down rose hot and fierce in his chest. He was halfway to the gangplank when duty nipped at his heels.

Hell and damnation!

He had a wife not three miles away…and a marriage to end.

As usual whenever Kit thought of the sickly little heiress he'd married, a grimace flitted across his face. He'd met her ailing father through Drake, who had engineered the match. The bold, brawny young captain agreed to give his name and protection to the little girl who would soon be orphaned. In exchange, Kit's father-in-law financed construction of the *Gull*.

Given the great disparity in ages and temperament of the bride and groom, though, Sir Danvers had inserted a clause into the marriage contract that made it null and void if either party should decline to consummate it within seven years.

Sir Danvers had died before the first timber had been cut, and the marriage had proved a disaster from the start. Kit's timid little bride had been so frightened of her oversize husband that she'd cast up her supper in his lap at their wedding feast, and shaken like a blancmange the few times she'd been forced to endure his presence afterward. The last time he'd seen her she'd been desperately ill and covered in spots. Pathetically, she'd begged him to leave her presence forthwith and forever! Kit had ignored her pleas and stayed until her fever broke, but had complied willingly enough with her fervent wish in the years since.

Despite the odd little note she'd sent him a year ago, all reports from Lady Margaret's steward indicated that she still found her marriage repugnant. Her cousin, Robert Clive, had reinforced those reports. Kit had little use for the unctuous, ambitious courtier, but when they'd conversed at court some months ago, Clive had been most frank about his cousin's distaste for her absent husband.

In another week, thank the Lord, the timorous Lady Margaret would be free to seek a husband more to her liking. In the meantime, Kit owed her at least the courtesy of a visit.

The prospect did little to lighten his foul humor.

Some three miles distant, Meg stood at the top of the cliffs that edged Oak Manor's sloping west lawn.

The sea crashed and roiled far below. The wind whipped up her skirts and tugged her hair from its net. From the curve of shore to the south came the booming echo of canons.

Meg closed her eyes. Relief and a contrary emotion she refused to acknowledge as regret coursed through her.

He was gone, for who knew how many weeks or months or years this time.

Her husband was gone.

Seven hours ago the weight of his outflung arm had pinned her to a feather mattress. She'd breathed in his rich, masculine scent. Listened to the steady drum of his heart against his ribs. Wondered at the changes his hands and mouth and hard, driving thrusts had made in her body and in her mind.

Now, she told herself with a resolute breath, she must deal with the consequences of those changes.

Windblown and disheveled, she made her way back to the manor house. Its mellow brickwork and sturdy timbers welcomed her, as they had all her life. She followed the cobbled passageway that led past the stables and kitchens. Without taking the time to remove her muddied clogs or the warm if somewhat shabby cloak she wore for her morning walks along the cliff, she hurried through the house. She needed to write a letter and dispatch it before her cousin made his morning appearance.

A shudder that had little to do with the chill December air rippled down her back. She'd not invited

Robert Clive to spend Yuletide at Oak Manor. He'd simply appeared a week ago, informing her that he'd come to share the festivities…and to celebrate with her the termination of her marriage. His black eyes had gleamed as they roamed the richly appointed furnishings and polished oak paneling that gave the house its name. They'd held far too much possessiveness for Meg's peace of mind.

Well, Robert Clive would not have Oak Manor, nor its mistress.

Not taking time to stoke the fire in the small sitting room just off the main hall, Meg seated herself at the desk and sharpened a quill. Hurriedly she dipped it into the inkwell and scratched out a note begging Lord Brough to attend her this morning, if he should be so kind. With her father's oldest and most respected friend as witness, Meg would inform her cousin that she was no longer free to wed him or anyone else.

Despite her resolve, she shivered at the prospect of Robert's rage. He was not a man to cross lightly. Hence the witness…and the proof, should her cousin demand it.

Setting the quill aside, Meg dug into the deep pocket of her cloak and drew out the jeweled dagger she'd taken from the Bird and Crown. Her fingertip traced the inscription at the cross of the hilt.

Elizabeth Regina, to her most bold Sir Kit.

Meg's mouth curled. Pah! If she didn't fear that she'd need evidence to support her claim of lying with her husband last night, she'd fling the damned thing into the fire. It would appear the rumors Clive had brought about the rogue she'd wed were true, after all.

She swept up the note and rose, intending to call a servant to deliver it. At the muted sound of a male voice in the great hall inquiring after her whereabouts, she halted in her tracks. Her breath caught in her throat.

Robert!

Involuntarily her fingers tightened on the dagger's hilt. Meg glanced around the room, seeking escape even though she knew there was none. The sound of footsteps came closer. White-knuckled and breathing hard, she lifted her chin.

Expecting her thin, dark-bearded cousin, she stumbled back a step when a golden-haired giant appeared in the doorway.

"Holy saints above!" she gasped. "What are you doing here?"

He didn't speak. Didn't move, except to rake her with narrowed eyes from her windblown hair to her muddy clogs. His gaze snagged on the dagger clutched in her hand.

In two strides, he crossed the room. Before Meg could do more than take a single step back, he banded her wrist and yanked it upward. A hard wrench took the dagger from her fisted fingers.

"Wait!" she gasped. "Allow me to explain!"

"Oh, you'll explain all right," he agreed, shoving the dagger into the sheath attached to his belt. "As will your mistress, who undoubtedly doused you with the costly scent that clings to you even now and sent you to my bed last night. For what reason I'll soon know.''

''My mistress?''

Meg gaped at him. He thought her a servant! A servant of the very wife he didn't recognize, even now! While she searched frantically for a way to explain the damnable coil she'd wrought, he twisted her arm down, then up again behind her back. With a single jerk, he brought her against him.

Meg gasped again and tried to pull back. ''Hold, sir! You mistake the matter most grievously.''

''The mistake was yours, wench.''

In the cold light of day, she could not but agree. Merciful heavens, how had her scheme gone so awry? Why was he here? How could she...?

''Had you stayed until I wakened this morning,'' he drawled, cutting into her chaotic thoughts, ''I would have paid you far more than I suspect your mistress did. I may yet, but this time I'll make damned sure you give full service for your coin.''

''Full service!''

Twin sparks of embarrassment and indignation heated Meg's cheeks. She had no other experience to measure last night against, but she couldn't imagine giving...or receiving...a greater measure of service. Even after drinking of the powdered wine, this man had brought her to a shuddering, shattering, sobbing state she blushed to remember.

''Aye, sweeting,'' he mocked. ''Last night but

whetted my appetite. You've a long, hard road to ride to satisfy it now.''

As if to prove his point, he lowered his head and stilled her stammering protests with a kiss. When he lifted his head again, Meg's lips throbbed and her heart all but jumped from her flat bodice. She gulped in an outraged breath.

''Do not…do not dare to use me thus!''

His blue eyes glinted like polished steel. ''I'll use you as I will, woman. You might have yielded your maidenhead to me last night, but you'll yield more, much more, afore I'm—''

''Her maidenhead!''

The low, infuriated snarl spun them both around. Meg's stomach, already twisted into tight knots, cramped even more.

Her cousin stood rapier thin and rigid in the doorway. His coal-black hair gleamed with the unguents his body servant combed into it, as did his pointed beard. A deadly fury shone in his black eyes. Without realizing that she did so, she shrank back against Sir Christopher.

''Clive,'' the man behind her acknowledged in a clipped tone.

Robert didn't seem to hear the terse salutation. His whole being was riveted on Meg. His face pale with anger and disbelief, he advanced into the small, paneled office.

''Did I hear aright?'' he raged. ''Did you lie with this man last night?''

Meg stiffened. This was the moment she'd been

anticipating and dreading. Now that it was here, she'd not cower and whimper in fear like some knee-less lack-bone. Wrenching free of Kit's hold, she stepped forward.

"Yes, I lay with this man last night."

She'd known Robert wanted her and her lands with single-minded avariciousness. Still she was unprepared for the violence her taunting reply unleashed.

His backhanded blow sent her stumbling into the man behind her. Before she could blink, before her shocked mind could even register pain, her husband exploded. Surging around her, he twisted a hand in Robert's starched ruff. With one hand, he lifted the courtier clear of the floor and shook him as easily as a terrier would a rat.

"If you strike another woman in my presence, even a doxy such as this, I'll break both your arms."

His face purpling, Robert clawed at the strangling hold.

"Do you hear me, you craven little court bait?"

"Y…yes!"

With a contemptuous flex of his arm, Kit flung him away. Robert stumbled backward, caught his legs against a wooden stool and went crashing down. When he scrambled up, Meg saw murder in his black eyes. His beringed hand went to his sword.

"If that blade clears the scabbard," her husband warned with a smile that raised the hairs on the back of her neck, "I'll put three feet of Toledo steel through your gut, and gladly."

No one in the room mistook the threat for an idle one. If Robert should be so foolish as to draw his blade, Meg didn't doubt for a minute that her husband could run him through. Sir Christopher carried a good four inches and a stone more weight on his tall, muscled frame than her cousin. Moreover, he'd spent the past twenty years or more living by his sword.

Slowly Robert's hand dropped.

"Your presence offends me, Clive," her husband drawled. "Get you gone from my wife's house before I wring your scrawny neck."

Her cousin's face contorted at the contemptuous dismissal. "I'll go, but you'd best look to your own neck, Walsh."

"My neck need not concern you."

"Mayhap not," he spit, "but it concerns the queen. Do you forget I was present when she professed such pleasure that her own dear Kit would soon be free of his wife? All at court heard her remark that you deserve better than a mere country baron's daughter. 'Tis said she thinks to arrange a match for you herself..."

Meg sucked in a swift breath.

"...someday. When she's done playing with you, mayhap. As all know, Elizabeth much mislikes to share her toys."

His mouth twisting in a sneer, Robert turned his gaze to Meg. "I can but wonder how she will react to the news that you've upset her plans, Cousin."

"Cousin!"

The startled exclamation was low but violent in Meg's ear. She dared not turn to look at her husband, hardly dared to breathe.

Robert had not heard the muted exclamation. His eyes on Meg, he executed a short, insulting bow. "I'll come to visit you in the Tower, when you've had time aplenty to regret your foolish, foolish action."

He started for the door, only to stop at the threshold and turn. His black eyes glittered with malice.

"I can but hope you live long enough to climb the steps at Traitor's Gate, Cousin. Remember what happened to Dudley's first wife when she came between the queen and her lover. The fall that broke the poor woman's neck was ruled an accident, but all have ever wondered…"

His thin, evil smile finished what he dared not say aloud. Satisfied with the way Meg's face drained of all blood, he turned and left.

For long moments, a heavy silence hung over the room, broken only by the sounds of the crackling fire and Robert's fading footsteps.

Then slowly, so slowly, Meg turned to face her husband.

Chapter Three

Kit had not risen to command of a fast-built galleon without learning to discipline both himself and his men. Still, it took every ounce of self-control he possessed to keep his hands off the black-haired witch who pivoted to face him.

She took one look at his expression and quickly stepped back a pace.

"Aye," he said through clenched jaws. "You'd best put some distance between us, *wife!*"

She wet her lower lip. Kit's back teeth ground together at the sight. Last night, a mere glimpse of that small pink tongue had stirred him to lust. This morning, it caused a far more violent emotion to rise in his chest.

"I had to do it," she began, her voice low and distinctly nervous.

"Why?" The single word cracked like a whip.

"Christmastide is less than a week hence. I...I had become desperate."

"Why?"

"My lands...the revenues..."

Kit's temper slipped its iron manacles. He surged forward, his anger exploding.

"I haven't touched a penny of your revenues in all the years we've been wed! You could not believe that I would rob you of your inheritance now."

Hastily she backed around the stool that Clive had tripped over. "No, no, not you! But my cousin would, had he his way."

Kit slowed his advance. "Clive thought to take what is yours?"

"He thought to wed me...and bed me."

At his short, vicious oath, she flung her head back. Spots of color rushed into her paper-white cheeks.

"Do not sound so disbelieving. Just because you hold my person in disgust does not mean that all men must."

Kit's mouth curled in derision. "You have it back to front, *wife*. You were the one with such a disgust of marriage that you tossed up your supper in my lap at our wedding feast."

"I was only a child!"

"Aye, a skinny, sickly child. I'm relieved to see you've lost your spots, *wife*."

"Stop calling me 'wife' in that disparaging way!"

"Do you dare to issue orders?" he asked silkily.

Kit took another step closer, Meg, another pace back. With her hips pressed against a table, she could retreat no farther.

He fully expected her to burst into tears, as she had whenever he'd approached her in the past, or, more probably, cast up her breakfast all over his shoes. To his considerable surprise, her chin went up. Her eyes met his, striking like flint to stone.

"Yes, sir, I do."

God's toes! Could this tumble-haired wench in wooden clogs and shabby cloak really be the pasty-faced little girl he'd wed so many years ago? Or the same lush female who'd waited, naked and perfumed, in his bed last night?

Suddenly Kit had to see how the two had come together. Before she realized what he was about, he yanked at the strings of her cloak and dragged it from her shoulders. She shrank from his touch, bending backward over the table. Her quick, indrawn breath mounded her breasts above the board-flat bodice and starched ruff. Her eyes darkened to a green as deep as the sea.

"You've lost more than your spots," Kit observed dryly. "You've lost all trace of the child you were."

"Thank the Lord for that much, at least!"

Her heartfelt reply eased some of the knife-edged tension between them. It dissipated for mere seconds, only to return in even greater force as Kit considered the implications of those hours at the inn.

Clive had not missed the mark by far when he'd warned of the queen's possible anger. She did not tolerate rivals well. Many still wondered at the "accidental" death of Dudley's first wife so many years ago. More recently, one of the queen's ladies-in-waiting had spent a long, nervous month in the Tower for daring to wed without consent.

Kit didn't flatter himself that he ranked higher in the queen's heart than casual affection. Still he'd gained enough measure of the vain, magnificent Elizabeth to know she'd not approve of his wife's brazen conduct.

He dared not leave the Lady Margaret alone to face the consequences of her rash actions.

Stepping away from the table, he held out a gloved hand. She stared at it with the same suspicion a fattened Christmas goose might regard a smiling goodwife with a hatchet in her hand. Hesitantly, as if fearing a trap, she laid her fingers on his.

Kit drew her upright, his grip tightening reflexively when he caught her scent. From this day forward, he suspected, a chance whiff of frankincense would bring an instant picture of this woman to his mind.

Instant, and most erotic.

His stomach knotted at the memory of how she'd taken him into her soft, silken body last night. How she'd cried out at the moment of her breaching, and again when he'd brought her to pleasure. As hazy as his recollections were after that, the image of her tangled hair spread across the pillows and her white throat arched in ecstasy would be forever imprinted on his mind. With some effort, he dragged his thoughts from the night just past to the present.

"Tell your maid to pack what things she can in a single trunk," he instructed briskly. "We have not time to wait for more."

She stared at him stupidly. "What do you say?"

"The *Golden Gull* sails on the afternoon tide. You sail aboard her."

"Are you mad?" She snatched her hand away. "I do not sail anywhere, this day or any other."

"No, lady wife, I am not mad. Only determined to save you from the disaster you've wrought."

"Disaster?" Her eyes flashed. "Is that how you regard our union?"

"You'll find out soon enough what I think. For now, we must deal with the fact that Elizabeth will not be best pleased when she hears of this."

The fire in her eyes quenched. She stared at him in gathering dismay. "It's true, then? You...and the queen?"

Kit's jaw hardened. "There are varying degrees of truth."

"I thought...I thought..."

"You thought what?"

Exhaling a long breath, she shook her head. "I thought my cousin enlarged upon those tales to reconcile me to the dissolution of my marriage."

Kit started to tell her the truth. That the whole court, in its tangled jealousies and intrigues, enlarged upon tales about the queen to suit their own interests. The words had just formed on his lips when his wife drew herself up to her full height, which came to an inch or so below the tip of his chin. Once more her eyes flashed, this time with a message of unutterable contempt.

"I should have listened to Robert. As little as I wanted marriage to him, I want the queen's leavings even less. I can't believe I was so rash, so foolish, so damnably *stupid* as to bind myself to you last night!''

The scorn on her face spiked any desire Kit had to lay out the truth. Let her believe what she would. He had no time and little inclination at this moment to convince her otherwise.

"I'm not best pleased with your rash, foolish, damnably stupid act, either. Be that as it may, you will pack your trunk and come with me.''

"I don't wish to go anywhere with you!''

"Your wishes are beside the point, Lady Margaret. I tell you for a fact that I will truss you like a goose and haul you aboard the *Gull* over my shoulder, if I must.''

"You would not!''

"I would, and at this moment, the prospect holds considerable delight.''

She stiffened in outrage, and once again Kit was struck by the difference between the termagant who faced him now and the pale, sickly child he'd wed so many years ago. A fleeting regret for the time he'd missed with her darted into his mind…along with the realization that the woman she'd grown into now most definitely needed her sails trimmed.

He folded his arms across his doublet front. "The minutes pass, Lady Margaret, and with them your chance to gather your things.''

She saw that he was indeed serious. Her protest took on an urgent note.

"I cannot leave! Christmas is almost upon us.

There is the Yuletide feast to prepare for my tenants and their families, and alms to dispense to the poor. And after Christmas, I must arrange for the blessing of the plows and the—''

''Your steward can see to those tasks.''

''There speaks a man whose feet are planted not in the dirt, but on a deck,'' she scoffed. ''I am mistress of Oak Manor, and my steward takes direction from me in all matters regarding the farms and flocks.''

''Then you may pen your directions from the *Gull*. Whether you wish it or not, wife, you'll accompany the husband you were so determined to bind to you.''

''But...''

Kit ran out of patience. With a quick step forward, he dipped slightly and slung the woman over his shoulder.

She shrieked in protest. Her lower legs thrashed up a foam of skirts and petticoats. Digging her fists into his back, she levered herself up and panted her outrage.

''You great, rude oaf! You rug-headed clodpoll! Put me down at once! At once, I say!''

Ignoring her furious command, Kit dipped again to scoop up her cloak, then strode into the hall. The slap of feet sounded from all directions as house servants came running to see what was amiss. Kit swung around, causing his burden to shriek anew. He searched the gallery of astonished faces until he found the one he sought.

''Mistress Violet?''

"Sir Christopher?" The plump, raisin-eyed matron gripped the banister in astonishment. "Wh…what do you with my Meg?"

"I take her to the *Golden Gull*. We sail with the evening tide."

Violet clapped her hands to her cheeks. "Do not say so!"

"Pack a trunk with what she needs," Kit instructed, "and send it swiftly to the *Gull*, or your mistress shall spend the next weeks washing out her shift."

The wiggling weight on his shoulder twisted frantically around. "Violet! Worry not about a trunk. Send a message to Lord Brough! Bid him come at once and…oh!"

The solid whack to his wife's bottom, cushioned as it was by layers of velvet, wool and lawn, could cause no pain. It did, however, cut her off in midcry.

"We don't need Lord Brough to wish us godspeed, *wife*."

"Dolt!" She thumped a fist against his back. "Heavy-handed skimble-skamble!"

Ignoring her outraged invectives, Kit sketched a short bow to the gallery. "Farewell and happy Christmas, Mistress Violet. Send Lady Margaret's things to the *Gull*."

Hitching his burden up on his shoulder, he strode to the door. A wide-eyed manservant hesitated, then jumped to open it for him. Kit turned left, taking the cobbled walkway to the stables. As he passed the outbuildings, dairy maids, dovecote tenders and stable hands all poured from the outbuildings to gape at the spectacle of their mistress being carried off by…good gracious, was it really her husband!

Kit smiled wryly at the wave of shocked whispers that flowed around the stable yard like a tidal wash. When he set his furious burden atop the mount he'd borrowed from Drake's own stables, his smile widened into a grin.

'Struth, she might just make a wife worthy of a sea rover. Black as a storm-filled night, her hair whipped in the morning breeze. Flags of color rode high in her cheeks. Her eyes spit green fire, and her bosom threatened to spill from her bodice with the force of her anger. He didn't doubt she would cheerfully and most thoroughly gut him and leave his entrails for the crows to feast on if she could.

Kit tossed up her cloak. "Here, wrap yourself. I don't want you to catch a chill. As I recall, you made a most whining, petulant patient."

Flinging the cloak around her shoulders, she glared at him. "I was but a child!"

"So you were." Kit took the reins from the gawking stable boy and swung into the saddle. "Which, as you took pains to demonstrate last night, you are no longer. Let's away, wife, and I'll soon see what other changes you have wrought."

Wheeling his mount, he took it through the manor gates. Once clear, he kicked the bay gelding into a trot. Perforce, the Lady Margaret had to wrap her arms around his waist to keep from jouncing off her makeshift pillion. Once Kit was sure she had a firm seat, he gave the gelding his head.

The sea called to him.

He would away, and his wife with him.

The *Gull*'s crew were no less astounded to see their captain escort a disheveled, muddied female up the gangplank than her servants had been to see him carry her off.

Word flew about the main deck and to those below faster than a rat fleeing the ship's cat. One seaman after another poked his head out of a hatch, or scurried down the ratlines to hit the deck with a plop of soft-soled shoes.

As with all sailors of the time, the *Gull*'s crew wore such clothing as struck their fancy. Some had purchased their baggy breeches and embroidered doublets with their share of plunder. Most adorned themselves with ruffles and plumes and velvets taken from captured ships. Such riches sat ill with faces that sported an assortment of puckered scars, missing teeth and black eye patches.

Kit's second in command adorned himself with even more finery than the rest. A short, bandy-legged Greek stolen from his native land as a mere babe by Moslem slavers, Xanthos wore gold rings in both ears and a black and red doublet studded with diamond buttons. His Venetians were of the finest wool, his ruff of Flemish linen. He strode forward with the rolling, sure-footed gait of one who'd spent his life on the sea.

Xanthos had joined Drake's crew the same year Kit had. Although a good ten years separated them in age, Xanthos claiming to be the older and the wiser, the two men had fought side by side, drunk side by side, and wenched with equal enthusiasm over the years. Kit would trust him with his life... and had in many a pitched battle.

The Greek's dark eyes gleamed as he measured the woman at Kit's side. "So! You've broken your so silly rule at last, my friend, and brought a wench aboard to pleasure you on this voyage. She looks a bit skinny in the shanks to mount one of your size, but..." His gaze lingered on the swell of bosom showing through the cloak's folds. "She'll do, Kristo, she'll do. How is she named?"

Before Kit could set Xanthos straight, his wife gave a little huff and shook off his hand. Stepping forward, she raked the Greek with an angry glance.

"You, sir, will address me as Lady Margaret, and if you don't take the lechery from your gaze at once, my husband shall run you through or toss you overboard or do whatever he usually does to men who offer insult to women aboard his ship."

Xanthos snatched at only one word in her stiff speech.

"Husband!" His incredulous gaze swept from the woman before him to the man at her side. "Do not tell me you are this husband who shall run me through or toss me overboard, Kristo!"

"I am."

A huge grin split the Greek's face. His black eyes roamed the lady's length once more.

"And this is the whey-faced little chit you wed? The one who puked in your lap at your wedding feast."

"One and the same," Kit drawled.

Xanthos rocked back on his heels, grinning even more at the disgusted expression Margaret turned on her husband.

"Have you told everyone about that awful day?"

"Not everyone." He cast his lieutenant a quelling look. "Only those I thought to call friend."

"And the spots," his supposed friend added. "He tells me, too, about the spots."

Margaret's eyes became glacial. "Indeed!"

With a gleeful look that said he was evening the score with Kit for every lost wager and real or imagined slight, Xanthos swept off his hat and bowed.

"May I say, Lady Margaret, you are much improved upon Kristo's memories of you."

"No, you may not."

Ice dripped from every syllable, but her coldness didn't faze the Greek. Crooking his arm, he offered it with a polish that would have done credit to one of Elizabeth's courtiers.

"I beg forgiveness if my clumsy tongue offends. Please, allow me to show you to the captain's quarters while he meets with the harbormaster who—" he tossed blithely to Kit "—awaits him even now on the quarterdeck."

Framed between the two men, the lady hesitated.

Taking her lower lip between her teeth, she glanced toward the hills that surrounded Plymouth. Uncertainty and worry clouded her eyes.

Kit felt a twinge of remorse at having pulled her from the only home she'd ever known, but he quickly hardened his heart against it. If either of them were to emerge unscathed from the tangle she'd wrought, he had to put some time and distance between his wife and the queen. Kit could only pray that any anger Elizabeth felt as a result of his wife's actions would have run its course by the time the *Gull* returned from its patrol.

If it did not...

His eyes went hard. He'd been content enough to let his marriage dissolve. Now that the Lady Margaret had given herself to him, however, she was his. And his she would remain.

"Go with Xanthos," he told her, more gruffly than he intended. "His mouth runs away with him at times, but he'll not offer you insult again—" he flashed the Greek a warning "—or I'll string a line through the rings in his ears and use it to hoist him to the topgallant."

Meg grimaced at the gruesome promise, but Xanthos merely laughed. "Come, lady, take my arm. I'll show you to the captain's cabin and you will tell me how it is you come to the *Gull.*"

"Your captain brought me," she said coolly, placing her fingers on his sleeve. "Much against my will."

"Oh so?" He shrugged. "Ah, well, for all his

handsome face, Kristo was ever cow-handed when it came to women.''

''That's not how I hear of it,'' she huffed.

Her tart reply held a touch of the same scorn that had infused her voice earlier. Xanthos clucked his tongue.

''I could tell you tales, lady. I could tell you tales.''

''I doubt it not! Whether I wish to hear them, though, is another matter.''

He led her off, grinning.

Shaking his head, Kit made his way down to the quarterdeck. He didn't doubt that by the time he got to his cabin, Xanthos would have dug a hole so deep for him with his wife that it would take every trick he knew to climb out again.

Ah, well, he'd learned a good many such tricks over the years. He didn't despair that one or two of them would work on the prickly wanton who'd bound herself to him. The idea of using them on his wife brought back a slow, stirring heat.

Forcing himself to attend to the business at hand, he ducked under the neatly roped rigging and made for the gentleman who waited impatiently for the payment that would drop the iron chain guarding the entrance to Sutton Harbor.

Kit paid the harbor fees and was making a last-minute check of the stowage of their additional supplies when a shout brought him out of the hold and back on deck. Like monkeys, his crew dropped from the shrouds all around him and gathered once more to gawk at the unusual sight of a female making her way up the *Gull*'s gangplank.

Kit hurried forward to offer his hand and help her to the deck. "You've come just in time, Mistress Violet. I thank you for bringing my wife's trunk, but you could have sent it with a groom and spared yourself this journey."

With a quick nod to two crewmen, he sent them to unload the wagon that had pulled up on the stone quay.

"I did not bring only my Meg's trunk, Sir Christopher." She waved a hand to cool plump cheeks heated from her climb up the gangplank. "I brought mine, too."

"What?" Kit's brows slashed together. "Surely you don't think to sail with us?"

"I do."

Her reply raised a wave of muttered comments from the crew. The captain's wife was one thing. But a second petticoat aboard? That was another kettle of fish. Women had no place on board a fightin' ship.

Privately Kit agreed. Unlike many captains, he didn't allow the harbor trollops who serviced his crew to ply their trade below decks. Nor had he thought until today to bring his wife aboard, as many captains did. The *Gull* was built to fight, and fight it did. Kit had no desire to see any woman gutted by splintered spars or torn apart by grapeshot. Nor would he have forced Lady Margaret aboard had not his orders sent him north into the Atlantic, when he believed with every bone in his body the Spanish fleet, when it came, would come south through the channel.

"You need not scowl at me," Violet said with unruffled calm. "Where my Meg goes, I go. As Huthburt often said, you must take the curds with the cream or you get no cheese."

"Who the devil is Huthburt?"

"He was my husband, sir, and a stout heart he was." She gave her linen coif a little tug to straighten it. "Now show me below that I may see to my charge. And send the cook to me, if you will. I've brought recipes for possets and potions to make sure Meg keeps down the contents of her stomach on this voyage."

That convinced Kit to agree to her presence. Summoning the ship's boy, he instructed the lad to escort the berry-cheeked goodwife below.

Chapter Four

Contrary to everyone's expectations, her own included, Meg took to the ship's movement like one born in a longboat and cradled in a sea chest.

To be sure, she clutched Violet's arm when she heard the groan of the capstan and the shriek of the anchor chain being winched up. And she would be the first to admit that her stomach lurched when the wind caught the running sails and the *Gull* heeled hard to one side. Yet her legs were as steady as her resolve when she slipped on a warm, fur-lined cloak and wool mittens and climbed the stairs that led from the captain's quarters to the poop. She could not, would not, sail away without a last glimpse of her beloved Devon hills.

December darkness had already begun to cast long shadows across the sky. In a blur of purple shadows and flickering lights, Plymouth's buildings and battlements slipped past. When the great chain that guarded the harbor splashed down and the *Gull* glided into the sound, her gloved fingers dug into the rail. She lifted her gaze to the pastures and fields dotting the hills above the gray cliffs. A lifetime of responsibility weighed heavy on her shoulders, and her mind whirled with thoughts of all she'd left undone at Oak Manor.

How would her servants and tenants manage without her? Without Violet? Would Cook see to that nasty scald on the third kitchen maid's arm? Would Tom Longshanks, her least dependable crofter, make sure that the ditches dividing his fields from Will Butterman's were cleared of winter rubble so the fields might drain? Would her steward collect the rents in time to meet the spring assizes?

And the Yuletide festivities!

Who would see them done? Who would send the maids to gather sprigs of rosemary, holly, ivy and mistletoe to string throughout the manor? Who would oversee the baking that sent the mouthwatering scents of mince pies and currant cakes curling through the house. Who would order the Yule log cut and pay the mummers and musicians?

Despite the fact that Christmas also brought the anniversary of her marriage to an absent husband, Meg always strove to make it a happy time for all at Oak Manor. For the first time in her life, she would not be there to celebrate with them. She'd miss Christmas, and mayhap Epiphany as well.

Dear Lord, would she return home even in time for the plowing? The lambing?

She was so caught up in her worries that it was some time before she realized that the *Gull* had skimmed around Hobbs Point. The sea had grown more choppy, the wind more brisk. But her stomach had stayed firmly fixed in place!

She was not the only one who appreciated that gratifying fact. When he made his way to her side some moments later, her husband eyed her wind-whipped hair and tingling cheeks with some surprise.

"I didn't expect to find you standing upright this far from shore."

"Nor did I," Meg admitted truthfully.

A smile tugged at his mouth. "Just to be safe, I wouldn't advise you to partake of anything more than ship's biscuits and wine for supper."

Her face fell. In her anger and resentment at her abrupt removal from Oak Manor, she'd barely touched the bread, cold beef and cheese the ship's boy had brought her and Violet for a belated dinner. She didn't fancy the prospect of going without supper, as well.

She angled her head back, eyeing her husband. "Perhaps by the time we sit down to table you'll see that I have, indeed, outgrown my childish ill humors."

"Perhaps," he returned noncommittally. His gaze lingered on her face, as though he expected it to go green at any moment.

While he studied her, Meg made bold to study him in turn. She had to admit that he made a most impressive sight. She'd never seen a man more suited to the fashions of the times. Some might think the gold ring in his ear a bit rakish, but his trunk hose molded firm, muscled calves and strong thighs. His black doublet drew the eye from his lean hips and waist to his wide shoulders. With the wind rifling through his tawny hair and his legs spread wide against the pitch and roll of the deck, he looked like what he was…the absolute master of his ship and all those aboard her.

The thought added to the hollowness in Meg's stomach. Did he think to master her, as well? Was that why he'd forced her aboard? Did he think to ease between her thighs tonight and ride her as he'd ridden her last night at the inn?

Without warning, her womb tightened. The intense sensation startled Meg, as did the idea of joining with her husband again.

Did he plan to lie with her during this voyage?

Did she wish him to?

No, no, of course not! She'd done what she'd done of necessity. Nothing more. She barely knew this man. Had not the least understanding of his nature or his ways. Until she and Sir Christopher resolved the course their marriage would chart through the murky waters ahead, she'd insist that they keep to separate beds. Violet, not the captain, would share the great cabin with her.

Mayhap someday, though, she'd taste again his mouth. Mayhap she'd feel his muscles bunch under his skin as he took her in his arms and…

Her womb spasmed again. Disgusted with the carnality of her thoughts and her traitorous body, Meg groped for distraction.

"May I poke about the ship a bit? I've never been aboard a galleon before. I would see her nooks and crannies."

"There are nooks and crannies even I don't like to poke into," he replied with a wry smile. "I'd best send the ship's boy with you, lest you stumble upon a sight that offends your sensibilities."

Meg lifted a brow, thinking that little could offend one who'd spent her entire life on a country manor. She suspected few ladies at the queen's court could fry a mess of tripe and onions, or stitch a stable boy's head with a steady hand. But if her husband preferred to think her still too delicate to sustain the sights she might encounter aboard the *Gull,* she would not convince him otherwise with argumentation.

Summoning the bright-eyed lad who seemed to lurk always within hailing distance of his captain, Kit instructed him to escort the Lady Margaret where she wished to go, other than the bilges, the head and the crew's quarters.

Accompanied by the boy, John Smallwood by name, Meg soon discovered a fascinating world where every rope, every knot, every sail, yard, mast and deck had its own special name and place. Pride swelled the boy's chest as he pointed out the gold leaf gilding the *Gull's* elaborate figurehead, the sixteen pounders on the main gun deck, the black-and-white tiles painted on the canvas stretched across the floor of the officers' mess.

Halfway through her tour, Meg caught the tantalizing scent of roasted meat rising through a grate in the floor.

"Is the kitchen below?"

"The galley? Aye, ma'am."

"Can we go down? I would see it." And perhaps snatch a bite of beef and bread.

"Well..." The boy hesitated, reluctance written clearly upon his face.

"Are you not allowed in the galley?"

"Oh, aye. I fetch the captain's meals, after all." His brow darkened. "'Tis just that the butcher's boy an' me is at odds, so to speak, an' the clophead ever keeps his great hams on a cleaver. I had to hop sprightly to dodge 'im just afore we sailed."

His tale of woe reminded Meg of the running feud between the towheaded lad who fed slops to the hogs and the second under dairyman. A galleon was not so different from a manor, after all.

"Well, I'll be at your side this time," she said, hiding a smile. "I don't doubt the butcher's boy will behave most circumspectly in my presence."

John brightened. "Aye, that he will. An' whilst we're there, I can fetch the captain's dinner. Yours and Mistress Violet's, too, if you tell me what you be wishin' to eat."

Considerably cheered by the prospect of filling her empty stomach with something other than ship's biscuit, Meg clambered down a set of stairs and spent a fascinating hour in the company of the *Gull*'s cook and his minions. She inspected ovens, store lockers, goat pens and chicken coops, and admired the ingenious roasting spit he'd devised, turned by the heat rising up the chimney that vented smoke above the decks. To tide her over until the dinner hour, she graciously accepted a bowl of pea soup brimming with thick chunks of fresh-cured ham and a currant pastry with the steam still rising from its flaky crust.

When she left, John Smallwood trailed behind with a heavily laden tray. Meg knew better than to offend his dignity by offering to assist him up the stairs.

Darkness blanketed the sky around them by the time she reached the quarterdeck. The air carried a wet chill that made Meg clasp her cloak tight about her shoulders. Three great lanterns mounted on the stern rail had been lit…to avoid a night collision, John informed her.

The men she passed didn't try to hide their curiosity. Some stared rudely, others touched their knuckles to their forehead in a sort of salute. Meg was breathless from the cold and running the gauntlet of their scrutiny by the time she climbed another short set of stairs and ducked through the portal that led to the captain's quarters.

John Smallwood set his burden on the polished oak table that took up most of the private dining room and began to lay out the dishes. Stripping off her cloak as she walked, Meg strolled into the bedchamber.

"You'll never believe how neat the kitchens are, Violet. Cook showed me the ovens and a roasting spit that turns with—"

She halted abruptly, her words sticking in her throat. Instead of her companion's plump, comfortable figure, she spied her husband, naked to the waist and bent over an intricately carved and outfitted washstand.

While he splashed away the soap lathered on his face, Meg looked hastily about the cabin for her companion. The area was almost as large as her own chamber at Oak Manor, and far more richly appointed with the plunder of many voyages. Exotic red silk covered the wide bed built, she suspected, to the captain's overlarge proportions. The great carved chair with its velvet-covered cushions could have graced a lord's withdrawing room. And the books! She'd never seen such a collection of leather-tooled, gilt-inscribed volumes.

She spotted her trunk stowed against one wall, and the little sandalwood casket, in which Violet had packed her brushes and what remained of the costly perfume she'd doused herself with last night. But she found no sign of her companion.

Stiffening, she waited until her husband finished his ablutions.

"Where is Violet?"

He scrubbed the wetness from his face with a linen towel and tossed it aside. "She's retired to her quarters."

"Her quarters? But I desired her to share these."

"Did you?"

With a lazy grace, he selected a clean shirt from the clothespress built into the far wall and pulled it over his head. Meg waited impatiently for it to settle on his shoulders.

"Yes, I did."

Shrugging, he reached for a richly embroidered doublet. "Our desires in that matter ran counter to each other."

"Our desires in *most* matters appear to run counter to each other," Meg retorted. "You did not wish to keep me to wife, and I did not wish to come aboard your ship."

Across the black-and-white painted floor, his eyes caught hers. "You chose to remain my wife, Meg. Now you must live with the consequences."

Lifting her chin, Meg met her husband's eyes. "By consequences, you mean I must bed with you?"

"Yes."

The bald reply took her breath away.

"And if I don't wish to?"

"As you said, our desires in most matters appear to run counter to each other."

"You...you would force me?"

"No, lass, I would not." His mouth curved. "But I should warn you that I'm not above slipping you a hair of the dog you slipped me last night."

"A hair of the...? Oh." Her cheeks heated. "You mean the potion."

"Aye," he drawled. "The potion."

Strolling forward, he curled a knuckle under her chin and tipped her face to his.

"From what I remember of last night, you came afire in my arms. And I...I lost myself in your silken heat.'' Like the slow ebb and flow of the tide, his thumb brushed across her lower lip. ''I think we could spark the same flame again, should we put our minds to it.''

Suddenly, Meg couldn't breathe. The thin whalebone reinforcing her bodice cut into her waist. Her heart thumped against her ribs so fast and hard she was sure he would hear it above the creaks and groans of his ship.

Before she could protest his familiarity, or even decide if she wished to, he took her cloak from her hands and hung it on a peg. Then he clasped her elbow and turned her toward the dining cabin.

''Come, have some wine and biscuit to take the edge off your hunger. Then we'll talk about this marriage of ours.''

Meg took the chair he held for her at the table and waited while he dismissed John Smallwood. The sound of the bolt sliding home made her start, as it had at the inn last night.

Then, she'd been an untried virgin screwing up her courage with wine and Violet's powders. Now she had a fair idea of what could occur between her and this man if he should insist upon it.

Would he?

Did she wish him to?

Awhirl with confusion, she reached for the wine he poured her and took a long swallow. The rich, sweet port slid down her throat and warmed her belly. The sight of her husband sprawling lazily in the chair opposite heated it even more.

His black doublet gaped open, as did the white linen shirt beneath. The base of his throat showed a swirl of gold hair. The ring in his ear glinted in the lamplight. Even in such careless pose, he had the look of coiled power and the confidence of a man who knows his worth. And the roguish handsomeness to steal a woman's heart. Any woman's.

No wonder the queen had taken a fancy to him, Meg thought with a touch of despair. Who could not?

Deciding to lay the bone bare upon the table, she met her husband's steady gaze. "Will you divorce me?"

"No."

"Even if the queen wishes it?"

"No."

The succinct reply made Meg blink. He was a man of direct words, this husband of hers.

"Why not? King Henry divorced two of his wives. His daughter might urge you to divorce yourself of your inconvenient spouse." Her fingers tightened on the stem of her goblet. "Or should I fear a tumble down a flight of stairs and a broken neck?"

He little liked her question, she could see. A wash of red rose up the column of his neck, and his blue eyes took on the chill of the sea outside.

"You have naught to fear from me, Lady Margaret."

Even before he growled the words, she knew they were true. Kit Walsh could have abused her last night at the inn. He could have used her even more roughly this morning, when he'd discovered the trick she'd played on him. True, she'd not liked being tossed over his shoulder and carted away from her home, but aside from a sorely dented dignity, she'd suffered no hurt.

There were more players in this game than Meg and her husband, however. Holding his gaze, she forced the question in her mind to her lips.

"And the queen? Have I aught to fear from her?"

When he did not immediately reply, her heart skipped a beat.

"Holy Mary!" she murmured, shaken. "What intrigues have I overset?"

"None." He leaned forward, his face grave. "I'm nothing more to her majesty than a bold, brash rogue she finds amusing. I want no titles nor high offices that would keep me from the sea and my ship."

He held her eyes. "There are those who believe otherwise, however. They would fan the flames of the queen's jealousies to oust me from her favor. I fear those flames could singe you, as well, Meg. You may yet lose the estate you hold so dear."

If not her head!

"I didn't know," she said faintly. "I didn't think…"

Never had she spoken truer words! Guilt crashed down on her with the force of the waves breaking against the cliffs below Oak Manor. She hadn't thought. She'd given no concern to any but her own selfish interests. Now she would pay the price for that selfishness, and her husband, too.

"I'm sorry," she whispered. "I meant you no harm. I swear it."

He muttered an oath under his breath and thrust back his chair. In two strides, he came around the table and pulled her up. His arms closed around her.

"And I didn't mean to frighten you. I only wished you to understand why I removed you so precipitously from Oak Manor."

His big hand stroked her hair. Shivering, she pressed closer, seeking comfort in his strength as if she were still the child he'd wed. His voice rumbled in her ear, deep and soothing.

"Elizabeth's rages burn fierce, but they burn fast. By the time we return, any anger the queen might feel toward either of us will have spent itself."

Meg tipped her head back. Tears trembled on her lashes. "I'll explain what happened to her. Tell her it was all my doing, not yours."

To her utter astonishment, his cheeks creased in a wicked grin.

"It wasn't *all* your doing, lass. My memories of last night fuzz a bit at the corners, but I seem to remember playing some part, too."

Meg blinked. Their very lives might turn on what had occurred at the Bird and Crown, and he jested about it? Was he mad?

She didn't realize she'd muttered her thoughts aloud until he slid a hand around her throat. Heat passed from his flesh to hers.

"Yes," he murmured, his grin softening into a roguish smile that made Meg's stomach flutter. "I must be mad, to desire above all things to take a skinny, sickish wife to my bed.''

Her breath caught. Could she yield to the invitation in his eyes? Did she wish to?

Yes! God help them both, yes! Fire kindled in her belly at the thought of lying with this man again. She ached to feel his hands on her once more, and his mouth on her flesh.

She tried to rationalize the sudden weakening in her knees. He was her husband. For this night. For these weeks. Who knew what uncertain future they would face when they returned to England?

Throwing her cap to the winds, she answered the question in his eyes with a shaky, tremulous smile.

''I've tried to tell you, husband, I'm no longer sickish.''

''Are you not, wife?''

''No.'' Her lashes fluttered down. ''Nor, do I think, most would consider me skinny.''

''Would they not?''

In response, she leaned forward, pressing her body to his. Her breasts mounded above her square-cut bodice.

''No,'' he said, his voice of a sudden low and husky. ''Mayhap not.''

He searched her eyes for a moment longer, then framed her face with his hands and bent his head.

Meg had not the least idea how desperately she'd wanted his kiss until his mouth took hers. It consumed her, lifted her, fired her with a need that sprang full force to life.

She could not be sure whether she pushed aside his doublet and shirt, or he did. If her life depended on it, she could not say how her hairpins came to scatter about the floor and her hair tumbled down her back. All she knew, all she wanted to know, was the taste of his mouth on hers and the feel of his hands swift and sure on her body.

Long, long aeons later, he broke the kiss. His eyes ablaze with a need that fed her own, he swept her into his arms and carried her to the bed.

In mere moments, she was naked and trembling. In only moments more, he joined her in the bed. Strong and full and ready as any of the stallions at Oak Manor, he held himself back until he'd brought her to gasping readiness.

Even then, he would not join with her.

She tried. In her untutored way, she tried most desperately to bring him into her. Her legs wrapped with his. Her hips lifted against his.

"Oh, no, lass."

The devilish whisper tickled her ear.

"This time, no ale or wine or potions dull my senses. This time, I would hear your every moan. Watch your every arch and twist. Taste your mouth…"

He did. Most thoroughly.

"Your throat…"

She threw back her head and offered it to him.

"Your breasts…"

Sweet heaven! She was afire!

"Your very essence…"

Never, ever had Meg dreamed that she could endure such exquisite torture and survive.

Not only did she survive, she woke in the small hours of the dawn with the burning desire to undergo such torture yet again.

She thought to nudge awake the gently snoring giant beside her, or drop a kiss on the shoulder pinning her to the bed, but her inexperience as a wife made her hesitate. How often could a husband rise of a night?

Uncertain about such matters, she eased out from under his weight and slipped from the bed. She needed wine to ease a throat raw from the groans she'd so shamelessly emitted, and time to consider how to go about this matter of wifehood.

The painted floor felt cool to her feet, the wine soothing to her throat. She was contemplating her next move when her gaze snagged on the little sandalwood casket Violet had brought with Meg's things.

She hurried to the chest. Raising the lid, she eased aside a jumble of combs and pins and lifted out the vial of blue Venetian glass. Its stopper tinkled in the quiet. The scent of jasmine and musk and frankincense rose to tease her nostrils. She daubed the perfumed oil sparingly on her throat and breasts. She didn't want to stink with it, as she had last night.

Wrapped in a cloud of scent and nothing more, she padded back to the bed and tried to slip under the richly embroidered silk coverlet. Her movements disturbed her slumbering husband. He muttered, curled his arm around her waist and pulled her to him. Slowly he came awake. When he rolled her over and inserted his leg between hers, Meg felt his shaft hard and rampant against her thigh. Swallowing a laugh at having doubted his abilities, she opened to him.

He mistook the strangled sound and froze. "Do I hurt you?"

"No." She saw the hesitation in his eyes and reached up to wrap her arms around his neck. "No, truly."

He rested his weight on his forearms. His muscles quivered with restrained strength. "Are you sure?"

His gentleness fanned Meg's burning desire to something higher, something purer. Something she might have called love were it not too soon and she too untutored in such emotion.

Yet the strange feeling tugged at her heart. For all she'd duped him and drugged him and forced him to remain in a marriage he had not wanted, Kit Walsh had used her with such consideration that she ached with it.

"Yes," she whispered, "I'm sure."

Still unconvinced, he bent his head and buried his face in the hollow of her shoulder.

"I'll take this scent with me to the grave," he murmured against her skin. "You near drowned me in it last night."

"I near drowned myself." She hesitated, then said shyly, "'Tis oil of Araby. You gave it to me."

"Did I?"

His mouth roamed lower.

"Yes," she gasped. "As one of my bride gifts."

He lifted his head, his eyes twinkling.

"Ah, sweeting, I make no claims to being as wise as the kings who brought gifts to Bethlehem. But all unknowingly I chose the right scent for you. Frankincense and jasmine. So exotic. So rare and—" he smiled down at her "—so precious."

Meg gave a swift, silent prayer that the oil in the glass vial would last the voyage. Sighing with a happiness she would not have imagined a week, even a day ago, she pulled his mouth down to hers.

She could not know that her fragile, fleeting happiness would shatter the next afternoon.

Chapter Five

Meg stood on the poop deck, her cheeks pinked with cold and her eyes alight with laughter at Xanthos's banter. Having taken it upon himself to explain to her and Violet the fine art of seamanship, the curly-haired Greek had spent the past half hour extolling the *Gull*'s superior qualities.

"Now Mistress Violet, you must see it. Yes, you must. The *Gull* has the grace of a lady and the heart of a bold, brassy strumpet. What man could not call himself content to live his life aboard a ship like this?"

Violet tut-tutted at his blatant foolery and took refuge in quoting her dear Huthburt. With a silent groan, Meg turned her attention to the two men who stood some yards away. One, a short, leathery seaman, squinted through some instrument Xanthos had called an astrolabe. The other…the other made her heart thump.

By the stars, he was a man to make any woman's heart go wild. The weak winter sunlight added a haze of gilt to his wind-tossed hair. He disdained a hat, even in the nipping cold of the Atlantic and had exchanged his fine velvets for a doublet of padded leather lined with warm wool. Once again, Meg was struck by his unconscious air of command. To her surprise, she felt a dart of something very akin to jealousy.

The sea was his life. This ship was the only reason he'd wed her. In exchange for his name and his promise to abide by the strict agreements Meg's father had written into their marriage contracts, Kit Walsh had gained a sickly little wife and a strong, sure ship.

Was it but yesterday that she'd stood on the cliffs behind Oak Manor and listened to the boom of cannons? Just short hours ago that she'd breathed a sigh of relief at the mistaken belief that her husband had sailed away from Plymouth for who knew how many weeks or months or years?

Now the realization that she'd put him and the ship he so loved at risk gnawed at her like a dog at a bone. Surely Elizabeth wouldn't punish Kit for Meg's precipitous action. Surely the queen's anger, if she felt any, would have blown over by the time—

"Sail ho!"

The faint cry carried down from high above. Shielding her eyes against the hazy noon sun, Meg craned her neck and squinted up at the figure clinging to a rope with one hand and waving wildly with the other.

''Hard astern!''

She barely had time to grasp the words before all aboard the *Gull* sprang into action. Shouting for John Smallwood to fetch his glass immediately, Kit whirled and strode to the rail.

Xanthos abandoned the two women without a backward glance. He ran for the rail and bellowed out the promise of an extra ration of grog for the first man to spot the colors. Those of the crew above decks scrambled aloft. Those below came pouring out of hatches as word spread. Faces tight and eyes intent, they crowded the rails to peer into the swirling mists.

Meg's lungs seemed to freeze in her chest. Of a sudden, the ship's true purpose burst upon her. The *Gull* was no graceful lady, nor even the bold, brassy strumpet Xanthos had named her. She was a ship of war, built to prey upon England's undeclared encmy. An enemy who, despite his false promises of peace, even now gathered the greatest fleet ever seen to attack her.

Was this distant ship part of the fleet?

Did more lurk behind it in the mists?

Scarce breathing, Meg clutched Violet's hands and waited for one of the crew to win his extra ration of grog. The *Gull* dipped and rose on the waves. The mists gathered, parted. The crew strained and mumbled among themselves.

The sound of the captain's brass spyglass snapping shut cracked through the air like a whip. He turned and strode to the rail that edged the poop deck.

"I have her colors, lads. She's of Spain."

A great fist seemed to squeeze Meg's heart, but not the crews'. To her astonishment and dismay, they gave a wild cheer. Evidently the prospect of a fight ahead banished all disappointment at missing a double ration of grog.

Kit stilled them with a raised hand. "Until we know if this ship sails alone or is part of the vanguard of the accursed armada, we'll dance around it."

"The devil with such dancin'," a broad-bellied crewman protested. "We can take any slow-bottomed scow launched by the papists."

"Aye, Cap'n! Let's have at 'er. Let's have at the whole bloody fleet!"

Grinning at their bravado, Kit shook his head. "Our orders are to bring word if we spot the Spanish fleet, not take it on."

His glance slid sideways. For a moment, his eyes met Meg's. His grin seemed to tighten, but was once again wide and cheerful when he faced his crew.

"We'll take her, lads, if she sails alone. If not, we'll lead her and any that follow her a merry chase. Gunners, get below and open the gun ports. Xanthos, take the deck."

Passing the spyglass and a few private words to his second in command, he made his way to the two women.

"You'd best go below. It could get lively above decks."

"Lively!" Gulping, Meg fought down her sudden

panic. "Do you...? Do you think this ship is really part of the armada?"

Kit's gut wrenched at the question. With every instinct he possessed, he believed the Spanish would sail south through the Channel to embark their vast army in the Netherlands before turning to attack England. So said the many English spies in Spain. So said every seasoned commander and sea captain worth his salt.

But...

A cold sweat chilled Kit's brow. What if they were wrong? What if the hundred or more ships Philip of Spain had been readying for over a year were even now rising on the *Gull*'s stern? What if they intended to attack Ireland, or perhaps land in Scotland to rally those Scots still loyal to their dead queen against England? What if the vast Spanish fleet was even now sailing north through gray Atlantic waters?

What if he had plucked Meg from one possible danger, only to expose her to another, even more grave? Damning himself a thousand times over for bringing her aboard, Kit forced a reassuring smile to his face.

"I don't know if this ship is part of the Spanish fleet or not. If it is, we'll sight other sails soon enough and speed back to port with the news. If not, well, she's a fine prize ripe for our picking."

"Prize?" Meg's eyes rounded. "You mean you'll attack her?"

"I must. I would know why she's in these waters."

His smile came more naturally at the thought of taking the gift that had unexpectedly fallen into his lap.

"The *Gull* can outmaneuver and outshoot any ship the Spanish put to sea," he said with the confidence of one who has proved his words many times over. "What's more, she carries a layer of lead sheathing between her double hulls. No Spanish ball has yet penetrated her inner skin, nor will it."

"So I should hope," his wife said faintly.

Beside her, Violet wrung her hands. "Hope maketh a good breakfast, as my Huthburt would say, but a thin supper!"

"Your Huthburt would be wrong in this case," Kit replied with a grin. "Get below now, mistress, and make yourself at ease."

His gaze shifted to his wife. Imperceptibly his grin softened.

"You, too, lass. I'll send John Smallwood to let you know what's apace."

Her green eyes huge, she stared up at him. Then, to Kit's great surprise and the lusty cheers of his watching crew, she threw herself onto the tips of her toes, wrapped her arms around his neck and bussed him soundly.

Curling an arm about her waist, Kit gave as good as he received. Color filled her cheeks once more when he at last released her.

"If you send John Smallwood to keep us apprised," she said breathlessly, "send him to the surgery. Violet and I shall offer your ship's doctor what assistance we may.''

His eyes glinted with approval. ''Now there speaks a brave captain's wife!''

Ha! Little did he know!

Never, ever, in all her years, had Meg endured such cowardly terror as she did in the next three hours. Not even her father's slow, agonizing death and her subsequent marriage to a towering stranger had prepared her for such gut-wrenching, heart-knocking fear.

The first inkling of what was ahead came from John Smallwood.

''It be a great, wallowing warship!'' the boy shouted. Barreling through the portal to the surgery, he skidded to a stop a few feet from Meg. ''New built, too, from the look of her shiny gilt and un-patched sails.''

''Warship!'' Meg felt the blood drain from her face. ''Then it's truly the armada!''

''No, no! The mists have cleared, and we can spot no other sail anywhere on the horizon. The cap'n says this one most likely blew off course. We'll know soon enough when we takes 'er.''

Meg swallowed. ''So we're going after her?''

''That we are,'' the boy replied with great good cheer.

A groaning shriek that could have raised the dead on All Hallows' Eve cut through Meg's tumultuous thoughts. Slowly the *Gull*'s massive helm brought the rudder around. The ship began to list.

"We're coming about!" John Smallwood exclaimed. "I'd best get myself topside or I'll miss the first broadside!"

Spinning on his heel, the eager lad dashed out. Meg lifted her gaze to meet Violet's round, black eyes. Her friend and companion essayed a weak smile.

"Come, child, we must trust Sir Christopher to know what he's about. Your husband's a good man and, I suspect, an even better captain. One worthy of the queen's regard…and yours."

"Yes," she whispered. "He is. He'll bring us home."

In a determined attempt to shake free of her fears, Meg turned to the chest of medicines the ship's surgeon had opened for their inspection.

"Come, Violet, let's get to work. We'd best know what's at hand before…" She gulped. "Before the first broadside."

It came not twenty minutes later. Roaring out of the portside cannons like the screams of hell. Booming across the water like a broken roll of thunder. Shaking the entire ship.

Meg began to pray.

She was still praying when John Smallwood came running into the surgery some two hours later. Skirting around the surgeon and his cursing patient, he hurried to where Meg stitched a lacerated scalp.

"The Spaniard be striking her colors!"

As black faced with powder and grime as Meg was chalk white with fear, the boy hopped from foot to foot in his excitement.

"The cap'n says for you to gather your things, ma'am. You and Mistress Violet. He be puttin' you both aboard the Spanish ship as soon as we secure the prisoners."

Without meaning to, Meg jerked around. "What?"

The injured seaman she was stitching muttered a curse, then blushed brick red when Meg's apologetic gaze came swinging back to his.

"I'll finish," Violet said quickly, taking the curved bone needle from her hand. "You see what this is about."

The boy spun and raced out. Gathering her skirts, Meg followed him up the zigzagging flights of stairs. As soon as she stepped onto the open deck, cold air hit her in the face and blew away the smells of sweat and gunpowder that fumed the air below.

Her anxious eyes swept the *Gull*'s deck, then the rigging. She saw a great, gaping hole in one sail and noted a missing stretch of rail. Her untrained eye could detect little other damage.

Even she, however, could see that the ship riding the waves some fifty yards or more away had taken far more serious hits. A jagged hole showed just above the water line. Her main mast had snapped in half and dragged down sail, tackle and shrouds. A smaller mast had been shorn off just above the deck.

Holes peppered her sides and her rudder, which had lifted half out of the water.

To Meg's horrified eyes, the ship looked as though she would sink at any moment and take all men aboard with her. Including, she saw with a gasp, the golden-haired giant who braced himself on the slanting deck to accept the sword of a scowling Spaniard.

"Is that ship going down?" she demanded of John Smallwood in a voice of near panic.

"Naw. She's but listing a bit. She'll be right and tight as soon as we pump 'er out and patch the hole in 'er side."

Despite his assurances, Meg did not breathe easy until Kit climbed down the side of the tilting ship, into a longboat and up over the rail of the *Gull* once more.

Grinning, he started toward her. Only then did she see the patch that darkened his leather doublet.

Her stomach fell to the soles of her shoes, and in that instant she knew that she'd given not just her long-cursed virginity to the rogue she'd wed so many years ago. She'd given her heart, as well.

"We've taken a grand prize," he announced, his eyes alight with the joy of victory. "One of Philip's newest galleons, launched but a week ago and blown far north of its course by a winter storm!"

Meg cared not a fig about the galleon. Her hands went to the slashing tear in the leather doublet and came away red.

"You're hurt!"

"It's a scratch, nothing more. How do the men in surgery fare?"

"Well enough. Come, let me tend to this scratch that bloodies your entire front."

He caught her elbow when she started back to surgery. "There isn't time, Meg, nor any pressing need. The surgeon can see to me when the *Santa Maria*'s patched and you're away on her."

Her gaze flicked to the Spanish ship, then back to her husband.

"Why must I away? What's happening, Kit?"

He hesitated, as if reluctant to add to her fears.

"Tell me."

"The captain of the *Santa Maria* let drop that there are more ships in these waters. All new launched and still undergoing sea trials. I think it a bluff, a desperate ploy to scare us off before we could secure our prize, but I have to see if he lies or speaks the truth."

"No! You can't go hunting alone! You said your orders were to bring word of the invasion back to the queen, not take it on full force!"

"It's not the invasion. At most, it's a handful of ships blown north by the storm."

"What if it is not?"

"I must make sure, Meg. Neither my conscience nor my men would give me rest if I did not." He gripped her arms. "I will not take you with me, though. Not this time. I won't put you at such risk again."

"But…"

"I'm sending Xanthos back with the captured gal-leon. He'll take it to London to inform the queen of the circumstances of her capture."

"But—"

"Listen to me! Xanthos has instruction to turn the prize over to the queen for such use as she deems fit. Such an addition to the Royal Navy will go far toward soothing any anger she might feel toward me or mine."

Still racked with guilt over the havoc she'd played with her husband's life, Meg could only mumble, "And so I should hope!"

"Xanthos will put you and Violet ashore at Plym-outh before he makes all speed to London. Wait there until I come to you."

She drew in a sharp breath. A pain pierced her heart, so needle pointed that she could have cried with the ache of it. He would not divorce her, but he would send her back to Oak Manor and the hus-bandless life she led before.

It was what she'd wanted. What she had schemed for. So why did the prospect leave the taste of ashes in her mouth?

"I see," she said slowly. "I will abide in Plym-outh while you roam where you will, as we did these many years before."

To her surprise, the corners of his eyes crinkled with tender laughter. He used his hold on her arms to draw her forward.

"No, wife, not quite as before. Now that I've

breathed in your scent and tasted your tartness, I've developed a most contrary craving for both.''

The pain in Meg's chest became more bearable. Infinitely more bearable. In fact, she hardly noticed it at all.

''Oh, so?''

''Oh, so, my little witch.''

He kissed her, hard and swift and sure, then turned her toward the hatchway.

''Now ready yourself. As soon as we patch the *Santa Maria*'s hole, you will away.''

Chapter Six

Ever after, Meg was never sure when the notion came to her to go to Elizabeth.

Perhaps it was while she stood at the rail of the *Santa Maria,* watching the masts of the *Golden Gull* grow smaller and smaller in the distance.

Or the next morning, when the Spanish ship picked up the softer, warmer winds that blew from the South Atlantic.

Or when the lookouts perched atop the masts spotted Land's End and shouted down the word.

She only knew that she must do something by the time she joined Violet in the magnificent cabin that had once belonged to the Spanish captain.

"Xanthos says Sir Christopher will sail straight into the teeth of the armada if he should chance upon it," Violet said worriedly, stuffing garments haphazardly into the trunk.

"His orders are to report it, not attack it!"

"He will report it, Xanthos says, but not afore he sinks what ships he can."

"He would not be so foolish as to take on the armada. He could not!"

But he could. He would.

Meg's stomach clenched with fear for her bold, brash husband. Thinking furiously, she paced the cabin.

"Drake and the entire Royal Navy are patrolling the Dover straits," she said a moment later.

Violet snorted. "Much good *that* acorn does our goose!"

"Just so! Drake should send one or more of his ships to these waters to aid Kit."

"No doubt the queen would so command it if her counselors advised. The trouble is, Xanthos says that the landsmen who advise her don't know their arses from…" She broke off, blushing like a maid. "Well, he says they're not seawise."

Meg blinked in surprise at the red stains on Violet's plump cheeks. Belatedly, it dawned on her that her friend quoted the Greek even more than her own Huthburt these past days. Thrusting that curious circumstance aside, she concentrated on the truth of Violet's observation.

"This is not a matter for mere counselors." A few paces more brought Meg to a momentous decision. "I shall go to London and add my pleas to Xanthos's report."

"Margaret!" Violet gasped. "The captain told you to wait for him at Oak Manor."

"And so I shall." Meg's mouth set in a determined line. "After I have been to see the queen."

As might be expected, Xanthos vigorously protested this change in his orders, but Meg proved most stubborn and intractable. With Violet adding her reluctant weight to the arguments, he eventually gave way. Only after Plymouth had dropped far astern did he admit that he, too, worried greatly about the captain.

Two endless days later, *Santa Maria* dropped anchor in the Thames estuary and was greeted by an excited Royal Admiral who wanted to know how the Spanish ship came into English hands. While Xanthos explained and arranged for a board of inquiry to confirm the disposition of the prize, Meg waited impatiently for him to finish.

Snow swirled through the air and added a mantle of lace to yards and sheets. Shivering in her warmest cloak and finest gown, she at last bid a tearful Violet farewell and clambered down to the barge that Xanthos had hired to take them upriver. The bargemen oared vigorously, cursing the cold, the snow and the other boats that cut across their prow.

By the time they arrived at the sprawl of buildings on the banks of the Thames that formed Whitehall Palace, Meg's stomach had tied into a tight knot of apprehension. She'd never traveled farther from her birthplace than Exeter, to attend the Great Assizes. Yet now she stood on the very steps of the palace where King Henry had married his Anne Boleyn, already pregnant with Elizabeth.

Shivering, she and the wiry Greek hurried up the steps that led to the great, oaken gate. In the descending dusk, Whitehall blazed with the light of a thousand torches and candles. The sounds of revelry carried even to the distant gate, where Xanthos emptied his purse to have a note carried to her majesty's second undersecretary. Sir Barnaby, they were told, would determine whether Lady Margaret and her companion gained access to the palace grounds, much less to the Great Court itself.

The coins...and word of the prize that Kit had captured...worked magic. Adorned in diamond buttons and costly velvets slashed through with gold, Sir Barnaby himself came rushing through the outer courtyards.

His actions told Meg she was right to insist on accompanying Xanthos. Flicking the foreigner a dismissive look he hurried to her side.

"Lady Margaret? Is it true? Sir Christopher has captured a Spanish war galleon?"

"It's true."

Anxious questions tumbled from the queen's minister. "Are there more off our shores? Is it the armada? Why did he not alert the coast watchers, so they might light the warning beacons and sound the alarm?"

Swiftly Meg explained Kit's belief that the warship had been blown north by a storm while yet on its maiden sea trials, and that it was not part of the vanguard of the invasion. She also told of the Spanish captain's claim more ships lurked just over the horizon.

"My husband went to ascertain whether that was bluff or no," Meg reported, her throat tight.

"Strike me!" Barnaby muttered. "The queen must hear of this. It would be better if she got the news firsthand, but…" He eyed Meg, frowning.

"But what?"

He hesitated, then chose his words with obvious care. "Her majesty had formed the opinion that Sir Christopher's marriage would soon expire. She was most, shall we say, surprised when your cousin brought word to the contrary."

Meg's heart sank. Damn Robert to a thousand hells! He'd wasted little time in spreading his poison. Stilling her incipient panic, she forced her voice to calm. She could not, would not, let Kit bear the burden of blame for her rash act.

"I doubt not that our changed circumstances surprised the queen. They surprised my husband himself no little amount."

Barnaby blinked. Before he could offer further comment, Meg rushed on.

"I would speak with her majesty and tell her of my husband's great prize."

Barnaby studied her for a long moment, then lifted his shoulders in a shrug that implied 'twas her head. Her heart in her throat, Meg and Xanthos followed him through the maze of yards. With each progressive court, the buildings grew finer, the lights more brilliant, the soaring notes of trumpets more clear and clarionlike.

Leaving Xanthos to cool his heels in an antechamber, Sir Barnaby escorted Meg to a small withdrawing room just off the fabled Stone Gallery. With a promise to return immediately, he dashed away. Despite the trepidation that near choked her, Meg could not but gape as she gazed about the room.

Diamonds and other gems studded the painted ceilings. Precious silver tissue covered the walls. Gold and silver plate filled the massive chest that took up one whole wall. Elizabeth's royal arms were picked out in jewels and gold leaf above the fireplace.

And this for just a withdrawing room!

Only after she'd taken in the twinkling gems and shimmering metals did Meg notice other, less majestic touches. Festive garlands of holly, bay and ivy draped the sconces. Ribboned balls of mistletoe hung from the rafters. The scent of rosemary and Christmas spices carried above the sulfur of the flickering candles.

She blinked, counting the days in her mind.

Good heavens! Tomorrow was Christmas Eve. The day her marriage would have become null and void, if she hadn't taken it upon herself to see it consummated.

But she had. Now she was a woman well and truly wed.

The thought filled her with a satisfaction she could not have imagined a few days ago, and with a dread of the queen's reaction to the news that Sir Christopher's wife sought an audience with her.

She soon found that her dread was well-founded.

Elizabeth swept in just moments later, followed by several men garbed in furs and jeweled seals of office. Meg sank into a curtsy so deep her knee knocked the floor. The queen let her remain in that awkward position for what seemed like two lifetimes before bidding her to rise.

Trying desperately to hide her trembling, Meg straightened and waited for the queen to give her leave to speak. Elizabeth took her time about it. Eyes narrowed to mere slits, she raked Meg from the tip of her high-swept hair to the toes of her less-than-fashionable traveling shoes.

Meg, in turn, could do little more than gape at the magnificent apparition before her. No image stamped on a coin caught the queen's aura. No oft-repeated verse or paean to England's monarch captured her regal magnetism.

A less awestruck observer might have noted that the virgin queen had long since passed the first flush of her maidenhood. A more discriminating eye might have discerned the pockmarks on her cheeks left by a bout with smallpox early in her reign. Meg saw only red hair still bright with fire, a thin, aristocratic face framed by a ruff sparkling with diamonds, and blue eyes as cold as ice.

"We have heard much of you of late, Lady Margaret," Elizabeth said at last. "How dare you show your face to us?"

Meg shook with fear, but she knew she had to speak fast and bold. "I dare, because I'm told you hold my husband in some affection."

Elizabeth's mouth curled. "Oh, so? And you think to profit from this affection?"

"No! No, I swear! I seek nothing for myself, your majesty. I know I deserve nothing except censure for my foolish, foolish selfishness in binding Kit to me when he wished it not."

"He did not?" The queen's thin, penciled brows lifted. "Your cousin tells us another tale."

"Robert Clive wants to gain my lands and my hand. He was most displeased when I..." She swallowed. "When I..."

"When you played the whore to entrap your husband."

The stinging truth sent heat into Meg's cheeks. Swallowing, she could only nod her head.

"Explain to us why you come to Whitehall," the queen demanded imperiously. "Do you hope to soften our displeasure by bringing news of Sir Christopher's prize yourself?"

"I hope to convince you to send him aid, your majesty. Most swiftly."

"Aid?" For an instant, Elizabeth's haughty demeanor faltered. Her face paled beneath its dusting of white powder. "Is it the armada? Sir Barnaby assured me Sir Christopher believes it is not."

"And so he does," Meg hastened to explain. "But I fear... I worry... I would beg you send another ship, mayhap two, to guard his flanks...just in case."

Elizabeth frowned. "Did he send you here to make this plea?"

"No. He sent me back to Oak Manor, that I might

await upon his pleasure, and yours. It was my thought to come to you." She drew in a deep breath. "Just as it was my thought, and mine alone, to consummate our marriage."

"You take much upon yourself, do you not, Lady Margaret? You disobey your husband, and your whorish ways dishonor a man we admit to holding in some esteem."

There was no answer for that. None was expected.

"If...*when*...Sir Christopher returns to us, we shall speak to him about divorcing his sluttish wife. In the meantime, you may wait his pleasure in the Tower. Lord Burghley, you will see to this matter."

At the gray-haired earl's nod, Meg felt her knees go weak.

The Tower!

The queen lifted her pearl-encrusted skirts and turned to leave. Meg could not let her go. Not without assurance that she would at least consider sending ships to aid Kit. Shoving aside her choking fears, Meg fell upon her knees.

"I will agree most readily to a divorce, if that is what my husband wishes. But please, your majesty, please! Send him aid, I beg of you."

Elizabeth slowed her step, then halted. Once more, she turned. Her mouth thinned to a waspish line.

"Do you love him, you forward, foolish creature?"

Near sick with her own boldness, Meg nodded.

For a moment, a fleeting moment, she glimpsed a most curious expression on the queen's unlined face.

On another woman, it might have bespoken peevishness or loneliness or…could it be envy? It was gone before Meg could wonder how a queen surrounded from dawn to dusk by men who loved her could envy any woman.

"Attend to the Lady Margaret," she ordered the earl briskly. "Then come to me, that we may discuss this matter of dispatching ships to aid Sir Christopher."

With a whoosh of her skirts, Elizabeth swept out of the withdrawing room.

All her life, Meg had heard tales of the Tower of London. Constructed by William of Normandy and enlarged by kings and queens ever since, its turreted walls and massive fortifications served as royal residence, menagerie, treasure house, mint, armory…and as prison and burial ground for those who had incurred the sovereign's displeasure. Here, innumerable prisoners had been brought to confess their guilt. Here, traitors had died. Here, two queens had lost their heads, one of whom had been mother to Elizabeth.

Never, ever, had Meg dreamed that she would occupy a small, dank room in Beauchamp Tower, where John Dudley, Duke of Northumberland and his four sons had once awaited their fate at the hand of Elizabeth's older sister, Queen Mary. Never had she thought to stand, hour after hour, at a narrow slit of window and stare at gray prison walls and dirty snow tramped down in the bailey below.

For all the bleakness of her surroundings, her every thought was not for herself, but for a sleek ship riding white-laced waves and the tall, broad-shouldered captain who commanded her.

How did Kit fare? Had the *Gull* encountered only empty seas, or a huge flotilla? Had the queen sent other ships to its aid?

She had no news, no visitors except Violet, who came daily and brought fresh bread, hearty meat pies, and sweets. The matron confirmed that Xanthos had drawn upon his own and Sir Christopher's great wealth to ensure Lady Margaret's comfort as best as he could before he'd departed in search of Sir Francis Drake. Drake would come to Meg's aid, Violet sniffed.

Far better that he went to Kit's aid, Meg had cried.

Violet left each afternoon alternately awash with tears and fired with hope that she and her own dear Meg would soon go home to Oak Manor.

The days stretched endlessly. The nights were filled with a thousand bleak hours. Almost unnoticed by the Tower's residents, Christmas dawned cold and snowy. Throughout the long day, Meg would not let herself think of home. Of the Yule log that always blazed in the great hearth. Of the wassail bowl she ordered well filled. Of services in Plymouth cathedral, and visits to her friends.

That night, she stood at the slit window and looked not down, but up at the narrow slice of sky visible through the turrets. The swirling snows had cleared.

The stars shimmered in a black sky. One shone brighter than the others.

Was it the Christmas star? The same star that had guided the three kings to Bethlehem?

Meg could only pray that it was, and that it would guide Kit to a safe harbor.

Some two weeks after her fateful meeting with the queen, Meg's prayers were answered.

The sound of keys rattling in the lock roused her from an uneasy slumber. She bolted upright in her bed, startled and atremble. Clutching the blanket to her chest, she stared at the door with wide, apprehensive eyes.

The stout oak panel crashed back against the wall. A moment later, her husband ducked though the low portal. In the light from the flickering torch carried by the guard who'd accompanied him, he loomed huge and so wonderful Meg would have cried out in joy if she could have pushed a sound past the monstrous lump in her throat.

He swept the room and spotted her immediately. The fierce expression on his face gave way to one of such mingled tenderness that Meg wanted to weep with joy and relief.

"Well, well, wife. I find you ever abed."

"So…" She fought for breath. "So you do."

The tenderness faded. A grim scowl settled on his face. "And bed is where I'll keep you, I think. Chained if necessary, so you don't take such foolish risks again."

Before Meg could think how to respond to that, he strode across the room and bundled her into his arms. "Come, Mistress Violet awaits outside. You're going home."

Trailing coverlets and coarse linen sheets, he carried her past the impassive guard.

"I'm free?" Meg gasped. "Truly free?"

"No, you are not." He glanced down at her, not breaking stride. "You have bound yourself to me, now and forever, and so I have told the queen."

Cold air sliced into Meg's lungs. "You've spoken with the queen?"

"Aye, earlier this night. It took awhile to get her seal affixed to the documents recognizing your services to the Crown and ordering your release."

"My services? What have I done, except bring shame upon you with my sluttish ways and force myself to the queen's attention?"

"And in doing so, you little baggage, you convinced her to send two ships to my aid." He hefted Meg higher in his arms and turned sideways to take a winding stair that led to the bailey. "If events had not transpired as they did, I would take your lack of faith in my judgment and my seamanship as insult."

"Wh...what events?"

His lips lifted in a slashing grin. "The very morning that Elizabeth's ships hailed the *Gull*, we sighted five more new-built Spanish galleons. They'd blown north like the *Santa Maria* during their sea trials, and we took them all."

"Each and every one?"

"Each and every one!"

He kissed her then, as Meg had been aching for him to do since the moment he burst into her room. When he lifted his head, the hunger in his eyes set her aflame.

"Damned if I didn't carry your scent with me in my dreams."

"Only my scent?" she asked breathlessly.

"That was enough, wench. If I live to be fourscore and twenty, every time I catch a whiff of frankincense I'll see you wide-eyed and naked."

At that instant, Meg swore to always, *always,* keep the little Venetian vial he'd given her filled to over-brimming with oil of Araby.

Still grinning, he hit the bottom of the stairs and crossed a cavernous entry. The yeoman guard in his red-striped uniform had obviously been awaiting the captain's reappearance. He threw open the stout door to the bailey and tipped his fingers to his hat.

Kit swept out, and Meg almost sobbed with joy at seeing more than just a narrow slice of stars. One in particular caught her eye.

"Look!" She dug an arm out of the enfolding blankets to point to the bright glow hanging low in the East. "The Christmas star still shines. I prayed that it would guide you home safely."

His arms tightened around her. He slowed his pace, then stopped. The guard escorting them went ahead to order the outer gate opened. For a moment, it was if they were alone in the vast palace that had seen so many regal celebrations and broken dreams.

"I'm sorry, Meg. I did not mean that you should spend the Yuletide in such dismal circumstances, so far from your home."

A shudder racked her. "Nor would I choose to do so ever again!"

"I'll make these dismal days up to you, I swear. I have the queen's leave to take you home to Oak Manor. We'll make a belated feast, and dance and laugh and gift each other with trinkets and kisses."

Taking her courage in both hands, Meg lifted her face to his. "I don't want trinkets from you, or feasting and dancing."

"What of kisses?" he asked, his eyes searching hers. "Do you want them, wife?"

Sighing, she slipped her arms around his neck.

"Oh, yes, husband. I've come to think them the greatest gift of all."

* * * * *

A TOUCH OF MYRRH

Suzanne Barclay

To Ken, still the best Christmas gift
I've ever received.

Chapter One

London, 19 December, 1387

It was a perfect night for thievery.

The sky was dark and moonless, the streets nearly deserted, most folk having been driven indoors by the icy wind that whistled down the stone and timber canyons of the city. Even Cosen Lane in The Steelyard, normally abustle with traffic from the nearby docks, was quiet.

Which suited Rosemary's purposes exactly.

Of course, it was not actually robbery she was about, Rosemary mused with a righteous sniff. The goods were hers, bought and half paid for. She was merely recovering them.

Drawing her cloak more closely about her, she glared at the warehouse across the street from the dark alleyway where she'd been lurking for the better part of two hours. If that fool of a man had listened to her explanations, none of this would be necessary.

But Master Jasper Pettibone, dock reeve to the high and apparently mighty Lord William Sommerville had brushed her away like a bit of dirt.

Rosemary straightened as the double doors to the warehouse creaked open. The wind caught one, flinging the metal-banded wood against the stone structure and flooding the street with pale light. Rosemary drew back into the shadows.

A man surged after the door, swearing loudly. He was big and burly, dressed in a plain gray tunic and baggy hose. Stout John, by name, one of the guards who'd stood menacingly by while Master Jasper ruined her only chance to save her family. As John wrestled with the door, two more men exited the warehouse, another guard and a shorter man whose distinctive shock of white hair whipped about in the wind.

Jasper Pettibone, the heartless cad who had driven her off this morn. "Be gone, ye troublesome female," he had snarled at her. "If ye've not got a bill of sale, ye'll not get yer goods."

"But I've explained that I paid George Treacle half—"

"George is dead."

"I know." And her heart ached for loss of her friend. "Surely he told Lord William that I'd paid."

"He did not. And the thieves who killed him stole his ledger books, so there's no record." Jasper had glared at her as though it were her fault. "My master said no one was to get any of George's goods lest they had a bill of sale."

"I demand to speak with your master then and explain—"

"What ye'll get is clapped in the gaol for trespass."

Rosemary had gone, but she'd not given up. She'd get her part of the cargo—the pellitory powder and her precious myrrh. Eyes narrowing, she watched Master Jasper.

"Arnald, give John a hand securing the door," the reeve ordered. "Make certain 'tis locked tight." He turned his head to scan the dark, twisting streets and unlit buildings.

Rosemary retreated farther into the alley, pulling the cowl of her cloak close about her face. Shaking as much from fear at her own daring as from the cold, she watched while the door was made fast, listened as the scrape of their footsteps echoed off the buildings then faded away. Still she hesitated, watching the wind toy with the sign above the door.

Fashioned in the shape of a large shield, it bore three ships above the diagonal slash, and the coat of arms of the mighty Sommerville family beneath. This warehouse, its contents and three seagoing ships belonged to Lord William Sommerville. An arrogant sprig of nobility he must be, Rosemary thought, picturing a puffed-up old man with triple chins and flinty eyes.

Rosemary's resolve hardened. The myrrh was hers. She'd paid half for it on account with George Treacle, and she would take delivery one way or another. Her eyes swept the warehouse again.

Had they left a guard within? Her hand strayed to the knife at her waist. She knew well how to use it, for her father had insisted his little girl not wander wild, unruly London town without being able to protect herself. But could she use what she knew in order to reclaim what was hers?

Rosemary sighed. Pray God, she was not tested. And while she was at it, pray God, she'd succeed, for without the myrrh, she and her small family would face ruin.

Bolstered by desperation, she flung off her fears, and the cloak, which might impede her climb up the drain spout in the rear of the warehouse. Slinking from her hiding spot, she trotted across the street. The wind tugged at the cap concealing the braid pinned high on her head and pierced straight through the coarse wool tunic and hose she'd borrowed from Malcolm, her uncle's apprentice.

The numbing cold was another reminder of what was at stake. If she didn't succeed, they would lose the apothecary shop and be forced out onto the streets. She and Malcolm might survive the winter. Uncle Percy, old and infirm as he was, would not live a fortnight.

As Rosemary rounded the building, a cat screeched, leaped from behind a rain barrel and took flight. So did Rosemary's heart. Gasping, she leaned against the wall and hastily surveyed the area. It was surprisingly free of debris. More important, no guard patrolled.

She moved to the clay downspout that fed the barrel. It was slick and cold, but since there were no windows on the ground floor, she'd earlier marked this as her best way in. The drainpipe climbed up the building to the roof two stories above, bypassing a narrow, shuttered window on the second floor. The metal straps used to lash the pipe to the wall were close enough together so she could use them as a ladder.

Rosemary scrambled onto the lip of the barrel and tested her theory. The straps creaked but bore her weight. The climb was slow and tricky, but not overly so. Thankfully her parents, God keep their souls, had not curbed her childhood predilection for playing with the boys in their neighborhood. Of course, if her poor mother and father had known that one of their favorite dares was climbing onto the church roof and walking its peak, they'd have kept her locked inside the apothecary.

As she drew level with the window, Rosemary gauged the stone sill, though narrow, as walkable. Leaning out, she transferred her left foot to the ledge and drew the knife from its sheath. The point of her blade fit between the two halves of the shutters and caught on the metal hook that held them from within. Two flicks of her wrist and she lifted the hook.

The shutters opened inwardly on well-oiled hinges. Grabbing hold of the casement, she eased onto the sill and peered within. The darkness was alleviated by the glow of a banked fire in the hearth. This must be Jasper's counting room, for beneath her stood a table covered with stacks of papers and ledgers.

Taking care not to dislodge anything, Rosemary slipped through the window, onto the table and thence to the floor. It was covered by a thick carpet. Sommerville must be rich indeed to provide his reeve with such luxury. The soft wool soaked up her footfalls as she crossed to the door dimly seen across the room. Along the way, she passed a pair of high-backed chairs set before the fireplace and one wall lined with sturdy-looking chests, each sporting a huge lock.

Were they full of coin and jewels? If she'd been a true thief, she'd have attempted to find the keys, opened the chests and emptied them. But all she wanted was what was hers.

Surprisingly, the door was not locked. Master Jasper was either careless or arrogantly assumed the warehouse was impregnable. Which proved how wrong he was, for the building had been breached by a mere woman.

Chuckling, she opened the door. The musty scent of wool and the tang of spices proved Lord William dealt in a variety of goods. Warily she watched the feeble light play down the first few steps. It was not enough to show the way. Below her, all around her, the vast storeroom gaped like a huge black maw. The cold, heavily scented air vibrated with hushed expectancy.

Was someone below? Nay, they'd have called out when she opened the door. Returning to the counting room, she took a candle from the table and lit it on the embers. Odd how a small, flickering bit of light could inspire confidence.

Back at the top of the stairs, she held the candle aloft. Its pale fingers failed to reach the far walls of the warehouse, but did wash faintly over the sea of merchandise. From her visit this morn, she recalled neat rows of crates, barrels and casks awaiting transit to buyers in London and beyond. The shipment containing her myrrh sat one aisle away from the big doors, covered with canvas. Master Jasper had looked at it when she'd identified herself.

Spying the canvas-draped pile, she hurried down the stairs and knelt to peer under the cover. A dozen small chests lay lashed together, each secured with a large, sturdy-looking lock.

"Drat," Rosemary muttered. Pray God, Master Jasper did not decide to return before dawn, because it would take her till then to open them and find her myrrh. She set the candleholder on the hard-packed dirt, drew the knife from her belt and went to work on the lock of the topmost chest.

The faintest whisper of movement behind her warned Rosemary that she was not alone. Gasping, she turned.

Too late.

A long arm grabbed her around the waist and hauled her up against a rock-hard body. "Where is the rest of your cutthroat band?" a flinty voice hissed in her ear.

The words barely penetrated her terror. "L-let me

go!'' Rosemary lashed out with her feet. The right one connected with her captor's leg, sending a wave of pain up her own.

"Bloody hell!" The man's arm tightened on her ribs, driving the air from her body. "Be still. Tell me where they are!"

They? Black spots danced before Rosemary's eyes, and her lungs burned for want of air. Her uppermost thought, her only thought, was to get free. With the last of her strength, she turned her knife on the arm that imprisoned her.

The blade skittered on his chain mail sleeve, slipped between the links and bit. Her captor cursed, loudly and in some foreign tongue. His grip on her lessened fractionally.

Rosemary, used to seizing whatever advantage she could in life, slipped from his grasp. The knife still clutched in her hand, she stumbled toward the darkened pathway between the chests and barrels.

"Bitch!" the man exclaimed. His footsteps thudded after her. Too close. Another step and he'd grab her again.

Rosemary turned, the knife held before her, her breath ragged, her mind perilously close to panic. "Stay back. I'll not hesitate to use this if I must."

The man stopped, his breathing as harsh as her own. He towered over her, his face a thunderous mask in the flickering candlelight. She had a quick impression of ruggedly chiseled features framed by a shoulder-length mane of sun-streaked hair. It was his eyes that demanded her attention. So dark they seemed almost black, they sizzled with fury. His glaze flicked to her knife. "Did you use it on George Treacle?"

"Nay, of course not," she sputtered. "He was my friend."

"So you say." He stood motionless, yet the muscular body fairly radiated tension, like a cat about to spring.

Rosemary tightened her sweaty hand around the knife's haft. "George supplies, or did, herbs and such to my shop."

"Your shop?" He snorted, those hard eyes of his moving scathingly over her bedraggled person. "You are no merchant. Did your treacherous leader send you hither thinking I'd not punish a woman if I caught her stealing from me?"

Rosemary straightened, stung by his dismissal. "I am no thief, cither. I came for what is rightfully mine."

He snorted again. "You break in here and speak of rights?"

Rosemary glared right back at him, the temper she'd never learned to master set aboil by his contempt. "I was *forced* to break in here because the dumb, arrogant men your master employs will not listen to reason."

"My master?" His brows rose.

"Aye, that Lord William whom George did hire to import our spices. Though I'd not speak ill of my dead friend, I think George showed poor judgment in hiring such a vile man."

"Vile?" His eyes widened so the lines fanning out from them showed white against his bronzed skin.

"Vile," Rosemary agreed. All and all, she decided, the guard was not ill-looking when he stopped scowling and snarling. "He must be to employ such cruel and heartless servants."

"Cruel?" His fair brow drew together as he considered the word. "I think I've been more than kind considering you broke—"

"It would not have been necessary had Master Jasper honored my request this morn and turned over to me my shipment. But nay, he shoved me out into the street before I could half finish explaining." She shrugged. "I had no choice but to come back tonight and take what is mine."

"You could have taken the matter up with Lord William."

"I asked to, but Jasper said his master would not speak with a woman and would have me thrown in gaol for trespass."

"Hmm." The guard stroked his stubbled chin. "Jasper may have been a bit zealous in carrying out his duties."

Rosemary nodded. "He bade Arnald chase me off."

"Did he...chase you off?"

"Aye. Arnald looks like the sort who'd break my arm if he but touched it." She grinned ruefully. "But I did not go far."

His lips twitched, but he didn't smile. "Nor stay away."

"I could not." Rosemary looked deep into his cool brown eyes. She found no mercy there, no spark of compassion, but at least he seemed willing to listen, which was more than Jasper had done. "I must have the spices that George ordered for me." Unconsciously she took a step forward and touched the warrior's arm. It was hard as stone, but warm where his eyes were not. "If you would help me…"

"What are you offering me?" he growled.

"I can pay the other half of what I owed to George."

"Is that all?"

Eyes locked on his, Rosemary nodded. Beneath her palm, his sleek muscles shifted and bunched. The movement sent a strange ripple up her arm and made her belly clench. "I am not wealthy."

"You are young and beautiful. Would you trade in that coin?"

"Trade?" Rosemary blinked, trying to understand his quick shift from wary to contempt. "Oh!" she exclaimed as his words sank in. Stung, she snatched back her hand and retreated a step.

"Offended?" He stalked her, forcing her to back up till she bumped into a pile of kegs that smelled strongly of wine. "Or is your refusal intended to spark my interest? If so, 'tis a useless ploy. I have little use for women in general and no interest in them at all."

"Well, that is fine with me," Rosemary snapped. "For I have no use for men."

"Is that what you told George? Is that how you

inveigled your way into his home? Did you kill him before or after you learned he did not have what you wanted?''

"I did not kill George, you thickheaded dol—"

The door to the warehouse banged open.

"My lord?" Arnald charged in, followed by Jasper.

"Lord William, where are ye!" the reeve shouted.

"I am here," replied the man Rosemary had called dolt.

"Lord William?" Rosemary gaped at him in dawning horror, taking in what she'd missed before—the rich fabric and fine cut of his black tunic and hose. The aristocratic bend of the nose down which he'd stared at her. "Oh, my God!"

"Ye've caught the thief!" Arnald exclaimed.

Lord William glared at her. "So it would seem." Turning to look over his shoulder, he added, "Find a rope."

Rosemary didn't wait to hear more. She dashed around the pile of kegs, gave them a hard shove in passing and kept on running. The rumbling of wine barrels on the move, the sharp cracking and gurgle as one or more split open, made her smile. Lord William's shouted curses changed her smile to a whoop of triumph as she scrambled up the stairs toward the counting room and, with any luck, her freedom.

Chapter Two

26 December, St. Stephen's Day

William Sommerville, second son of the Earl of Winchester, owned three sailing vessels, a prosperous shipping business and a small manor inherited from his paternal grandfather. He was wealthy, well-connected, handsome…and miserable.

He had not, William reflected as he stared out the window of the bedchamber he habitually occupied in his parents' town house, known a moment's peace or happiness in nearly a year. Eleven months, two weeks and six days, to be exact.

On Epiphany of the year just past, he'd lost the most important thing in his life: his Ella. If Ella la Beaufort had lived, they'd have wed this past spring. With luck, she would have been expecting their first child by now.

But his luck, and his will to live, had deserted him that cold and frosty morn when Ella was taken from him.

"Stop torturing yourself," grumbled a dry voice.

Will spun toward the hearth where his older brother sat before the crackling fire. "I'm not," Will lied.

Richard sighed. "I cannot stand seeing you in such pain."

"Then leave. No one asked you to come."

"Mama did." Richard crossed to the window. "She worried when you did not come to Ransford for Christmas Day." He gently squeezed Will's shoulder. "Come home with me, at least till after Epiphany. We don't want you to face that day alone."

Will looked into the face so like his own they were often mistaken for twins. But for all their outward similarity, they were vastly different under the skin. Richard was the dedicated heir to an earldom, content to oversee the Sommervilles' vast estates. Will was the rebel, who'd taken after their mother's side of the family and become a merchant trader. "I'll not be in London come January 6. In a few days— as soon as this business with the spice thieves is settled—I will set sail for Italy."

Never to return. But he could not tell Richard. Their parents deserved to be the first to know.

"Taking your pain with you. Can you not let go of your grief and rejoin the living, Will?" Richard asked softly.

"Would you be able to go merrily on your way if, God forbid, something happened to your Mary?"

"I'd be devastated," Richard gravely admitted.

"I'd likely do as you have, rage and drink and wallow in my sorrow. But then I'd have to pick myself up and go on. If not for myself, for the sake of the family and my sons."

"Aye, you've got Gareth and Geoff, at least. Some bit of Mary to sustain you, to make you look toward the future, but I—"

"You have us." Anguish lining his face, Richard took Will's shoulders and shook him. "Is that not enough to live for?"

"I'm not dying, Richard." Though there'd been days after Ella's death when he'd prayed to join her. "I'm only going to Italy to oversee my business interests there."

Richard's dark brown eyes locked on Will's, seeing beyond the barriers. "You are not returning, are you?"

Will sighed. "I cannot stay. England holds too many memories. Everywhere I go, I see Ella. Jesu." He scrubbed a hand over his face. "I knew her all my life. She *was* my life."

"I am so sorry." Richard embraced Will and held him as he had years ago when they were lads of ten and twelve. Will had tumbled from a tree he'd been forbidden to climb and broken his arm. Richard, who'd trailed after his brother and seen him fall, had sent a page for help and held Will still till it arrived.

The pain Will had endured that day was nothing to what he still felt, nigh a year after losing Ella. It was part of his heritage, he supposed. The Sommervilles loved only once, and that for life. He'd found his Ella when he was ten and she five. They'd had a scant eleven years growing up together, waiting for her to be old enough so they could wed. Now he must somehow face the bleak despair of living the rest of his days without her. The tightness in his chest spread up to clog his throat.

"Thank you, Richard," Will said hoarsely. He slipped from his brother's grasp and forced his lips to curve up in what now seemed an unnatural gesture. "But I must go."

Richard cleared his throat. "We need you here."

Nay, they didn't. After thirty years of marriage, his parents were still deeply wrapped up in each other and their work. Raising warhorses kept Gareth Sommerville busy while the unlikely avocation of goldsmithing engrossed Lady Arianna. Richard had Mary and their sons to fill his days and nights.

Will had nothing except his trade. He had worked at it like a man possessed, searching foreign ports for new items to tempt his customers, overseeing their shipment back to England. The pace he'd set filled every waking hour and sent him to bed exhausted. Still peace eluded him. His sleep, when it finally came, was haunted by dreams of what might have been.

"I will write often and visit each year," Will offered.

But never during the cursed twelve days of Christmas.

"It is not like you to run away," Richard said cagily.

"I am doing what I must." *To preserve my sanity.*

"Ella would not want this for you. She'd want—"

"Do not say she'd want me to wed," Will snarled.

"I'd not be so cruel." But Richard's expression said he thought it. Everyone thought it.

"I have no interest in finding another woman." But into Will's head slipped a vivid image of bold hazel eyes and a beautiful, dirt-smudged face. The spice thief.

A week his men had searched yet found no sign of her. Will had gone himself to George Treacle's shop, hoping the sheriff's men had overlooked the merchant's ledger book. But the thieves who'd murdered George had taken it, so there was no way for Will to learn if his thief had been a customer of the old merchant's.

Bah. She was a thief, plain and simple. She was just better than most at appearing fragile and earnest. Much better. Though he'd railed at her and besmirched her character, part of him wanted to believe she had been telling the truth. That she wasn't a murderess, but a merchant desperate for her goods.

What goods? George had ordered thirty different herbs and spices bought for him. Some rare…myrrh and pellitory, whatever that was; others costly but less exotic, like mandrake root. What spices had the woman-child needed so desperately she'd braved the dangers of London's docks after dark, climbed the slippery drain spout and faced his wrath to obtain them? If he knew, it might provide a clue as to the sort of shop she owned.

If she did.

Absently Will rubbed the spot on his arm where her blade had pierced his mail and left its mark. A prick, no more. It bothered him less than did the memory of holding her in his arms. A few brief moments, yet he could not forget the odd, exhilarating sensation that had filled him.

Triumph, surely, at catching the thief. Aye, that must be why. The mystery woman intrigued him so Will had actually thought of *her* last night instead of Ella. He had been chasing the thief down dark, twisting alleyways, his pulse pounding, his lungs burning. Stronger, swifter, he'd caught her, but when he'd looked into her frightened face, the fury driving him had faded.

"Help me," she'd whispered.

"Tell me how. What do you need?"

"You," she'd murmured, and his frozen heart had lurched.

"What is it?" Richard demanded.

"What?" Shivering, Will shook free of the nightmare and refocused his attention on his frowning brother.

"What were you thinking just now?"

"Of finding George's murderer," he lied. "Why?"

Richard cocked his head. "Because you looked alive."

"I am alive." A state he'd cursed more than once this year.

"Nay, you live, you exist, but you are not alive."

"Richard, do not pick at me."

"All right." Richard sighed and shook his head. "I'll leave you to this half life of yours, but—" His expression hardened. "Promise me you will come to see Mama and Papa before you sail."

"Of course. I must stay in London for a few days to catch these thieves, then I'll go to Ransford."

"Why involve yourself in this? Surely the mayor and London's sheriffs are capable of catching—"

"They've not proved themselves to be. Three months this band of thieves has preyed on the city's spice importers. George is but their latest victim in a string of three." Will sighed in exasperation. He'd been in the Mediterranean, hunting the myrrh George had ordered when the first murder took place, returning to find George two weeks dead. "Nay, I am not being fair. London's peacekeepers are overworked and hampered by the lack of clues. Whoever they are, these bastards are clever. They strike quickly, leaving no trail and no living witnesses."

Was his lady thief one of them? The confidence with which she'd wielded her knife swayed him one way, her reluctance to use it, another. And she'd come alone. No lone person, man or woman, could have committed these crimes. It would take several, with a cart, to carry off the spices so swiftly and silently.

"This sounds dangerous, Will. I think—"

"I've plenty of men to guard me. Now," Will said as the city bells tolled thrice. "I pray you'll excuse me. I've promised to attend the festival being held at the Guildhall.''

''You are?'' Richard exclaimed. ''That is good. Excellent.''

''I am not going to enjoy myself. It is business.'' The business of catching these thieves. But he doubted that details of his daring, dangerous scheme would please his brother.

''Well, at least you are getting out,'' Richard said as he retrieved the cloak he'd tossed over the back of a chair to dry. The day had been seasonably wet, but just this hour the skies had cleared. ''And it looks a fine night for a fete.''

''Aye,'' Will replied smoothly. For a fete and, with any luck, for laying a trap to ensnare a band of murderers.

''Now are you not glad you agreed to come?'' chirped Lady Muriel FitzHugh.

Rosemary dragged her mind from the morass of problems besetting her and glanced about.

The air inside the Guildhall's great room fairly hummed with camaraderie, not to mention the scent of perfumed bodies and smoke from the fires in the huge hearths at either end of the vaulted chamber. Servants bustled about setting succulent roasts, pies and puddings on the tables placed along one wall. The merrymakers pounced on each offering, stripping meat from the carcasses and stuffing it down with wild abandon.

"They are like a flock of starlings," Rosemary muttered.

"Who can blame them? The forty days of Advent fasting ended yesterday. We are all starved for meat and sweets." Muriel popped a bite of roast hare into her mouth and snagged two wine cups from a serving maid. "Relax, enjoy. The twelve days between Christmas and the New Year are our only respite from work."

Rosemary nodded absently.

"Everyone is here," Muriel whispered. "The mayor, the city alderman and nobles of King Richard's court. My Herbert says His Majesty would be here himself had he not gone hunting in Kent." Her blue eyes danced; her round face glowed with excitement.

Rosemary smiled in spite of herself. "Aye, there's nothing to rival the Guildhall's Christmas banquet."

"How pretty the greens look." Muriel pointed to the fir boughs and holly hanging from the timbered ceiling two stories above. It was impossible to be glum in her company. Daughter of a wealthy draper, she had wed into the nobility—the third son of a baron, mind—but nobility nonetheless. Her Herbert was a minor court functionary, older and pompous, but a doting husband.

A pesky rash had brought Muriel to the Bainbridge Apothecary Shop a year ago. The skin condition had been banished by Rosemary's chamomile cream, but the friendship between the two had flourished. Dear Muriel had zealously undertaken to steer as many noble patrons as possible Rosemary's way. If not for their custom, the shop might have failed months ago.

That they could still lose it dimmed Rosemary's smile. "'Tis lovely. And I'm glad you convinced me to come, but I should get back to Uncle Percy."

"Bah! He had his nose so far into those moldy old scrolls of his he will not miss you for hours. Besides, there's someone I want you to meet. A new client." Muriel stood on tiptoe. "I do not see her yet, but we will make a search." Linking her arm with Rosemary's, she plunged through the crowded room.

Rosemary followed, hardly in a position to turn down a new customer, however much the boisterous throng grated on her nerves. A week had gone by and she was no closer to getting the myrrh. A week of watching the pennies trickle into her cash box and just as quickly out again for food and drink.

There'd be no celebrations at the Bainbridge house this year. No special Twelfth Night feast topped off with a bottle of red wine. No small gifts exchanged on Epiphany with Uncle Percy, Malcolm and Winnie, the housekeeper who had been with them forever. Every bit they could scrape together would be needed when the rent for the shop came due in February.

Head down, Rosemary stumbled along in Muriel's wake and ran straight into some hapless soul. "Pardon," she mumbled as she bounced off a fleshy chest encased in crimson velvet. The collision tore her from Muriel's grasp. Reflexively Rosemary looked up. "I did not see—" The rest of the apology stuck in her throat as she recognized the swarthy face glaring down at her.

Baldassare di Corrado, the Italian count whose potions and elixirs were all the rage at court. "You travel heedlessly," he hissed in his heavily accented English.

"Aye. I am sorry, I was—"

"Careless." His full lips curved behind the drooping halves of a black mustache as sleek as the hair framing his hawkish face. His glittering yellow eyes raked her from head to hem. "Still, I forgive because you are young and beautiful."

Rosemary shivered beneath the power of his gaze. Something in its hooded depths made her skin shrivel and her pulse thunder in her ears. *Escape! Flee!* The words rang in her head, but she could not move or tear her eyes from his.

"Rose?" Muriel took her arm and tugged. "We must go."

Baldassare blinked, breaking the spell. "We have only just met, and I would know your name, lovely one."

Rosemary pretended not to hear. "I cannot linger. Sorry I blundered into you," she said, careful to address the count's ornate, gold-encrusted belt. Grabbing Muriel's hand, she fled.

"Wait." Muriel dug in her heels as they passed a table laden with fruit tarts. "What did *he* want?"

"I—I do not know." Rosemary seized a cup of wine from a passing maid. The warm liquid eased the tightness in her throat but not the feeling she'd just had a narrow escape.

"Did he say something? Threaten you?" Muriel demanded.

"Nay." But there was something about him. Bah, she was being foolish. Baldassare was just a foreigner with odd eyes.

"I cannot blame you for being intimidated." Muriel leaned close. "They say he's in league with the devil. There's talk of unnatural rites and magic potions."

"Nonsense," Rosemary said tartly. The reply was an instinctive defense on behalf of a fellow practitioner of the healing arts. She had once been accused of evildoing because she went into the woods at night to gather plants. "Come, let us find this would-be customer so I can return to the shop."

"Very well. While you were, er, speaking with the count, I saw enter a noble party. The ladies wear tall headdresses glittering with gems. Lady Chandre may be with them, for she is wealthy and dresses to dazzle."

Rosemary hung back, intimidated at the notion of accosting such exalted company. "What would she want of me?"

"What we all want," Muriel said as she led the way. "To be the most beautiful, sought-after woman in the world."

"But I cannot give her that." Rosemary's protest was lost in the noise of the crowd. Grumbling about false promises, she followed Muriel to the front of the hall, where the mayor, Master James, the fish-monger, and Henry le Spencer, the alderman, were welcoming a dozen or so noble guests.

Muriel whispered, "That is Lady Chandre in the emerald green standing off to one side with that lord in black velvet."

"Ah." Rosemary dismissed the tall man whose back was to her and concentrated on the lady.

She was not only wealthy, she was breathtakingly lovely. The dark green velvet was a perfect foil for her pale skin. Her forehead had been plucked bare of hair, but she must be fair, for her eyebrows were the color of ripe wheat. Large blue eyes dominated her perfect oval face, the lashes fluttering like butterflies as she flirted with her companion.

"I do not see why she needs my creams," Rosemary muttered.

"She ages and cannot bear it." Muriel grabbed Rosemary's arm and herded her forward till they stood just behind Lady Chandre's companion. "My lady…a moment."

Lady Chandre turned her head, and the harsh torchlight played across her face, mercilessly illuminating every line and wrinkle, every sag and pouch and imperfection. Unaware she'd been unmasked, the lady raised a haughty brow. "Who are you?"

"Muriel…Lady Muriel FitzHugh, we spoke of face creams."

Lady Chandre paled. "I have no need of such things."

"Not for yourself," Muriel said swiftly, still a

merchant's daughter. "But you admired a lotion made for me by Rosemary and thought some of your, er, friends might profit by its use. You asked to meet her." Muriel propelled Rosemary forward, between Lady Chandre and the silent man in black.

"My lady." Rosemary dropped into a swift curtsy, then rose to stand tall before the haughty beauty.

Clearly torn, Lady Chandre inspected Rosemary's face.

"Where is your shop?" asked the man, his voice deep, resonant and oddly familiar.

Rosemary turned and looked up, a polite smile on her lips. It faded instantly.

Staring down at her, his face so still it seemed carved from stone, was the one man she'd hoped never to see again.

Lord William Sommerville.

His dark eyes reflected the image of her own stunned face. "You do have a shop, do you not?" he asked.

Rosemary gaped. Would he denounce her as a thief?

"Bainbridge's, on Fule Lane," chirped the helpful Muriel.

Chapter Three

She really was an apothecary.

William watched shock play over her pale face as he struggled to mask his own triumph. After his futile searching, finding his thief had been as easy as chancing to be waylaid by the annoying Lady Chandre. Had she not snagged him, he might never have found the little apothecary in this press.

Rosemary. The name was apt, considering her calling.

Rosemary for remembrance.

It shook Will that he had not been able to forget her.

The other night, filthy and clad in boy's clothing, she'd appealed to him. Now, dressed in a simple gown of blue wool, her face scrubbed clean, her shiny brown braids wrapped in a coronet atop her head, she moved him. Nay, it was not her quiet beauty that struck a buried cord. It was the vulnerability in those wide hazel eyes, the delicacy of the chin that lifted toward him in silent challenge. She was too fragile to best him. Powerless.

One word from him and she'd be arrested, thrown into prison, there to languish. She knew it, but instead of cowering or running or even pleading, she met his gaze with a calm courage he'd seen in few men and no women...outside his own family. Ella had been soft, gentle. Will had been her shield against her tyrannical father. This woman would fight her own battles.

And yet, in his dream she had cried, "Help me." Oddly, he wanted to do just that.

"You may call on me on the morrow, mistress," Lady Chandre said sharply, shattering the mood. "Now, William, I am parched." She grabbed hold of his arm, molding her generous breast against it as she steered him toward the refreshment tables.

William went. He'd been raised to honor women, even harpies like Chandre. And he detested ugly scenes of the sort she reportedly threw when crossed. Since his return to London a fortnight ago, Chandre had been angling to get him into her bed. He'd been mildly interested in the prospect. What man would not who'd been at sea a three-month? Honor Ella's memory, he did, but men, even those with broken hearts, had urges.

Meeting Mistress Rosemary has somehow shifted his.

"Who was that man?" Muriel whispered.

"I am sure I do not know." Rosemary wrapped

her arms around her waist to still her trembling. Mayhap he had not recognized her. If he had, surely he'd have denounced her.

"Well, he's a cold fish, that's sure. And rude. Did you note the way he stared at you?"

"Aye." Her heart sank. He *had* recognized her.

"He'd be handsome if he wasn't so hard looking."

Handsome? He was a cruel, emotionless devil. Had he gone to report her to the mayor or the sheriff? She had to leave.

Shuddering, Rosemary glanced over her shoulder. Despite the crowd, she spotted him instantly, for he stood a head taller than most men, calmly sipping wine with Lady Chandre. Even in profile, he looked remote, removed from the gay throng.

As though sensing her regard, Lord William turned his head. His gaze locked on hers, grim with the steely determination that sent dread skittering down her spine. Never had she felt more like a mouse facing a hungry, implacable cat.

"Well, at least you have leave to call on Lady Chandre," Muriel said excitedly.

Rosemary dragged her eyes back to Muriel, her heart thudding wildly. She had to escape. But where? *Oh, Lord. He knew her name, the name of the shop.*

"If your new cream takes the wrinkles from her skin, Lady Chandre vowed she'd give you a fortune."

"Muriel." Rosemary stared at her friend in dawning horror. "You did not tell her about my experiments."

"Nay, well, I only told her a little, that you'd come upon an ancient recipe that promoted youthful skin. I did not tell her about your uncle's scrolls or what the secret ingredient is." Muriel grinned. "How could I, when I do not know?"

Rosemary groaned. "Muriel…"

"I only wanted to help." Muriel's lower lip wobbled. "You must have money or you'll lose the shop. I have not the sum to loan you, so when I heard Lady Chandre ranting about the failure of the potions Count Baldassare had sold her…"

Oh, fine. Now she was in competition with the Italian. Well, actually, she was not. Not unless she could get the myrrh. "I may have to disappoint her, too, Muriel. I have had trouble getting the ingredient I need to make more of the cream."

"Oh. Is there no way?" Muriel wrung her pudgy hands. "I did not want to put undue pressure upon you, but Lady Chandre has promised a thousand pounds for the removal of her wrinkles."

"'Tis a fortune." Visions of a bright future danced in Rosemary's head. A learned physician to attend her infirm uncle. A larger shop. A maid to ease Winnie's burden. Mayhap even another helper so she would be free to develop new potions.

Reality shattered her hopes.

She had no coin with which to buy myrrh from another source, even supposing she could find one.

The spice was rare in England, considered useless and thus seldom imported.

William Sommerville was her only hope. And he was more likely to see her thrown in prison than help her. Unless...

Rosemary risked another glance at him, but the brooding figure in somber black was nowhere to be seen. Was he huddled with the sheriff? Or, horror of horrors, en route to the shop?

"I must leave," Rosemary exclaimed, thoughts of creams and money banished by concern for Uncle Percy.

"Nonsense, we just got here." Muriel threw a fleshy arm around Rosemary's shoulders. "Dieu, you are trembling something fierce." She frowned. "And white as new snow. Are you ailing?"

"Aye." She was sick with fear. "I must go."

"Let me find Herbert, and we will accompany—"

"Nay!" If she was to be arrested, she did not want an audience, even a sympathetic one. "Malcolm is in the courtyard celebrating with the other apprentices. He will see me home."

Her apprentice was less than happy to be dragged away from his drink and dice.

"We just got here." Malcolm kicked a stone before him as they went. He was tall for ten and four, with gangling limbs and a thin face, now sunk sullenly into the neck of his best russet tunic. "The Christmas fetes come but once a year."

"I know, but I am worried about Uncle Percy."

Malcolm lifted his head, pique gone. "Is his foot

paining him again? He didn't say so when I bid him goodbye, but then, he never does complain.'' The boy began to walk faster.

Rosemary hurried after him, stifling a pang at the half-truth. The gout had left Percy Bainbridge bed-ridden and in constant pain. A terrible fate for a man who had once sailed the high seas and gone explor-ing in foreign places like Cyprus and Egypt, where he'd chanced on the scrolls of the ancient healers. He never cried over his lot, but he did have such high hopes for the special cream they'd perfected together.

It was early yet, and the streets were filled with merrymakers. Lights shone from the shops still doing a brisk business in hot meat pies. Rowdy patrons spilled from the doors of the alehouses, blocking the thoroughfare and filling the night with raucous song. Things quieted and traffic thinned when they turned down Fule Lane.

The shop lay in the middle of the block, the front door shut, the shutter over the ground floor window likewise closed. A faint glow from the upstairs win-dows marked the room where Uncle Percy was doubtless still reading.

Rosemary was just reaching into the pouch on her belt for the front door key when a tall figure stepped from the alley. Though his dark clothes blended with the night, she knew immediately who it was. A soft, agonized groan left her lips.

Malcolm moved in front of her. ''Be off,'' he com-manded, the effect ruined by the break in his voice.

"I've business with your mistress." William Sommerville closed the distance to stand a scant yard away.

"We're closed." Malcolm drew a small knife, holding it before him with less skill than she'd displayed a week ago.

"'Tis all right, Malcolm." Rosemary laid a restraining hand on the boy's arm. "This man is known to me." Unfortunately. "What do you want?" *Have you come to arrest me?*

"The answers to a few questions."

"Oh." And then what? She looked beyond him.

"I came alone."

Rosemary sighed. "What do you want to ask me?"

His lordship's gaze flickered to Malcolm, armed and standing protectively before her. "Does he know?"

About her fling at robbery. "Nay."

"Do you want him to?"

Nay. "Malcolm, go inside and check on *things.*"

"I'll not leave you alone with him," the boy replied.

"Actually..." said Sommerville "...I'd prefer to come inside."

"You've not been invited." Rosemary crossed her arms over her rapidly beating heart. "Malcolm, do as I ask. I'll answer this man's questions and be along directly."

Malcolm cast a fulminating glance at the nobleman, who topped him by a foot. "I'll be watching from upstairs. If I see anything amiss, I'll scream for the watch.'' Taking the key Rosemary held out, he entered the house but left the door open.

''I admire the boy's loyalty.''

Rosemary stared at his lordship, trying to fathom what was going on behind those closed features of his.

''It speaks well of you,'' he added.

''Unless, of course, he is also a thief.''

''You said you were not one.''

''Nor am I. Why are you here? I took nothing.''

''I would know why you broke into my warehouse.''

Rosemary sighed. ''I told you. To get what was mine.''

''What, specifically, had George ordered for you?''

Inbred caution made her hesitate. Even in normal times, the apothecary trade was a competitive one. The makers of lotions and potions were always on the lookout for ways to steal or mimic another's wares. ''There were several items.''

''List them for me.''

''If I do, will you give them to me?''

''Mayhap.'' He waited, unmoving, unblinking. When she didn't reply, he pushed. ''Why the hesitation?''

''You could be in the employ of one of the other shops, out to steal my secrets.''

He blinked, and a wry smile tugged at his lips.

"I've been called many things, but never a merchant's shill."

"You look down on us?"

"Nay, I am a trader and merchant myself."

"With a noble name and lineage."

"On my sire's side. My mother was…is…a goldsmith."

"Is that supposed to put me at ease?"

"I am hoping something will." This time the smile was fuller, reaching his eyes, gentling his expression, however briefly. The change it made in his appearance was startling, like a ray of sunshine shooting out of a brooding cloud.

What had caused him to turn so grim and solemn? she wondered. She had the oddest notion that he'd been hurt by something. "Why would you care how I feel?"

"Because I've decided you were telling the truth about not trying to rob me, and I want to make amends."

"Really?" Rosemary took a step forward, her spirits lifting. "You will give me my spices?"

"Which ones?"

Rosemary pulled up short of the trap. "Let me into your warehouse. I will pick them out of the shipment."

Will looked into her stubborn little face and wanted to scream. Instead, he swept the neighborhood of sleeping shops with a critical eye. These people were too poor to employ guards to protect their shops. Chances were they did not even have members of the city watch quartered here. "'Tis too dangerous."

"That is for me to say."

"Fool!" Anger flared. He forgot caution and grabbed hold of her arms. "Whoever killed George was too early to get the spices I had brought back with me, but they took his ledgers, the records of his consignments. I think they are watching and waiting for me to make deliveries. Then they will strike."

Her eyes rounded. "But why would someone steal spices?"

"To sell, I would guess." Disturbed by the pleasure he felt in having his hands on her, he let her go. "Some of the spices taken recently were extremely rare and costly." Yet his men had not uncovered any activity in the black market for such things. It could be that the thieves were shipping them abroad for sale in Belgium or France. "I'd not want to endanger you and yours."

She nodded and glanced fearfully down the street where she'd undoubtedly felt safe. "Mayhap you'd better come inside."

William accepted the offer. Part of him wished it had been given under different circumstances. Part of him wished he were not here at all. Why did she intrigue him when no other woman had since Ella? Abstinence? Insanity? Aye, he was insane not to forget her and get on with his search for the thieves.

At the Guildhall, he'd dropped hints that he still had George's spices. He should be at the warehouse with his men, waiting to spring the trap if the bastards took the bait.

Instead, he'd followed Rosemary into her shop.

Like her, the narrow room was tidy, smelling of sweet spices and earthy herbs. She led him through it, past surprisingly imaginative displays of dried herbs and clay pots, to the workroom in the back.

"Pray be seated." She gestured toward a bench set before the empty hearth, but did not sit herself. Instead, she paced, her slender hands with their telltale plant stains clenching and unclenching as she walked.

William forced himself to look away and take stock of the room. Cramped, utilitarian. Books and papers were shoved into a hutch in the left corner. The remaining walls were lined with shelves, and these crowded with clay vessels, big and little. Herbs hung from the exposed wooden rafters. A clutch of mortars and pestles in varying sizes littered the small table behind the bench. He imagined her working here, grinding spices, adding goose grease or whatever to make a cream for some wealthy lady like Chandre to smooth on in hopes of catching a man.

Was there a man in Rosemary's life? William did not like the knot that notion put in his belly. Nay, no man would let his woman wander about London alone.

"I will be honest with you." Rosemary stopped beside the bench, her expression pained. Despite the shadows under her eyes and the down-turned mouth, she was beautiful and young. No more than twenty, he'd guess. "Our situation is rather desperate. If I do not get those spices so we can make more of our special creams, we will likely lose the shop."

We. This time William's chest cramped. He rose, unable to keep himself from taking one of her clenched hands. How cold and small it was. "And where has your husband been whilst you've been putting yourself in harm's way to save your business?"

"I've no husband. I live here with Percy, my uncle."

Unwed. The news, welcome and damned, put his mind at war with other, less discerning parts of his body. Lust, Will told himself. 'Twas understandable given his celibacy this year. When Ella was alive, he'd occasionally visited the whores to ease the passion he'd not share with her till they were wed. With Ella dead, it seemed wrong to find pleasure in anything. Aye, that must account for the intensity of his desire for the apothecary.

Still he did not like it one bit. He did not want to want anyone. "Well, your uncle should pay more heed to your safety." Will made to release her hand just as the door flew open.

A squat old woman hurtled in, her clothes in wrinkled disarray, a rolling pin held aloft. "Get away from her. Get back, ye villain."

"Winnie!" Rosemary stepped into her path. "'Tis all right. Lord William was just—"

"He had his hands on ye."

"Aye, well." Rosemary glanced at him, mouth

quirked in wry amusement. "There was a misunderstanding. Several. Winnie is our housekeeper," she added, as though that explained the woman's rash intrusion. Turning back to the maid, Rosemary smiled brightly. "Lord William is a spice importer, you see."

Winnie sniffed and looked him over as she might a mouse who'd invaded her kitchen. "Don't care if he's the king. Got no right being here alone wi' ye, touching ye."

"I could not agree more," William said stiffly. He moved to the door. "I only came to—" His voice trailed off as it occurred to him that he'd come solely because he had to see her. "You looked frightened when I recognized you tonight. I wanted to set your mind at ease." His gaze flickered to the glowering housekeeper. "I will do nothing about our *meeting* last week."

He was not going to have her arrested. The rush of relief left Rosemary weak-kneed. Then she realized he was leaving. "Wait, please." She brushed past the scowling Winnie and put her hand on William's sleeve to stop him. Beneath the black velvet of his surcoat, his arm was as warm and muscular as she'd remembered. But the heat that singed her fingertips was stronger. So was the sense of awareness that flooded her when he looked back and their eyes met. Clashed. "The spices," she murmured, though business seemed suddenly remote, unimportant.

"I cannot." His voice was hushed, his gaze, for once, unshuttered. The swirl of emotions that filled his eyes was painful to see: agony, guilt and regret. These she glimpsed before he blinked. When his lashes lifted, his expression was stark. "I cannot give you what you want." He shook free of her grasp and walked away.

"Wait," Rosemary cried again, dashing after him and ignoring Winnie's protest. She caught up with his lordship at the front door. "You must give me the spices. If you don't, I'll...I'll break into your warehouse again and—"

He turned on her, his expression so furious she retreated a step. "'Twould be a waste of time. My property is closely guarded. Not even a fly could get in unnoticed."

"I could," she retorted, furious and desperate.

"Step one foot on my property, and I'll have the lot of you thrown in prison." Wrenching the door open, he stomped out and vanished into the night.

Chapter Four

She was the most infuriating female he'd ever met, Will thought as he hurried away from the cursed shop. How could he have thought her intelligent, when she was so obviously lacking in common sense as to put commerce above safety?

"If we do not have the spices to make our creams, we will likely lose the shop," she had said.

Bah, she was doubtless exaggerating, as even his sainted mother and sister, Alys, were wont to do to get their own way. The profits from a few pots of lotion could not save a business.

Arnald emerged from the side of a nearby home. "Are we going, then?" he asked, falling into step with Will.

Will slowed his headlong dash and thoughtfully kicked a loose stone from his path. "Did you see anyone lurking about?"

"Hard to say. John—he's posted at the other side of the shop—thought he saw the same man pass by twice. But he could have been going out for ale or a quick toss with a whore.''

Will nodded morosely. He'd do well to find both himself. ''I'd like you and John to stay, for tonight at least.''

''But if ye put out the word that we've still got George Treacle's goods at the warehouse, shouldn't we be there in case the bastards try to break in?''

''I've men aplenty there, inside and out.'' Will glanced back at Bainbridge's. The shop was dark, save for a faint glow from behind the shutters of an upstairs window. Rosemary's room? Was she within, preparing for sleep? The thought of her removing the soft blue gown sent another unwelcome shaft of heat to his loins. ''Stay here, just in case. I'll be at the warehouse with the lads, keeping watch.'' And wishing myself here.

Damn, but he was a sorry case. Lusting after one woman with the anniversary of his love's death fast approaching. Furious with himself, Will stalked away from the apothecary shop. He'd not return here. Nor would he think of her.

Instead, he turned his mind to the fete at the Guildhall. A few of the merchants to whom he'd spoken had expressed interest in buying George's shipment of goods. He'd put them off by saying he had yet to take an inventory and fix a price.

''Tis sure to be high,'' one bewhiskered merchant had grumbled. ''What with the recent robberies, supplies are scarce.''

''To be sure,'' said Edward, head of the Peppers'

Guild. "But I'll not be stocking any of the rare, more costly spices till these thieves have been caught." While the others had nodded in agreement, their faces edgy with concern, Edward had added, "Who could be doing such a thing?"

"Someone who wants to drive up the price or drive some of you out of business," Will had speculated. "Is there one of your number who has continued to be well supplied during this time?"

The merchants looked at each other and shook their heads.

"It may be that the herbs are being made into potions. If we knew what sort had been stolen," added Edward. "it might give a clue as to who'd be likely to want them." At Will's insistence, he'd explained that while some shops sold raw spices, others turned them into medicines, tonics and the like.

The idea opened up another avenue for Will to explore. One he hoped would not only lead to the thieves' capture, but keep his mind, and his lustful body, from remembering Rosemary.

A thud jerked Rosemary awake. Disoriented, she sat up and glanced around, realizing she'd not made it to her bed in the narrow room upstairs next to Uncle Percy's. Instead, she'd fallen asleep at her workbench. Thankfully she hadn't knocked over the pot containing the bit of youth cream she'd stayed up making with the last of the myrrh powder.

Stretching her cramped muscles, she reached for the pot.

The thud came again.

Malcolm leaped up from his pallet in the corner. "It came from the back of the house," he hissed, eyes wide with fear.

Rosemary nodded. "Mayhap Winnie is having another bad dream and fell out of bed."

"Twice?"

Winnie stumbled into the workroom, a blanket clutched over her night shift. "There's someone knocking on the back door."

"Trying to beat it down, more like," Rosemary said as another thud reverberated through the room. "Mayhap 'tis a drunk who has got the wrong house."

"Or the spice thieves," Malcolm whispered.

Winnie cried, "We've naught worth stealing."

Nothing save Uncle Percy's recipes. Rosemary eyed the door that led to the kitchen where Winnie slept and thence to the outside door. Worried, she thrust the only crock of cream into the right pocket of her work apron. Into the left went the instructions written in Uncle Percy's bold script. "Surely the neighbors will hear and sound the alarm."

"That lot." Malcolm snorted. "Timid as sheep, they are."

Timid and old. "Aye, you are right. Quick, in here." She herded her frightened servants out into the shop.

Malcolm barred the workroom door. Winnie headed for the front exit, gray braids streaming behind her.

"Stop," Rosemary hissed. "There may be more out front."

"What can we do?" Winnie wailed. Victim of a husband who had beat her before mercifully drinking himself to death, she was terrified of any sort of violence.

"Go up to Uncle Percy," Rosemary said. "Malcolm and I will secure things here and follow." Working quickly, she and the boy pushed a tall hutch filled with crocks over to block the workroom door. They braced a long display table against the window shutters and dragged a heavy chest across the front door.

Another thud from the back, this one punctuated by the ominous cracking of wood, drove them through the doorway that led up to the second floor. After barring the door, Rosemary directed Malcolm to fill the stairwell with whatever he could find—chairs, her bedding, anything.

"If we make it difficult to get in, mayhap the thieves will weary of the sport or help will come," she said lamely before scurrying off to see how her uncle fared.

Leaning heavily on a crutch, Uncle Percy was filling a small chest with his precious scrolls while Winnie emptied his bookshelves into a sheet spread on the floor.

"Uncle Percy. You shouldn't be up." Rosemary rushed over to take the roll of parchment from his gnarled hands.

"Can't let the bastards get my library." His face

was flushed, his mane of snowy hair a wild tangle. Pain clouded the hazel eyes so like her own, but they were determined, too.

"There's no time for this, Uncle Percy. We must save ourselves. Winnie, open the window and tell me if you see anyone lurking in the street out front."

"What difference does that make?" Percy demanded.

"If the way is clear, we'll climb out onto the roof and—"

"My dear girl," her uncle said in that dry voice of his. "If I cannot walk down the stairs, how could I negotiate the roof? Still…" He tapped his lips as he did when puzzling with an old manuscript. "You and Winnie should get away. Aye, climb down and I'll lower my books and papers."

"Uncle Percy, how could you think I'd leave you?"

He smiled, deepening the lines in his pale, sun-starved face. "Death is friend, not foe to a man in my position."

"Uncle!" Rosemary cried.

"Mistress." Malcolm dashed in, panting with terror. "They've broken into the shop. They are pounding on the stair door and calling for ye. By name."

"By name! Sweet Mary!"

Winnie began to cry softly.

Her uncle cursed.

"Who are they? What do they want with me?" Rosemary whispered.

"Stay here, Rose," Percy said. "I'll go and try to reason—"

"Nay." Rosemary squared her shoulders. "I will speak with them. At the very least, I may be able to delay these brigands. Malcolm, help Winnie pack up Uncle Percy's things."

Her heart in her throat, Rosemary crept down the stairs. Malcolm had filled the bottom two steps with chairs and bedding. Over the rubble, she called, "Wh-who are you? What do you want?"

The pounding stopped. "Give us the spices," called a rough voice. "The myrrh and pelli... pellitory."

Rosemary gasped. How could they know. "I have none."

"Ye lie. We know ye'd ordered them from Treacle."

"Aye, but he died. The shipper refused to give them to me."

"Another lie. Sommerville was here. He bought ye the goods. Now tell us where they are, or we'll tear the door down and torture the information from ye."

"But I do not have them," Rosemary sputtered.

"I'll give ye to the count of three to tell me. One..." A heavy object hit the door, opening a crack in the thick oak.

"His lordship was here, but refused my request," she cried.

There was a pause in the assault on the door. On the other side, several men argued, their speech coarse and pungent with curses. Finally one said, "Let us upstairs to search."

"Nay, mistress," Malcolm whispered from the step above her. "If you let them in, they'll kill us, no matter what they find."

"Agreed." They were well and truly trapped. "I must talk this over with my uncle," Rosemary called to the villains.

"Be quick about it. We ain't got all bloody night."

Rosemary shooed Malcolm up the steps ahead of her. At the top, she grabbed hold of his arm, speaking softly but earnestly. "The rooftops hold the only hope of escape. Uncle Percy could not negotiate them, and I cannot leave him, but you and Win—"

"Nay, mistress! There must be another way."

Rosemary's heart contracted. She did not want to die, but neither could she abandon the old man who had given up his traveling to raise her after her parents' deaths. "There is not. I will help you carry Uncle Percy's things out onto the roof. I pray you can get his scrolls, at least, away and give them to Master Edward the Pepperer. He'll appreciate their worth. But if it comes to a choice between them and yours or Winnie's safety, look to yourselves, Malcolm."

Malcolm protested, as did Winnie and her uncle when they heard what she intended. But Rosemary stood firm. "It may be that I can reason with them if they do break in," she said. And if she could not sway them with words, she'd use the sharp knife her father had given her. "Come, we've not a moment to lose." She pushed open the window shutters, letting in the dawn light.

In accordance with the city ordinance that forbid thatch or straw, the roof was made of shingles, and was not as steep as some. The sill outside was wide enough to walk on...carefully. It took only a few moments to transfer the scrolls to the bedsheet, which Rosemary then slung over Malcolm's back.

"This will leave your hands free to climb and help Winnie."

"I am not going," said the old woman. "I'll not leave ye."

"You must," Rosemary said. Winnie would be utterly terrified if these men did burst in. And if things went ill... Nay, she'd not think of that. "Go, both of you," she commanded, just as the hammering on the door below resumed amid threats she was glad she couldn't understand.

Malcolm climbed out onto the ledge, then reached back to assist Winnie in awkwardly following. The pair stepped into the gutter they'd travel to reach the roof of the neighboring house. Rosemary had instructed him to pound on the upstairs window and see if the old couple living there would let him and Winnie in.

"If they do, I'll run quick for the watch," Malcolm said.

"Aye. Good." But it would likely be too late.

As the servants passed from view, Rosemary

turned away from the window, forcibly keeping her face calm, her spine straight.

"You should have gone with them." Propped up in bed, Uncle Percy shook his head. "Never could make you mind."

"Uncle." Rosemary sat beside him and laid her head on his shoulder, as she used to when she was ten and three, newly orphaned and fearful of the future. Now she was afraid neither of them had a future. "You said I was a model child."

"Model of impertinence and impatience," he said fondly. "But I'd not change one hair on your head." He stroked her tumbled curls. "The pounding's stopped."

Rosemary sat up, ear cocked toward the stairwell. "Aye, but the shouting is louder." A string of roars and curses echoed up to them, followed by sounds of a scuffle. "I suppose it's too much to hope they will kill each other fighting over Grandma's silver spoon." It was the only thing of real value they possessed other than the spice inventory and Percy's library.

"Aye." Percy's eyes twinkled, then sobered. "Damn, if not for this bloody gout, I'd go down and give them a thrashing." Indeed, he'd been a formidable swordsman in his time.

"I'm going to see if I can hear anything." Rosemary rose, evading her uncle's hand. "I'll be careful." She crept down to Malcolm's pile of chairs, sprinkled now with bits of wood.

The door was cracked clear through in the center,

showing a thin strip of light and the shiny tip of an ax blade. One more blow would shatter the door, but all was curiously quiet.

What had happened? Where had the robbers gone?

"Rosemary! Are you within?" shouted a deep voice.

Another of the robbers, doubtless. "Go away!" she called.

"Rosemary! Open this door at once, dammit, or I'll beat it down." A heavy weight smote the door, shaking it. "Open, I say."

Rosemary ran back upstairs, frightened but determined. She was not going to give up. She would move Uncle Percy's great bed in front of the chamber door to block it. She would hang out the window and shriek for help till someone came.

Chapter Five

"Quick, Uncle, get out of bed if you can," Rosemary cried as she dashed into the room. "I'm going to move it over."

The door to the chamber flew open, crashing back against the wall so hard it shook loose a cloud of whitewashed plaster.

Drawing the knife from her belt, Rosemary shouted, "Stay back! I'll—William?" she asked, belatedly recognizing the man who had catapulted into the room.

"Rosemary!" He reached her in two strides, sweeping her off her feet and into a crushing embrace. "Are you all right?"

"Mumph," she replied, her face pressed to his chest.

"Rosemary! Are you hurt?" He had one arm clamped around her waist; the other hand moved erratically over her back, patting and stroking. "Tell me where you're hurt," he demanded, his heart beating a wild, deafening tattoo beneath her ear.

Rosemary lifted her head and looked up into his distraught face. "I am fine."

"Fine? You are sure?" Some of the rawness left his eyes when she nodded.

"Only a little shaken." Truly, William's emotional outburst was almost more of a shock than the attack had been. Why was he so upset? "You came in time to save us."

"Thank God." He exhaled sharply. "When Arnald sent word someone was breaking in, I feared..." His eyes grew bleak again. "I feared we'd not arrive in time. Jesu, if anything had happened...if I'd failed to save another—" He broke off, looking distinctly uncomfortable.

"I am fine, as you can see." Rosemary kept her smile bland while her mind raced. What or whom had he failed to save?

He grunted and let her go, arms dropping to his sides as he turned stiffly away from her. "Well, that is fine."

Insane is what this was, Rosemary thought. First his rabid concern for her welfare, now a cool dismissal.

"I am Percy Bainbridge," her uncle said into the strained silence. Beaming at them from the bed, his inquisitive eyes darted back and forth between them. "Are you by chance the same Lord William who saw my Rose home last eve?"

"Aye. The streets are less safe than normal, what with all the drunken merrymakers about," William grumbled, doubtless annoyed by the implied intimacy.

"Uncle heard your voice and feared there were intruders," Rosemary said hastily. "I explained that…that…"

"Aye. She said you were an old acquaintance concerned for her welfare." Percy chuckled. "I was expecting a man of my years, or poor George's. But no matter. Now it seems I must thank you again. Your arrival was most opportune."

"Not at all." William inclined his head. "I am only thankful that I'd left men behind to watch the shop."

"How chivalrous," Percy said dryly, peering at William as he might a fascinating new scroll. "Unexpectedly so."

Rosemary groaned, familiar with Percy's probing mind and not at all certain she wanted it delving into this shadowy little corner of her life. Not until she knew how she felt about William and, more important, how he felt about her.

Before matters could worsen, a youth materialized in the doorway. "My lord. Both men got away, but Rodney wounded one."

"Damn," William muttered. "Did they take anything, Harry?"

"They weren't carrying any bundles when they ran from us, but there's nothing left whole below."

"Nay." Rosemary started forward.

William blocked her path. "Stay here till I see what—"

"Waiting will not change things," Rosemary whispered, but she bowed her head beneath the weight of the pain.

He touched her hair ever so gently. "You have endured so much tonight. Why not wait till you are stronger?"

Tempted as she was to burrow into his chest and agree, Rosemary looked up. The compassion in his usually remote eyes brought tears to hers. "Imagining would make it worse."

She was wrong, Rosemary discovered a few minutes later when she overrode the men's protests and went downstairs. Nothing could be worse than the reality of seeing the ruins of her shop and workroom. The robbers had smashed her hopes and her dreams along with the crocks, vessels and shelving that had held them. There was not one thing untouched. Even the dried herbs had been yanked down and ground beneath the thieves' heels.

"Do you think they were rivals out to ruin you?" William's hand rested protectively on the small of her back.

If not for his support, she feared her legs might fail her. "It could be, for they called me by name, but—" Rosemary frowned "—they also knew what I had ordered from George."

William cursed. "Tell me exactly what the bastards said." He swore again, more loudly, when he'd heard her tale.

"What is it? What does it all mean?"

"It means that you and your uncle are coming home with me," William said grimly.

"I cannot leave. There's too much work to be done."

"You are not safe here."

"Of course we are. The robbers know we do not have—"

"My lord?" Arnald stepped through the shattered back door. "There's a lad and an old woman trapped on the roof of the next house. I offered help, but the woman threw a book at me and screamed like a banshee." He rubbed the bruise on his forehead.

"'Tis Malcolm and Winnie," Rosemary said. "When things looked hopeless, I sent them away with Uncle Percy's library."

"You saved his books, but not yourself?" William growled. "Never mind. Arnald, go tell them we've driven the robbers off and have the Bainbridges safe. See if you can find a ladder to get them down while I take Rosemary and Master Percy home."

"This is our home," she exclaimed. "We're not leaving."

William's scowl was just as determined. "Your uncle would rest easier if you were safe behind my stout door instead of this." He waved his hand toward what remained of their portal.

"You would use a sick man to get your way?"

"If I thought it best." William flashed a wolfish smile. "We Sommervilles are a ruthless lot. But I take no unfair advantage. Your uncle's foot may keep him bedridden, but his wits are sharper than mine. Sharp enough to realize that whoever these brigands be, they will return for the spices.''

"But I do not have the cursed things," Rosemary grumbled.

"They do not know that. They will be back. I mean to see none of you are here when they do." He raised a hand to still her protest. His voice gentled. "Do not fight me on this. I am partly to blame for this attack. My visit last night obviously led them to believe you'd taken delivery of your goods."

"That is true, I suppose, but you need not feel obligated."

"But I do." Pain flickered in his eyes, like a ghost through a haunted house. "I'd not be able to live with myself if I failed to protect you."

Defeated, Rosemary nodded. "All right, but I do not like the idea of putting you out. Malcolm, Winnie and I can sleep on the floor, but have you an extra bed for Uncle Percy?"

William grinned. There was no other word for it. The smile revealed even white teeth and made him look years younger. "Oh, I think we can find someplace for him to lay his head."

"This is your home?" Rosemary's lush, expressive mouth hung open. Her head tilted back as she took in the timbered ceiling two stories above the carpeted floor of the great room. Bright tapestries worked by his Aunt Gaby enlivened the whitewashed walls, and the furnishings, tables, chairs and a large wooden chest were finely wrought. The servants, roused from their sleep by the message he'd sent on ahead, were busy moving a large bed from the upper story into a ground floor room beyond the hall he'd asked to have readied for Percy.

"This is my parents' town home, aye," Will replied. She looked so small, standing there in her faded gown, her eyes dulled by exhaustion and dread. So small and vulnerable. He had the oddest urge to sweep her into his arms and carry her upstairs. To his bed. But not so she could rest. Nay, because he desired her more with each passing moment.

Will watched pale dawn light spill through the windows onto her face and wanted to see her by candlelight. He studied the rise and fall of her breasts beneath the blue wool and thought silk would suit her delicacy.

Candlelight and green silk. He had a bolt the color of emeralds in his warehouse and maids aplenty here to stitch it into a fashionable gown.

Will killed the thought aborning. She was not for him. No woman was. "This is one of our homes, aye. Ransford Castle is four times larger and far grander," he added spitefully. It should have been Ella standing here beside him.

Rosemary spun toward him, her awe replaced by quiet dignity. "Will you show me the way to the servants' quarters?"

"Of course not. You and your uncle are my guests."

"I assume 'tis where your squire took Malcolm

and Winnie. Uncle Percy and I will join them, providing there's a bed.''

The notion of her sleeping on a pallet on the floor appalled him. ''You will lodge where I say.''

''Very well.'' She clenched her hands before her. ''But—'' Her proviso was interrupted by the arrival of Percy, carried by Will's servants in a sedan chair.

''Interesting trip,'' Percy announced. ''Been years since I was out and about in the city. So many new buildings I scarce recognized some of the streets. Especially nice this time of year, eh? Christmas and all. Did you see, Rose?''

Christmas. The word alone sent a chill of revulsion through Will. A reminder he had only nine days left to solve George's murder and quit London.

''I saw, Uncle.'' Rosemary smiled fondly, reminding Will of his mother's love for her aged great-aunt who'd lived with them.

''The greenery,'' Percy added. ''The displays in the shop windows. Lovely. Very lovely indeed.''

Rosemary flinched, no doubt thinking of her shop.

Will's heart contracted. Why did he feel so much for her when he'd been numbed this past year?

''Grand.'' Percy looked around. ''Very grand. Reminds me of the Knights Templars' hall on Malta. I nearly took orders with them.'' He winced as he shifted in the chair.

''Uncle, you should rest now,'' Rosemary said gently.

''I've had the servants set up a bed in the room beyond the dais,'' Will said. '''Twas the solar in my grandparents' time. I thought it would be easier for you to get to table for meals.''

''Ah.'' Percy's tired eyes danced. ''It's been some time since I ate at table instead of in bed like a puling infant. You are kind. Most kind. Is he not, Rose?''

''Aye, a veritable wellspring of kindness.'' Rosemary's wry glance reminded him of his earlier graceless remark.

Damn. He did not want to be affected by her beauty, her wit or her compassion for her uncle. '''Tis nothing,'' he said sharply. ''John, you and the lads can carry Master Percy through to my father's library.''

''Library!'' Percy's eyes went round as platters.

''My father is something of a collector of books.''

''Well, well.'' Percy rubbed his hands together. ''I shall be interested to see what he has. Mayhap some I've not read, though I'd be surprised. Most surprised.''

''Uncle, Lord William has kindly taken us in till we can set the shop to rights, but you cannot impose further on his good—''

'''Tis no trouble, I'm sure,'' her uncle said heartily. ''Books were meant to be read. How many would you say your sire has?'' he asked as avidly as a drunkard with a cask of ale.

''Hundreds, I should think.''

''Hundreds.'' He smacked his lips. ''Splendid. Splendid. It'll take a fortnight to make our house habitable again. Mayhap more,'' he added gleefully.

"Must not waste a moment. Take me through to the library, if you will, John. There's a good lad."

"We will be gone as soon as I can find a friend to take us in," Rosemary said as they bore the chattering Percy away.

The thought of her going made Will more miserable than did having her stay. "And cheat him of this gilded opportunity?"

"I do not like to. He never complains, you see. Not of the boredom or the confinement or the pain." Her gaze met his, challenging. "But our presence here disturbs you. Or is it me?" she asked when he did not reply.

"This is a difficult time of year for me. That, coupled with my inability to catch George's killer and put a stop to these robberies, has put me out of temper." Will braced for the volley of questions about his first statement.

She focused on the second. "Was George a friend of yours?"

"Both friend and mentor when I was new to the importing business. But come, you must be weary." Will motioned to a waiting maid. "Anna will see you to your chamber."

Anna stepped forward, her gown spotless—and likely more costly than Rosemary's—her graying hair drawn back in a tidy braid. "Which chamber, my lord?" she asked haughtily.

Will bit back a reprimand. Anna's family had been in service to his for generations, but he'd speak to her later. "Lady Alys's old one. I asked Walter to have it readied."

Rosemary stirred. "I can share a pallet with Winnie."

Stubborn girl. "Nay. Though Anna can show you where your housekeeper and apprentice are sleeping, if you like, I think you'll find my sister's chamber more comfortable. Consider it recompense for my having led the thieves to your door."

"I do not hold you responsible," she said stiffly.

"I blame myself for not realizing I'd be watched. Now, go along with Anna." Will let out a sigh of relief when Rosemary grudgingly followed the maid from the room.

Then, tired as he was, he put on his cloak and went down to the warehouse. Though it was not yet noon, the streets were clogged with traffic. Everywhere he looked, there were signs of the approaching holiday. Children stood with their noses pressed to the bakeshop windows, drooling over the cakes inside. A group of young men skipped past him, likely headed for the frozen Moorfields for an afternoon of fun.

A wagon full of greenery to decorate the altars was being unloaded at the side door of St. Paul's Cathedral. Spruce boughs, ivy and holly, the red berries shining in the sunlight. Red to protect against evil in the coming year. The old talisman had not protected Ella from an untimely death.

Will tucked his chin down and quickened his pace, shutting his senses to the joy and anticipation all around him.

Jasper opened the door to Will's knock. "What happened at the apothecary shop?" the reeve asked as he closed them inside.

"The place was a shambles when we arrived, and the stock a total loss, but thankfully no one was hurt." Will flung off his cloak and hung it on a hook with the other men's. Chafing his hands, he made for his counting room. "What of you?"

"No one tried to break in here." Jasper kept pace. "Mayhap they are a small group and all were busy at the apothecary."

"Hmm. Rodney wounded one of the bastards in the leg. Have the men make the rounds of the rougher taverns and see if anyone recently came up limping." Will entered his counting room and straight away unlocked the chest that held his papers. "Take a seat, Jasper. Let us compare the items George commissioned me to bring back with the stuffs stolen from the other merchants."

"What are we looking for?"

"Similarities." He told Jasper about Edward's theory, then they both fell to reading the lists.

"I've a bit of knowledge about spices and such," Jasper said after a time. "But many of these are unfamiliar. What the hell do you suppose pel…pellitory is used for?"

"Damned if I know." Will leaned back in his chair, rubbing at the bridge of his nose. "Nor do I know *nux vomica* or spurge, except that I have seen them on the ship's manifest. Time grows shorter and we are no closer to catching the bastards."

"What if we do not succeed by the sixth?" Jasper asked glumly. "Do we stay and see the thing done, or leave before—"

"I cannot remain in London for Epiphany." Not even so George's murderer could be brought to justice. "We must find someone to help us with—" Will broke off. "Damn, my brain grows addled." He stood and began gathering up the papers. "I know who will know. If not Rosemary, then her uncle. He is a learned man, much traveled in the foreign parts where these spices grow."

Jasper helped bundle the documents into a leather pouch. "Take with you a few of our men. If we are being watched, the robbers might waylay you and steal the only records we have."

Will agreed, grudgingly, used to going about on his own. The trip home was quick and uneventful. "Is Mistress Rosemary still abed?" he asked when Anna opened the door to him.

"Nay, nor has she been. She left right after you."

"Left?" Will roared. "Where did she go?"

Anna sniffed. "I'm sure I do not know."

"Why did you let her go?" he demanded, an inch away from shaking the maid.

"Why would I stop her?"

"Because the streets are not safe. Jesu!" He threw the pouch of papers on the floor. "Her shop was attacked and pillaged a few hours ago. God only knows what harm may befall her." Beside himself with terror, Will turned to the guards who'd accompanied him home. "Go back to the warehouse.

Gather as many men as you can. Return here and fan out. Search every street, every alleyway and building.''

"In what direction?'' asked the boldest of the men. "Where would she have gone?''

Will raked the hair back from his face with a trembling hand. "To her shop, mayhap. I'll go there myself now.''

Chapter Six

Lady Chandre sat at a long table, eyeing herself in the largest, most highly polished mirror Rosemary had ever seen. After grilling Rosemary about the youth cream, the imperious lady had ordered her maid, an equally haughty if terribly plain Frenchwoman, to remove the layer of flour that gave Chandre's complexion its fashionable pallor. Beneath the coating of white, the lady's skin was mottled and lined with fine wrinkles.

"The cream feels cool and soothing," the lady muttered.

"Aye." Rosemary stood at a respectful distance, waiting for the verdict that could spell the salvation of her family.

Lady Chandre frowned at Rosemary in the mirror. "Should it not burn and itch as it eats away the wrinkled flesh."

"Nay," Rosemary said quickly, understanding now what had caused the rough, red patches on my lady's face, but too seasoned at dealing with fragile egos to mention it. "While the lotion I sometimes use to purify the skin does tingle a bit, the skin is fragile and easily harmed by harsh potions." Of the sort someone had sold to the lady. Count Baldassare, mayhap?

"Hmm." Lady Chandre touched a particularly sore looking spot beneath her left ear. "I do not welcome pain, but at least I know the potion is doing something."

"Something destructive," Rosemary dared to say. "You see," she added, launching into the explanation put forth by the ancient Greeks and garnered by Percy from reading their scrolls. "The reason skin wrinkles with time is because it grows dry." *Like old leather*, which the lady's certainly resembled beneath her costly cosmetics. "The effectiveness of my cream lies in its ability to soften the skin, while returning the youthful moisture and holding it in."

The goose grease did the lubricating. The myrrh the preserving. The unusual ability of the rare spice to preserve living skin had been noted by the Egyptian embalmers seeking to preserve their dead kings for posterity. Uncle Percy had grinned wryly when he'd read that to her. "Mayhap we should smear on the youth cream and wrap the old harridans up like mummies."

It was a suggestion Rosemary thought best not to pass along to the aging woman who sought eternal beauty.

"I do not notice any difference," Lady Chandre grumbled, leaning close to the mirror.

"'Twill take a few days to work. Pray keep the jar I brought as a sample. If you are not completely satisfied, you need pay me nothing. If you are and would like more…"

"My lady?" A homely maid dressed in Chandre's colors of blue and silver, had crept soundlessly into the room, and now stood a few paces away, wringing her hands.

"What is it, Betty?" the lady snapped. "You know I'm never to be disturbed when I am occupied with matters of my health."

Health. Rosemary squelched a smile.

"I—I am sorry, my lady," the hapless Betty stammered. "But Count Baldassare is here asking to see ye, and—"

"Baldassare? Here?" Lady Chandre gasped. "Dear God, he must not find you, or this." Her beringed fingers fluttered over Rosemary's cream, the plain crock standing out in the horde of fine vessels that crowded her table like a frog in a flock of butterflies. "He will be most upset if he learns I've become dissatisfied with his cures and sought another's help."

"I could take it away and come back later," Rosemary said, her bright dreams fading.

"Nay. I am intrigued by your cream and would try it as you suggest. But he must not see it." Chandre shoved the ugly crock behind a wall of lovely soapstone jars. "Betty! Escort Mistress Rosemary down the back stairs and out through the kitchen.

Then bring the count up. I will receive him in my solar.''

Dismissing both Rosemary and Betty, Chandre turned to the maid who'd been hovering at the edge of the room. "Get out my green velvet cotehardie. And the necklet with the emeralds.''

"Come along, mistress.'' Betty took Rosemary's sleeve and dragged her toward the door.

"Betty!'' Chandre cried, stopping them. "As soon as the count is above stairs, bring us refreshments. Wine mulled with sweet spices and some of those poppy seed cakes he likes.''

Betty bobbed a curtsy and shoved Rosemary out the door.

"The count is obviously an honored guest,'' Rosemary muttered as she was hustled down a narrow stairwell and along corridors whose walls were lined with fine tapestries and floor covered by costly carpets. Testimony to the lady's wealth.

"Oh, aye, the lady is fair taken with him. Me, I'm terrified just looking at him.'' She shivered. "'Tis his eyes, ye know. Dark and evil they are.''

"Aye,'' Rosemary murmured, understanding completely.

Betty paused at the open kitchen door. "Folks say he's in league with the devil. There's talk his potions are made from the bones of dead folk.''

"Hmm,'' Rosemary said noncommittally. It was the lot of those who sought to heal to be accused of witchcraft by the ignorant, suspicious folk they tried to cure. But his lotions appeared to be somewhat caustic.

"I'm friends with a maid who lives two streets over from his house," Betty whispered. "She says there's folk coming and going in the dead of night."

Shy clients, mayhap. "Your friend is something of a gos—" Rosemary gasped as the object of their discussion appeared in the doorway behind Betty, a half-eaten poppy seed cake in hand.

"Dieu, who is this?" The count looked Rosemary over as though he intended to devour her, too. "You are an improvement over the drabs Chandre usually hires," he said in his thickly accented English. "Wait, I have seen you before." He dropped the cake and grazed her cheek with fingers that stank of sulfur. "Your skin is soft as a child's." He took her chin and tilted it toward the candle in a nearby wall sconce. "What is your secret?"

Secret. Rosemary felt the blood drain to her feet.

"My lord," Betty interjected. "Lady Chandre said I was to escort ye to her solar."

"You dare interrupt!" Baldassare turned on the maid, his eyes burning with a brilliant, ruthless light.

"Nay." Betty threw one hand up as though to ward off a blow. "'Tis just she's waiting, and my lady hates to wait."

"Baldassare does not hurry for any woman, but—" he shrugged one velvet-clad shoulder "—Chandre pays most handsomely." He whirled on Rosemary again. "A fortune she has promised me for making smooth her skin." He touched Rosemary's cheek again, his finger moving down her neck, making her shiver with distaste. "'Twas at the Guildhall I saw you. Do you work for one of these clod-witted Pepperers? Does your master try his lotions on you? Is that how you came by such grace, or were you born so? I must know. Come, work for me. I would cherish you as you deserve."

"Nay!" She wrenched free and ran into the crowded kitchen.

"I will have you," the count called out.

Nay, you will not. Dodging scullery maids and serving wenches, Rosemary headed out the back door, into the garden. She paused only an instant, glancing frantically about at the trees and bushes set in orderly rows. A path cut between them. She took it. Gravel crunched beneath her heels as she ran past elegant statues, secluded stone benches and a small pond to a wooden gate. It was locked. Desperate, she hiked up her skirts, put her foot on the latch and clawed her way up and over.

A passing couple eyed her oddly, but Rosemary didn't stop to explain. Like a wounded animal seeking familiar shelter, she headed for her shop. The sight of the back door, sagging on its hinges, drove all thought of Baldassare from her mind. Picking her way through the rubble, she hesitantly went inside.

Her heart sank further as she looked around. Seen in full light everything appeared so much worse. So much more hopeless. Even with Malcolm's help, it would be beyond her to repair the doors. The shutters might be fixed, but they would need new tables and shelves. Where would she get the money?

Strong arms grabbed her from behind, dragging her back against a wall of solid muscle.

"Nay!" Gasping, she lashed out with her feet.

"Rosemary! 'Tis I, William."

"William." She ceased struggling to look over her shoulder and up into his scowling face. Nothing had ever looked dearer. Sagging in his embrace, she whispered, "I am so glad to see you, but what are you doing here?"

"Looking for you." He spun her around, captured her shoulders and gave her a little shake. "Why did you run off?"

"I did not run. I had business to conduct."

"Business? Your shop is ruined, your stock scattered, how—"

"I managed to save a pot of the cream I was preparing the night before the attack. I had an appointment to give it—"

"Bloody hell. You should not have gone anywhere alone. 'Tis too dangerous." He dragged her against his chest again, but this time he held her as he had the night before, tenderly.

"Why are you worried about me? I am nothing to you."

His hand stilled on her back, and he moved so he could look down at her. "I feel responsible for you."

"So you've said." She wished she knew what was going on behind his shuttered expression. "I absolve you of whatever—"

"Idiot. I am trying to keep you from winding up dead like George. Why will you not cooperate? Do you think I want another woman's death on my conscience?"

Another woman? One he'd failed? Was this the cause of his bitterness? "Nay, I do not want to die."

"Fine." He let her go and stepped away, raking a hand through his hair. "Then you will come home with me and promise not to return here without me or, indeed, to go anywhere without telling me and securing a suitable escort."

Rosemary bristled. "I come and go as I please."

"You *did*. Once this matter with the thieves is settled, and I have left England, you may do as you bloody well please. But while they are still at large, you will do as I say."

He was leaving. For some reason the notion saddened her. *You can leave,* she thought, studying his haunted eyes, *but you will not outrun what plagues you.*

"Agreed?" he demanded.

"I agree not to leave without telling someone where I am going," she said, thinking of her confrontation with the count. What if Betty had not intervened and he'd taken it into his head to spirit her away? No one would have known.

"*Me.* You are to tell *me.*"

Rosemary bristled, glancing up at the cold, austere man who had her cargo, and her family's future, in his hands. "I will agree, if you give me two things."

"What?" he snarled.

"The spices I ordered from George, and a place where I might use them to replenish my stock."

"Which spices?" he asked silkily.

Rosemary hesitated.

"I will not steal your secrets."

"Mayhap, but…"

He smiled, and she was again struck by how handsome he could be. "Little skeptic. I did not save your life last night to betray you today." His smile dimmed; his eyes locked on hers. "I swear it on the soul of a man we both called friend. Can we not work together to catch George's murderer?"

"Of course." Rosemary sighed. "I am sorry to doubt you. You've been both kind and understanding." She grinned ruefully. "Especially considering the way we met."

William chuckled. "Well, let us say my opinion of you has changed since that night."

"I am glad," Rosemary whispered. Simple words, but the air around them seemed suddenly charged with possibilities. Awareness hummed inside her, making her blood heat, her heart beat a little faster.

He felt it, too, she thought, his eyes darkening till they looked nearly black in the quiet, shadowy room. He lifted his hand, as though to touch her, then dropped it again.

"William?" she murmured. "What is it?"

He shook his head, like a man coming out of a daze. "Nothing." His voice was hoarse. "I…" He shook his head again and turned away, walking to the empty hearth. "We were speaking of the spices," he muttered, his back to her. "If you will tell me what you'd ordered from George, I will have them brought to the house and provide you with a workroom."

"You would do that?"

"Aye." He turned slowly, his expression remote once more. "I would ask your help in return, and your uncle's, too, if he is well enough. I need to learn who might use the spices George ordered and also those stolen from the other murdered men."

"To what purpose?"

"It is my understanding that some apothecaries and pepperers specialize in certain types of goods."

Rosemary nodded. "I sell many things, but am primarily known for creams and lotions that appeal to ladies. The apothecary in the next block is especially skilled in tonics for the gravely ill. You hope that knowing who might most want these things will narrow your search?"

"Aye. Whoever robbed the other merchants passed over some costly spices like saffron and cinnamon, and took instead some obscure things I cannot even pronounce."

"Of course I will help, and Uncle, too."

"Excellent. There is a workroom in the cellars of our house. My father had it built for my mother so she might pursue her goldsmithing without interruption, or —" he grinned "—setting the house ablaze. She tends to forget herself when the urge to create is upon her."

"It is the same with Uncle Percy when he has his

nose in a scroll. The world could come down about his ears, and he'd not notice a thing. I wager that we'll return home to find he has not slept a wink for reading your sire's books.''

''Is there anything you need from here?''

Rosemary looked around doubtfully. ''There does not seem to be much left whole, but mayhap something escaped.'' They spent nigh an hour sorting through the rubble, with only a dented mortar and mismatched pestle to show for their trouble.

''I am sorry,'' William said softly as they prepared to leave. ''We will buy whatever else you need.''

''I could not take your charity.''

''I offer none. If not for my carelessness, you would not have been attacked. I will have your shop rebuilt and your furnishings replaced.''

''There is no need for you to feel obligated to have us in your home. Especially since our presence upsets you.''

''That is not true,'' he growled. But something made his eyes turn bleak. ''It is not you, it is me. I would solve George's murder, and my time grows short. I did not mean to upset you.''

He did a great deal more than upset her; he made her feel things she'd never expected to. At times, she thought he also felt drawn to her. Nay, it must be her imagination.

''I apologize, too, my lord,'' she said coolly. ''I fear recent events have made me overly sensitive. I am not upset, merely, like you, frustrated by circumstances. Of course I will help you catch these brigands." Drawing a deep breath, she looked around her shop, then straight into his assessing gaze. "Pellitory and myrrh. They are what I ordered from George."

"What the hell is pellitory used for?"

"Gout. Uncle Percy has read that an unguent made from the powdered flowers does ease the swelling caused by gout."

"Hmm. I'd never heard of it."

"Nor have most people, I'd wager. My uncle has learned a great deal about ancient healing, mostly from reading Greek and Roman scrolls. If it helps him, he may live pain free."

"And the myrrh?"

Rosemary sighed. "According to Uncle Percy's readings, a cream made with myrrh can restore youthful vigor to the skin."

"Hmm. In a court as vain as King Richard's," William said dryly, "that would indeed earn you a fortune."

"I suppose." It was what she'd wanted, but if Lady Chandre was any example, Rosemary would rather eke out a living providing creams for gentler, if poorer, folk like Muriel.

Chapter Seven

29 December

It was a mistake being here with her, Will thought, studying Rosemary as she sat beside him at the workbench, her head bent over the lists of spices. The hour was late, and they were alone in a corner of his mother's atelier.

For two days he'd watched her ply her trade, working with the implements and common ingredients he'd bought from sympathetic members of the Pepperers' Guild and the more exotic spices he'd fetched from the warehouse, secreted in a bag worn under his clothes so no watcher would be the wiser. Doubtless the stout guard he'd mounted here had discouraged the thieves from trying to break into Sommerville House.

Rosemary had started with the pellitory. "Uncle Percy's gout is more important than Lady Chandre's wrinkles."

"If the lady is pleased with the cream, your fortune will be assured. But I've heard she can be difficult if crossed. She is a stickler for perfection and tolerates no mistakes."

"Nor any competition. Her clothes, her jewels and her home are beautiful. Her serving maids are homely, poor things."

Will had smiled, absurdly pleased she'd confided in him about her youth cream. Though she denied it, he sensed she held back something about the visit. Still he did not press, oddly content to sit by while she ground the dried pellitory flowers into a pungent powder and mixed it with goose fat.

"Uncle's scrolls recommend hog's lard, but the thought of smearing that on..." She'd giggled and shuddered delicately.

He'd wanted to hug her and kiss her smiling mouth.

But Will had held his desire in check. He should have left her alone and busied himself at the warehouse, but for some reason he couldn't bear to. So he'd found himself helping her pick through reddish brown lumps of myrrh. Rough and powdery on the outside, the walnut-sized hunks of plant resin were very brittle, yielding easily to Rosemary's mortar and pestle. The resulting powder she had dissolved in a mixture of sweet oils and lanolin to form a creamy lotion.

Setting it aside to cure, she had turned her attention to the lists they'd pored over each evening.

He should not be here with her, Will thought again.

By candlelight Rosemary's skin shimmered, smooth as finest silk. Did some special potion of her own devising make it so? Or had God blessed her with such fairness to compliment her wit, humor and bravery? It was a heady combination, that, which put him much in mind of his mother and two aunts. The longer he was with her, the more he wanted her.

"The problem," Rosemary said, frowning as she glanced up at him, "is that these herbs and spices can have several uses."

Nay, the problem was that he could barely gaze at her mouth without wanting to find out if it would taste as sweet as it looked. "I see." His voice came out tight and strangled.

"You are frustrated by this."

Will smiled ruefully. "You have no notion how frustrated."

"Oh, but I do. 'Tis tedious work with little to show for our hours down here. Except stiff muscles." Sighing, she arched her back. The innocent motion pushed her small, high breasts against the bodice of a green wool gown that had once been his sister's. He'd not appreciated it half so much on Alys.

"Stiff muscles," he agreed. Some more so than others. He wanted to sweep her into his arms, kiss her till they were both senseless. But he could not, in all honor, touch her. She was here under his protection. She was an innocent, judging by her demeanor. And, most important, he had nothing to offer her save a few moments of mindless pleasure.

A woman as rare and wonderful as Rosemary deserved better, a husband who would cherish her and love her all their days. He could not love her or any woman. His heart lay buried with Ella.

"At least we know that whoever took these things is a skilled apothecary, for no ordinary person—no customer—would have use for them in their natural state."

Will stifled his lustful urges. "Do you know of any in the trade who might stoop to robbery and murder?"

Count Baldassare. Nay, it was not fair to condemn the man for making advances toward her. It was for that reason she'd not mentioned the incident to William. "There are some I could name who are more ruthless than others, cheating their customers by adulterating their pepper with grit or their ground herbs with dried grass, but murder..." She shook her head.

"Well, if you can give me a list of those who might use these things, I will send my men to scout their shops."

How tense he was, Rosemary thought. His body fairly vibrated with suppressed emotion as he sat beside her. It was, she supposed, the pressure of trying to solve this case. The need to soothe him welled naturally inside her. Less familiar was the heat that filled her when he was near.

Desire. She'd read about it in the French romances, heard other girls giggle about it, but never had she dreamed it could be so powerful, so tempting to lie with a man. She was glad William was remote and cool, for if he'd touched her, she'd undoubtedly have melted. Gathering her wits, she asked, "Could you not turn what we have over to the sheriff?"

He snorted. "He and his men have had months to solve these robberies, yet they've made no progress."

"And now they are busy keeping the Christmas revelers from wreaking havoc with their drunken mischief."

William flinched, then grunted noncommittally.

"Why do you dislike the season?" She had noted the lack of holiday preparations, and Anna, who had warmed toward her, said Lord William would not be keeping Christmas this year. But the maid would not say why. "'Tis a time of joy and hope, a time to celebrate the birth of our dear Lord."

"There can be no joy in it for me." Will hesitated. He never spoke of Ella, not even with his family. But mayhap doing so now would help him maintain the distance he needed from this tempting woman. "My betrothed died last year. On Epiphany."

"Oh, I am so sorry. I know how it hurts to—"

"Nay. You cannot know." Will surged up from the bench, the bitterness he'd held inside bursting like a blister, filling him with renewed pain. "No one can." He paced the dim room, his anger raging. "I'd known her all my life and loved her as long. She was but ten and six. So young. So filled with hope and dreams. We both were. They died with her on that snowy street. I tried…''

Will jammed his hands into his hair and bowed his head as the memories of that black day assaulted him.

Ella laughing, running ahead of him toward the little house she'd found while he was away at sea. Even without seeing it, he knew he'd buy it for her. Anything to make her happy.

The weather was cold, the snow crunching beneath his boot heels as he followed where she led. Ahead of her, he saw the patch of ice, but his warning cry came too late.

It happened so quickly. Her feet slipped, flew from under her. Will screamed her name and started to run. But he was too slow. Too late to catch her before she went down.

It tormented him still. Vivid nightmares of running after her, of arriving too late. Always too late.

''Ella's head struck the curbstone.'' A soft thunk. So slight a sound to do so much. A little sound that had ended her life and destroyed his world.

Blood in the snow. Blood on Ella's head. So much blood.

''I carried her here,'' William whispered. ''To my family. Aunt Gabrielle was with us. For the holiday. But skilled as she is, she could do nothing to wake my Ella. All that night, I sat by her bed, talking to her, begging her to wake. In the end, she slipped away without ever opening her eyes.''

Rosemary went to him, wishing she dared put her

arms around him to try and absorb some of his pain. But his rigidity kept her at a distance. "I know how hopeless you must have felt."

"Do not say that!" He turned on her, eyes wet with unshed tears. She guessed he'd not cried for his Ella.

"Aye, I do," Rosemary said gently. "Seven years ago my parents caught the blood fever that swept through the city that December. I nursed them myself, certain that I alone could save them, for my mother had taught me all she knew of healing and told me I was most skilled." She looked down at her hands. "Not skilled enough, though. They died within two hours of each other, Mother first, then Father."

"Rosemary." He took her hands and squeezed them. "I am sure you did all you could."

She lifted her eyes, his image blurred by her tears. "I tried, but I failed them."

"My God, you were only, what, ten and three? And the fever claimed many victims that winter."

"Aye, but I will always wonder if I doomed my parents with my pride. Would they have lived if I'd called in another apothecary or even a physician to tend them?"

His grip on her tightened. "You cannot know that."

"Nay, I cannot. 'Tis something I've had to learn to live with." As you will learn to deal with Ella's death, she thought. But his grief was too raw for such platitudes. She blinked away her tears, part of the river she'd shed for her loss. "But it was hard at first. I missed them so. It seemed a great hole had been ripped from my life, from my heart."

"Aye." He whispered the word, his eyes meeting hers, filled with shared anguish. "It is the same for me, but I thought no one else could understand. To lose Ella was hell, to lose both your parents...God, I am so sorry." He reached for her.

Rosemary went into his embrace, the feel of his arms wrapping around her as natural as breathing. For a moment, they stood still in the quiet, shadowy corner of the workroom, locked together by a bond that went beyond the physical. His unspoken compassion eased her pain if not her lingering guilt. Would that she could bring him peace, but that was something he must find within himself. Raising her head, she murmured, "I am sorry to weep all over you." She was more upset to see he had not cried.

"Do not be." He cupped her cheek, wiping away her tears with his thumb. "You lost much."

"My whole world, or so it seemed." The feel of his hand on her face was soothing yet rousing.

"Were you alone?" His voice was low and husky. His eyes were different somehow, darker, more intent.

Mesmerized, she nodded. "If not for George Treacle, I'd have been truly lost. He took care of me, even sent one of his own clerks to run the shop till his letter found my uncle in Malta and Percy returned to raise me."

"George was a good friend to both of us." Ordinary words, absently spoken. His gaze slipped from her eyes to her mouth.

He was going to kiss her. Rosemary's whole body seemed to vibrate with anticipation. She was suddenly, acutely aware of how close they were, his arm around her waist, her hands splayed on his chest. Beneath them, she felt his heart race as his face dipped toward hers. Nearer. Nearer.

Her lips parted of their own accord. A sigh gusted between them as his mouth brushed over hers, light and fleeting as butterfly wings. Oh, but it was wonderful, she thought as her blood heated and her bones melted. Wanting more, needing to get closer, she wrapped her arms around him and stood on tiptoe.

"My soft, beautiful Rose." Will deepened the kiss, groaning as she opened to the questing tip of his tongue, like a flower before the morning sun. She tasted even better than he'd dreamed, sweet yet earthy, her responses shy and bold, generous and greedy by turns as she came alive in his arms. Her little sighs of pleasure, the feel of her body straining against his tore at his control.

William. Oh, William, my love! The words sang in Rosemary's heart as he took her far beyond her girlish dreams. This was what she'd been born for. This was why she'd been spared by the fever—to love and be loved by this man.

"Easy. Easy." Will wrenched his mouth free and buried it in her chestnut curls. He was trembling like an untried lad with his first woman. And indeed, she did not feel like any woman he'd ever held before.

There was a newness, a freshness to being with her that threatened his good intentions. "We must not," he murmured, but could not make himself release her.

"I know." Rosemary's voice was as raspy as his own. Even their hearts beat in wild concert. "But I never thought to find anyone who made me feel like this."

"'Tis lust." Somehow Will found the strength to put her from him. "Lust, pure and simple."

Her mouth still wet from his kisses, her eyes dark and wounded, Rosemary looked up at him. "I do not know."

"Well, I do." Unable to bear her pained expression, Will turned away. "I've had experience in such matters. You are a beautiful woman, and I've been long without one."

"Oh."

That single word affected him more than would a river of tears. "We must fight it. I must fight it." Jamming a hand into his hair, he walked back to the table.

"Why?"

"Nothing can come of this passion." He turned on her, hoping anger would quell his need for her. It didn't. Worse, she'd come to stand beside him. Hands clenched to keep from reaching for her again, he snarled, "Nothing!"

She nodded, her eyes grave but sad, so sad. "I know, you are a nobleman and I just a—"

"That has naught to do with it. If my father, who

was heir to an earldom, could wed a goldsmith's granddaughter, I, who am only his second son, could wed where I pleased.''

''Then why…?''

''Why? Do you think I am so dishonorable that I would seduce a woman I'd sworn to protect?''

She smiled. ''What if I seduced you?''

''You?'' Will stared at her, agog.

''Well, I admit I am new to this, but I do think I'd have a good idea how to go about it.'' She fluttered her lashes.

The muscles below Will's belt tightened in response, making him very glad of the long tunic he wore. ''Have you no shame?'' he asked scornfully. ''Do you want to be left carrying a bastard babe when I sail away?''

She flinched as though he'd struck her with his palm instead of words. ''Of course not,'' she said in a hollow voice. ''I had forgotten you were bent on leaving.''

Will grunted. So had he for a moment. When he'd held her, he'd forgotten everything, even his beloved Ella. ''Aye, I am. And the sooner we solve George's murder, the sooner I may be about quitting this cold, accursed city. If you will prepare that list of apothecaries and give it to Walter.''

''Where are you going?''

''Down to the warehouse.''

''At this hour? It must be nearly ten.''

''I've hopes that our thieves will take the bait I've spread about and try to rob me.''

"What bait?"

"George's cargo. I've put it out that I am preparing to move the goods he ordered from me."

"Oh, William. That is too dangerous."

"To them, mayhap. I've men concealed within the warehouse. A mouse could not get in without being caught."

"Well, I will see you tomorrow, then. We can go over the list and—"

"I will be busy on the morrow." And every moment till he sailed, since he obviously could not trust himself in her company. "You may give the lists to Walter."

Rosemary frowned but nodded. "What if there is a battle with these thieves?"

"I only hope there is," Will said with relish. Aye, a good fight was just what he needed to vent his frustration. Spinning away from her, he headed up the stairs.

"You will be careful," she called after him.

Will did not answer.

He would not be careful.

Rosemary shivered with foreboding as she listened to William's footsteps fade away.

He had a death wish.

Chapter Eight

With Ella gone, William did not care to live. Rosemary had seen the hopelessness in his eyes, heard it in his voice when he'd spoken of his anguish over Ella's loss.

Rosemary understood. She'd felt the same after her parents died. It had been hard to face each day without them, but somehow she'd found the strength. Nay, George had forced her to it. Tears welled as she recalled her dear friend cajoling and, finally, bullying her into not just surviving but learning to enjoy life again. The shop had been her salvation, as shipping had William's. But with the anniversary of Ella's death nigh, he was consumed by a cold morass of grief and guilt.

And yet he had not been cold or remote when he'd kissed her, Rosemary mused. For a few precious moments he'd come alive in her arms. Lust, he'd called it, but she'd seen other things in his gaze: tenderness and a loneliness she knew instinctively she could

ease. If he would let her. But guilt and loyalty to
Ella's memory drove him to reject her.

How could she fight a ghost?

Rosemary ground her teeth in frustration. Her first
thought was to rush down to the warehouse and make
certain he did nothing foolish. Nay, she would only
get in the way, mayhap distract him at a critical moment.

Her gaze fell on William's lists. At least she could
carry on his investigation. Gathering the papers and
the candle, she left the workroom for the old solar,
her steps brisk and purposeful. Despite the late hour,
her uncle was awake, sitting up in the great bed, the
counterpane covered with books.

"Uncle, may I come in?"

"Hmm," he said without looking up.

Smiling fondly, Rosemary crossed to him. A tray
of food left untouched on the table beside the bed
bore mute testimony to his interest in the Sommerville library. "Uncle?"

"Hmm." Two books lay open on his lap. His eyes
darted between them as he muttered in what sounded
like Greek.

"I am sorry to intrude, but I need your help, Uncle."

He blinked at her owlishly. "Ah, Rose. Shop all
locked up?"

"Uncle, the shop was destroyed days ago."

"Hmm. So it was." He patted her hand. "Sorry
about that. You worked hard—so hard. I'll help you

set things to rights as soon as I've finished with this."

"William has hired workmen to do that." She had not wanted his charity, but William had secured her uncle's permission to make the repairs. Not that Percy remembered.

"Good. He's a good lad, if a bit stiff." Percy looked down, ready to disappear into the books again.

"Uncle." Rosemary touched his arm. "I hate to drag you away from all this, but I need you to work out a puzzle for me."

"A puzzle? Ah, of course. Love a puzzle." Carefully setting the books aside, he asked, "What is it?"

Rosemary spread the lists before him. "William and I are trying to determine what sort of person would make use of the spices taken from the London merchants. The costly saffron, mandrake root and pomegranate could be used for many things from cooking to medicines."

"Mayhap the thieves sold them."

"William's men found no flood of them on the black market." She shuffled William's manifest to the top. "These things George ordered. The myrrh and pellitory were for us, of course."

"Hmm." Percy glanced at the lump in the covers. Beneath it lay his gouty foot, slathered in pellitory ointment, wrapped in bandages and elevated on a pillow. "I do believe the Greek physicians were right. The foot seems less swollen."

"Oh, I am so glad. And the pain?"

"Hmm." He gingerly flexed the foot. "Less. Definitely less. Not that I'm ready to get up and dance."

"'Tis a miracle." She beamed at him through happy tears.

"Just tenacious research. What of the myrrh cream?"

"I do not know. I sent Malcolm around to tell Muriel what had happened to us." Her friend had returned with the boy, filled with sympathy and apologies that her small home could not accommodate them. "Muriel promised to act as go-between with Lady Chandre, but there's been no word if she liked the cream."

"Ah, well. Time will tell."

"Time is in short supply. We must catch the thieves before they strike again. Some of these items on George's list are not familiar to me. Do you know what they might be used for? It might help us to narrow our search."

Percy scowled as he read the items. "Find me ink and parchment, and I will make a list of all possible uses first."

Rosemary got the supplies and stood by while her uncle worked, frowning, muttering and scribbling. The minutes dragged by. Her mind drifted to William, waiting in the warehouse for the thieves to strike. The worry that had plagued her earlier grew. She pictured him stepping in harm's way, risking the life he no longer valued. Finally she could stand it no longer.

"I am going down to William's warehouse."

"Hmm. Take Malcolm with you."

Rosemary nodded. She had no intention of rousing the apprentice, but she would ask Walter for an escort. She eased out of the solar and tiptoed across the darkened great hall, taking care not to step on any of the Sommerville servants who slept there, rolled in their blankets. In the entryway, she paused, uncertain where to find the steward.

Footsteps echoed down the stairwell that led to the sleeping quarters on the floor above. Quickly she stepped back into the shadows. A pair of muddy boots came into view, followed by muscular legs and then a broad chest encased in blue wool. The face that topped the body drew a gasp from her.

"William." Rosemary leaped at him. "I am glad you have not gone." She wrapped her arms around him and clung. "I feared—"

"I can see that, but—" a warm hand slid under her chin, lifting it so their gazes met "—I am not William."

"Oh!" Horrified, Rosemary let go and stumbled back from the man who was like William but different.

This man grinned, his eyes dancing in the light of the candle he held. "I am Richard, William's brother."

Richard, heir to the earldom. Anna had made certain Rosemary knew all about William's exalted family. "My lord." Rosemary tried to curtsy, but her legs were so weak she'd have toppled over if he hadn't caught her shoulders to steady her.

"No need for that. But I would know who you are."

"Rosemary. I…we…"

"The family whose shop was destroyed. Walter told me when I came in." Richard's smile deepened, his gaze frankly curious. "I've just settled my two sons for the night. We were delayed on the road, and both were nigh asleep in the saddle. They teased to see the city all dressed up for the holidays—" he looked around the entryway with its display of ancient weapons "—and were most disappointed to find our house bare of decorations."

"William, er, Lord William ordered that no holly be hung and no Christmas cakes baked."

"Damn him," Richard growled.

"He is in mourning for his Ella," she replied defensively.

Richard cocked his head. "Will told you that?"

"Aye. He loves her very much."

"I am surprised he spoke of her to you."

Rosemary averted her head, her cheeks heating at the memory of the kiss that had followed their mutual confidences.

"What is my brother to you?" he asked sharply.

"A friend." Rosemary whipped her head up. "Nay, less than that. He helped my uncle, servants and myself. He—"

"Less than a friend." Richard's voice was gentle; his eyes warmed suddenly. "I'd say from your greeting when you mistook me for Will that he is rather *more* than a friend."

"I was worried about him. I..." *William.* Rosemary drew in a sharp breath. "I must go to William." She spun away.

Richard grabbed her arm. "Why? What has happened to him?"

"He is at the warehouse, waiting to spring a trap for these spice thieves, the men who murdered George Treacle and the other merchants." The knot in her chest tightened. "I fear he may not care if he survives so long as the brigands are caught."

"Dieu. Mama was right to insist I find a pretext to visit Will. She thought that being with my boys might lift his spirits." Richard cursed. "I was with Will only a week ago. He talked of moving to Italy, but suicide...Will is not the sort."

"Nay, but he may not fight very hard to stay alive."

Richard whispered, "He would not..."

"I mean to make certain he does not do something foolish." Rosemary slipped from his grasp.

Richard stepped in front of her. "It's late. In the morning, I will speak with Will and judge his mood."

"If the thieves attack tonight, morning may be too late. I am going to the warehouse to make certain he is all right."

"'Tis too dangerous. Stay here, and I'll find Will."

Rosemary looked up into a face so like William's, yet vibrant with strong emotions. Richard was concerned, surely, but beneath it he was at peace. He had his sons, his wife, his family. She'd not be able to make so content a man as Richard understand what it was like to feel you had no reason to go on living. But she knew. Dear God, she knew. "Nay, I must go."

Richard hesitated, then nodded in grudging acceptance. "I'd say you are much more than a friend to my brother. And 'tis glad I am that you came into his life just now."

"He is not, I think," Rosemary said softly.

"Then once I've made certain he is all right, I'll have to beat some sense into him." He grinned at her gasp of horror. "Fetch your cloak, my lady, while I gather up the men I brought with me. If the thieves do attack, an extra thirty men-at-arms and two knights may come in handy."

Chapter Nine

30 December

Sitting in a dark warehouse, waiting for something that might or might not happen gave a man too much time to think, Will decided, hunkered down beside the chests containing George Treacle's last order.

And regret.

He regretted Ella's death. That was foremost, a pain he'd lived with for so long it seemed a part of him, like his arms or his legs. But mingled with that old regret was a new one.

He wished he'd never met Rosemary.

She made him feel things he had no business feeling. Especially with Ella not dead a year. The lust he could understand and deal with. The tenderness, the near obsession to be with Rosemary was inexcusable.

"What was that?" Jasper whispered from behind a crate.

William perked up. "Rodney, do you hear anything?"

"Aye, there's someone outside," Rodney hissed. He and John were crouched at either side of the main door. "I think—"

An explosion shattered the night. The warehouse's big double doors with their metal bands flew open as though propelled by some giant hand. The force of the blast knocked Will onto his back and tossed barrels into the air. Stunned, he lay there as it rained chests of pepper and bales of wool.

A scream rose over the chaos, a high, hideous shriek of pain that ended as abruptly as it had begun.

Will struggled to his feet. Dazed, he gaped at the ruins of his warehouse. Smoke, thick and stinking of black powder, billowed in through the open door. Orange flames crackled around the framework. Beyond it, a dozen or more figures lurked, their faces hidden by black masks.

The thieves.

Will drew his sword. "Jasper?" he called softly.

"Here," came a hoarse whisper. "Are ye all right?" Jasper materialized out of the sooty pall, eight men on his heels.

"Aye." Will took stock of the grimy, blood-spattered men, one holding an apparently broken arm. "Where are Rod and John?"

"Dunno. They were close to the door." Jasper looked toward the charred ruin. "Bloody bastards likely killed them. Jesu, who'd have thought they'd do such a terrible thing? And there they stand, waiting for us to roast. What'll we do?''

"The noise is sure to bring someone," Arnald muttered.

"Aye, but how soon?" Will glanced around at the jumble of barrels and chests. There were plenty of places to hide and ambush the thieves when they came in. But his men were outnumbered and several were wounded. "We'd best go up to my counting room. Mayhap one of us is slim enough to go out the window and summon help."

Jasper snorted. "I'd not count on it."

"Then we'll barricade ourselves in and hope we can hold them off till someone comes to investigate the explosion."

"By then, the thieves'll have made off with yer goods."

"Aye." Will gritted his teeth as he led the way to the stairs. Damn but he hated to let them get away with this. Nor would he likely get another chance to try and trap them. He hurried his men up the stairs, the whole assisting those who were wounded. Jasper went to assess the size of the window.

"There's no way that any of us can get out this."

Will cursed. "I want you to bar the door after me, then pile the table and all the chests in front of it."

"Where are you going?"

"Back downstairs. I'm going to wait till they come in."

"Ye'll be no match for them alone," Jasper exclaimed.

"I don't intend to fight. While they are looking through my warehouse for the things they want, I'll sneak past and run for the warden of the watch."

"'Tis too risky," Jasper grumbled. "Let one of us."

"Nay." That was precisely why Will was going himself. The other men had families and sweethearts. "Do as I say, and be quick." He left, with Jasper's whispered protests still ringing in his ears. Vaulting down the stairs, he crept along the aisles of chests and hid behind a wall of wool bales. From there he had a good view of the door and an easy path to reach it.

Grimly he studied the burly figures outside. One of them had a white swath around his upper leg and walked with a limp. Doubtless the one poor Rodney had wounded at Bainbridge's.

"Come on. We're going in," ordered a gravelly voice.

Another whined, "The fire's still burning."

"We cannot wait for it to go out. 'Tis only the door frame that's aflame, ye coward." The tallest of the men, who must be the leader, grabbed hold of the foremost thief and shoved him toward the opening. "Go quick, and it'll scarcely singe ye."

Cursing, the first brigand plunged through the ring of fire and stumbled into the warehouse. "I made it, Rene," the man called, brushing ash from his clothes.

"Aye. Get going, the lot of you," Rene growled.

So, at least he had a name, Will thought. And an

infamous one at that. This was undoubtedly Rene Renard, owner of a string of brothels and, according to the sheriff, a brigand so clever he'd been often suspected but never convicted of a crime. This time, Will vowed, Rene would be caught and hanged.

One by one, Rene urged his men inside till only himself and another remained.

"Odo. Stay outside and keep watch." With that, Rene dashed through the flames and began issuing orders. The first sent his men scrambling to light the torches they'd brought in. Finding fire was no problem. In moments, each held a lighted brand.

Will groaned in frustration, sinking lower into the shadows. How the hell would he get out now?

"What are we looking for?" asked one of the men.

"Mandrake root, myrrh and a passel of others. They'll be all together in several small chests," Rene added. Hands on hips, the Frenchman surveyed the warehouse. "Spread out. Fetch all the small casks and pile them here. I know what to look for. I'll open them till we find that for which we came."

"Have we time?" ventured one man. "What if someone comes?"

"Then we'll kill them," Rene snarled. "If we fail tonight, we'll all be gutted and left for the rats as Andre was when he came back from the apothecary shop empty-handed."

"*Dieu,*" Will whispered. He vaguely remembered the sheriff mentioning a body found disemboweled in an alley. Rene truly was a fiend. Obviously the grisly deed had made an impression on his men, for they scattered like stricken rabbits. Their torches sent fingers of light streaking down the aisles and between the stacks of goods. Exclamations of triumph marked the discovery of each small chest and casket. How long before they found him?

Gut tight with dread, Will crept to the other side of the wool bales. Grimly he gauged the distance to the door. It was only a dozen steps, but Rene stood in full view of the opening. Even supposing Will could make it that far undetected, could he disarm the man who waited outside?

He had to, for every second that passed lessened his chances of capturing the thieves. Crouching low, his sword in hand, Will made for the door.

"Hey! Who are ye?" Rene shouted. "Get him!"

Will stood and ran for his life, expecting at any moment to take a blade in the back. If he could just reach—

"Will?" A man appeared in the doorway. Not just any man.

"Richard! Beware! Thieves!" Will shouted. Behind his brother, he spied a throng of Sommerville soldiers and realized the tide of power had shifted. "A Sommerville. To me!" Will cried, turning back toward the brigands.

"Ye'll not live to take us!" Rene boasted. He drew back his arm and threw the knife he held.

The blade gleamed wickedly in the torchlight as it whizzed across the warehouse. Time seemed to freeze.

Dully Will watched it come, realized the knife flew straight at his heart. What did it matter? Richard was here. He would see Rene's band captured and punished. Will's work was done. Mayhap it was better this way. Soon he'd be with Ella in—

"William!" Rosemary's voice, high and hysterical.

Rosemary here? He must be dreaming.

A solid little body slammed into his, driving Will to one side. Something whizzed past. The sound ended in a soft grunt of pain. He looked down into Rosemary's pain-contorted features. Blood welled from her shoulder.

"Nay!" Will cried, catching Rosemary as she fell.

"Tend to her," Richard ordered. "We'll deal with the rabble. After them!" Richard roared.

A horde of men in Sommerville red and black poured into the warehouse, swords upraised, screaming for vengeance. The thieves dropped their torches and drew their weapons. Lit only by the hellish fire from the burning doorway, the battle was joined.

Oblivious to the hoarse grunts and clashing steel, Will laid Rosemary on the floor. Her limpness, the blood on her shoulder catapulted him back a year. Terror cramped in his gut.

"You cannot die. I cannot lose you, too." He repeated the words like a mantra while he flung back her cloak and ripped away the sleeve of her gown.

Unlike Ella, who had lain unmoving, Rosemary opened her eyes. "Are you all right, William?" she whispered.

"Aye. Whatever were you thinking?" he growled, frantically tearing strips from her cloak, for his own was upstairs.

"I was afraid for you." She winced when he pressed the woolen pad he'd fashioned to the wound. "Easy. I know this hurts, but we must stanch the blood."

"Adder's tongue is good for that." She smiled faintly. "But I do not suppose you have any with you."

"Rosemary, now is not the time for levity. You are hurt." Mayhap dying. Nay, he'd not think of that. "Rest, love." He brushed a shaky hand over her brow. "I'll carry you home."

Love. Rosemary smiled up at her worried Will. It was worth the burning pain in her shoulder to hear him call her that. "Is the cut very deep?"

"I do not know. You should not be hurt at all. Dear God, Rosemary." He bent to lay his forehead against hers. "Whatever possessed you to come between me and that blade?"

The knowledge that you would not move from its path. But Rosemary hesitated to destroy the moment by reminding him, however obliquely, of Ella. "I had to save you."

He raised his head, staring deep into her eyes. "I am not worth the spilling of even one drop of your blood."

"To me, you are."

"Rosemary, I cannot be what you deserve. I—"

"How is she?" Richard knelt at her other side, his face sweaty, his breathing raspy.

"Alive." Will looked over his shoulder. "The thieves?"

Richard grinned. "Dead or dying. They fought like fiends, but were no match for skilled warriors in ar—"

"Dead!" William shouted. "I wanted Rene, at least, alive so I might turn him over to the sheriff for hanging."

"Unfortunately, they left us no choice. What difference does it make if they died tonight or hanged on the morrow?"

"I had hoped to find out what they had done with the spices," Will snapped. "What good to cut off the tail of the snake and leave the head to strike again?"

Richard sighed. "You are right, but they refused to surrender. I will sit with Rosemary while you go and see if any are yet able to answer your questions."

"Nay," Will replied, though he looked tempted. "I'd not have her lie here in the cold, her wound untended."

"Go," Rosemary said, touched by William's concern for her. "I do not think my wound is—"

"Nay. You are my first concern." Will looked to his brother. "I will leave the questioning to you and Jasper."

31 December

Rosemary awakened to a dimly lit room and the sight of William sitting vigil at her bedside in a high-backed chair.

"How do you feel?" he asked, leaning forward. His jaw was darkly stubbled, his rumpled clothes the same ones he'd worn at the warehouse. More telling was the fear haunting his eyes.

"Better." If you discounted the grinding ache in her shoulder, which she was willing to do to alleviate his guilt. "Was the wound a deep one?"

"Nay, according to Anna, who has been healing our hurts for years and insisted on tending you, the blade only grazed you. She bound it tightly and said no stitching was necessary."

"That is good news." Rosemary shifted, gingerly flexing the shoulder. It pained, but not overly much. "A few days and I will be back at my worktable concocting potions."

"You could have been killed." William bolted up and began to pace, dragging a hand through his disordered hair.

"But I was not," Rosemary said gently.

"Damn, when I think how close I came to losing you, too."

"Would it have mattered so greatly?"

He spun to face her, expression haggard. "Of course it would. How can you even ask such a question?"

"Because I know that part of you is sorry we met."

Will stared at her beautiful, if too pale face, framed

by a cloud of chestnut hair and dominated by those wise hazel eyes. His heart contracted. Some force stronger than his will drove him back across the room. Sinking down beside her, he took both her slender hands in his. "I cannot regret knowing you, but—"

"Shh." Rosemary freed one of her hands and stroked his cheek. Her palm was prickled by his beard as her heart was by his suffering. "I understand." But she did not like it one bit. They belonged together. Sensing their time slipping away and desperate to make every moment count, she slid her hand around to his nape and urged his head down.

"I should not." But the temptation of her ripe mouth a breath away was irresistible. Groaning, Will gave in and kissed her. She tasted better than he'd remembered, the sweetness of her lips parting beneath his the only antidote for the bitter moment when he feared he'd lost her, too. Desperate to forget, to celebrate life instead of death and danger, he cupped her face and slanted his mouth over hers, hungry, demanding.

Rosemary recognized the pain that fueled his ferocity and tempered it with the instinctive compassion of a born healer. Wrapping her good arm around his neck, she opened herself to him, heart and soul.

Will knew he must leave before he gave in to the passion she roused in him and sullied what honor he had left. But how could he leave her with her eyes filled with such poignant yearning? "You should be sleeping."

"I am not tired. How could I be when you are near? Being with you makes me come alive."

Will frowned. "Do not read more into this than there is."

"Lust you called it, but I know 'tis love I feel."

"You must not. There can be no future for us."

She raised her chin to meet his challenge. "Then let us at least have the present." She matched her mouth to his again.

The sweet intensity of Rosemary's kisses tore at Will's control. Desire had never bit this sharply nor passion flared so hotly. He burned with the need to bury himself in her welcoming heat, to give them both the release they strained for.

But he could not.

Even though his body ached for hers, some inbred sense held him back. The fragile woman trembling in his arms was not only an innocent, she was precious to him.

He could not take her and leave her. And leave he must.

Groaning, Will wrenched his mouth from hers. "I have to go," he rasped.

"Go!" Rosemary clutched at his shoulders. "Where? Why?"

"To see my ship readied to sail." Slipping free from her grasp, he stood, his expression bleak. "We leave for Italy as soon as she's provisioned, and I have bid farewell to my family before I go."

Rosemary's spirits plunged. "When will you return?"

"I am not certain." *Never,* his eyes said. London held too many memories of Ella.

How did one fight a ghost? Rosemary thought miserably as William walked to the door. It closed behind him with a soft click, yet that sound shattered her bright dreams.

Chapter Ten

4 January

"Wait till ye see the new shelving and all." Malcolm dragged Rosemary into the workshop. "It's ever so grand."

It was. Rosemary smiled, but she wanted to weep when she saw what William had done to restore their home: stout new doors and shuttered windows, sturdy yet handsome tables and benches, and even a high-backed chair beside the hearth in her workroom. "He's given us more than we had before." And taken her heart.

"His lordship's very fond of ye," Malcolm said, beaming. "Walter and the rest of his servants were always whispering about how he'd not taken an interest in anything since his betrothed lady died last year. Not till ye came along."

"Aye." But his love for Ella was stronger than his attraction to her. Anguished, Rosemary turned away from the mortar and pestle sets, the chests of spices and bunches of fragrant herbs hanging from the rafters. "How is Uncle Percy?"

"Very well, indeed." Malcolm followed her out into the shop. "That pellitory cream has eased the pain in his foot. He's above stairs sitting in the new chair and padded footstool Lord Will bought him, reading the books his lordship lent him. He—"

A knock at the front door stilled Malcolm's gush of words. They exchanged nervous glances.

"'Tis nigh dark," the apprentice whispered.

"Who is there?" Rosemary called.

"I've a message for Rosemary Bainbridge from Lady Chandre de Cressy," replied a male voice.

Rosemary moved to the door, then hesitated. Before leaving, Arnald had reminded her to be cautious. Renard was dead, but a search of his houses had not turned up any cache of spices nor clues to what he'd done with them. "What message?" she demanded.

"Her ladyship would buy all you have of a certain cream. She said you would know what was meant by that. I've instructions to pay whatever you want. In advance."

Rosemary smiled for the first time in days and gave Malcolm a quick hug. "It worked. It worked," she whispered. "Praise be to God and Uncle Percy, the cream worked. Our fortune is made." She lifted the bar and opened the door. "Come in, good sir, I—" She stumbled to a halt as she recognized one of the dark-clad figures lurking on her doorstep. "Count Baldassare!"

"Ah, you remember me. How nice." He brushed past her into the shop, followed closely by two hard-faced giants with arms as thick as tree trunks. "Lord William's workmen were most skilled. One would not know your establishment had been so thoroughly wrecked a few days ago."

"What are you doing here?" she demanded.

The count turned in a swirl of fine black wool. "It is as I said. Chandre wishes a cream that will diminish her wrinkles."

"But you were making one for her."

Baldasarre scowled. "Much as it pains me to say so, your cream is vastly better. A miracle. I must know how it's done."

"The recipe is not for sale." Rosemary backed up a step.

"All things have a price. 'Tis a matter of determining—"

"Be gone." Malcolm moved in front of her, looking rather like a mouse facing down a surly black cat.

"Oh, I shall go." Baldassare said. "And your lovely mistress with me."

"Nay!" Malcolm leaped at the count. Baldassare backhanded him into a display table, scattering red and black peppercorns. The boy landed in a heap among them, eyes closed, unmoving.

"Malcolm!" Rosemary started forward.

"Hold there." Baldassare grabbed her arm. "What say you, do I have my men—" he gestured toward the lurking thugs ''—pry the information from the boy, or will you give me what I want?''

''Malcolm knows nothing.'' Rosemary shuddered, thinking of Uncle Percy, who possessed information the count would doubtless value greatly. ''I have some of the cream made up. In the workroom. Let me fetch it, and—''

''How fortunate. Chandre will be pleased. Tell me where it is, and I will have Edgar bring it along.''

''Along where?''

''Did I not mention you were coming to work for me?''

''Nay. I cannot leave.'' Rosemary tried to tug free, but his grip on her arm turned bruising.

''I insist. I've never had a female apprentice. It should prove interesting,'' he drawled, eyes bright and glittering. ''And I simply cannot have you in competition with me.''

''I swear I will make no more.'' Rosemary was truly frightened now, her mouth dry, her palms slick. ''I—''

''How nicely you beg.'' His smile became a leer; something evil moved through his eyes as they traveled over her body. ''You must do it for me again, when we are in private.''

5 January, Twelfth Night

William reached London midday to find the city in the grips of the usual Twelfth Night rowdiness. The sun shone in defiance of his bleak mood. The shops were hung with holly, the streets clogged with boisterous revelers, some in lavish disguises.

The year before, he and Ella had joined them. She had gotten a little tipsy on the wine he'd bought from the street vendors. Giggling, she had pressed her nose to the bakeshop windows, admiring the dark fruit-cakes decorated with knights, castles and dragons fashioned of marzipan and spun sugar.

The memory choked him. The urge to ride by Bainbridge's for one last glimpse of Rosemary mocked him. Truly he was cursed, mourning one woman, loving another.

Aye, he did love Rosemary. He'd admitted that to himself the night before as he'd watched his parents, still deeply in love after all these years. If something happened to one of them, the other would not stray as he had.

Disgusted with himself, anxious to depart, Will turned off Westchop and rode quickly toward the warehouse. He had hoped to sail yesterday, but when he'd announced his plans to live in Italy, his mother had begun to cry and his father to argue. He'd been lucky to get away at all, Will thought morosely as he dismounted before the warehouse.

Jasper ran out to greet him with the welcome news that all was in readiness for their departure. "The sky was so clear last night ye could see the Christmas Star," the old man remarked as they went aboard ship. "If it's the same tonight, the moon should provide good light to guide us down the river."

Will nodded, then, like a man possessed, harried

everyone through the final stages of making ready to sail. Still, daylight had deepened to dusk before the last water keg was stored and the anchor weighed. As the *Lady Sommerville* glided away from her moorings, he left the deck for his cabin, unable to bear the sight of London fading from view.

London and Rosemary.

Nay, he'd not think of her. But as he paced the narrow confines of his cabin, his restless mind kept jumping back to her. Ella had gotten sick just looking at the sea, but he'd wager Rosemary would take to it. He could picture her reading or writing at the desk bolted to the floor. Easier, even, to imagine was Rosemary reclining on the bed built into one wall, her arms open, her eyes beckoning him to join—

"Stop!"

Will whirled away from the bunk, snatched aside the heavy drapes that covered the stern window and stared bleakly out. The moon was indeed up, painting phosphorescent whirls in the ship's wake. Lifting his eyes to the heavens in search of some measure of peace, he easily found the Christmas Star.

How bright it was, how dazzling, filled with hope and promise. As he continued to stare at the brilliant star, the turmoil in his breast began to settle. He could well imagine Ella gazing down at him from on high.

"Ah, Ella, I have missed you so," he whispered.

Instantly his peace was shattered by the memory of the horrible moment when he'd lost her. He tried to push it away, but the scene continued to roll through his mind like a mummer's play. The too-familiar horror when she began to fall. The race to catch her. The gut-wrenching agony of holding her in his arms, feeling her life drain away.

"Ella. Ella, do not leave me," he cried softly.

Miracle of miracles, her eyes opened.

"Will." She gazed up at him with such sweetness, her eyes paler than he recalled. Blue-white, like the Christmas Star.

"Ella, my love, you are restored to me."

"Nay, I fear not." The lips that had smiled at him so often turned down at the corners. "You must let me go."

"Nay. I cannot. I loved you."

"And I you. I would have been a good wife, but God had other duties for me. Let me go, Will, so I can be about them."

"I—I do not understand."

"Your guilt and grief have trapped me between two worlds. Set them aside and you set me free."

"How can I?" he cried out. "How can I forget you?"

"I am not asking you to forget me any more than I will forget you, but it is time to move on. For both of us. I have my work. You have Rosemary."

"I—I can explain about Rosemary."

"There is no need." She smiled again, very gently. "I have looked into your heart and seen the love you try to stifle. For the sake of my memory. It is not necessary. I rejoice in your happiness, my dearest friend. Go to her. She needs your help."

"What is it? Has something happened?"

"Go to her. Be happy, you and your Rosemary. When you think of me, let it be with joy for the youth we shared. Be at peace, knowing that I am, too." Ella's voice and image slowly faded.

"Wait." Will reached for the star and rapped his knuckles on the leaded glass window. Was what he'd seen real? Or a figment of his imagination?

For a moment he stood there, staring at the bright, magical light that had led three kings to a manger in Bethlehem. They had followed the star out of faith. So, too, must he follow what was in his heart.

Bent over a table littered with the tools of her trade, Rosemary carefully mixed ground myrrh with melted goose grease. It was imported from France and of the finest quality, as were all of the supplies she'd been given to work with. Thick tallow candles burned in sconces over her head. A brazier in the corner chased away the chill. Beneath her feet, a thick carpet warmed the stone floor. Even the simple gown she wore had been woven from fine, costly wool.

No expense had been spared to make her comfortable. But a prison was still a prison. Rosemary had spent her first night here praying that Percy, Winnie and Malcolm were all right. Baldassare had assured her they'd be safe so long as she cooperated. But the man was utterly ruthless, without morals or scruples.

Behind her, she heard open the door to the subterranean chamber she occupied. Likely it was the menacing Edgar with another meal or a query on her progress from his master.

"Well, is it yet done?" demanded Baldassare.

Rosemary gasped, nearly falling off the stool as she whirled to find him at her elbow. "A-almost."

"Excellent." He leaned forward, dipping a blunt finger into the cream and spreading it on the back of his hand. "'Tis soothing. I can see why Chandre was skeptical as to its effectiveness, but the results are dramatic, as you will soon see."

"She is coming here?" Rosemary asked hopefully. If she could somehow tell the lady she was being held prisoner.

"Aye. When the other hags at court see that Chandre's coarse and lined skin is now as soft as a newborn babe's, they will pay dearly for even a small dram." The count fairly drooled as he lined up the small jars she'd filled with the youth cream. "How much more can you make?"

"None. I have no more myrrh." She had already made three batches of the cream, which the count had taken away.

Scowling, he went to rummage through the neat stacks of chests lining the walls. This had been his workroom and was crammed so full of the raw materials he used for his potions—everything from sweet chamomile to noxious sulfur—that there had scarcely been a place to set the cot on which she slept.

Not that she'd slept much. Mostly she'd dreamed

of William and prayed to find some way out of this horrible—

"Damn." The count slammed shut the last chest and stomped back over to the table. "No myrrh."

"I am not surprised. Few spicers use it."

"Whatever made you add a touch of myrrh to your cream?"

Rosemary stiffened. "The secret was passed down from my mother," she quickly lied to protect her uncle.

"Did she live in the East or study the ancient teachings?"

"Her father did."

"Ah. I wish I'd known them both, we might have exchanged information." Baldassare smiled. "I am also a scholar of ancient texts. I discovered in them the recipes for many unusual cures." Warming to the topic, he boasted of the fortune he'd made peddling his potions to Italian and French nobles. "Regrettably, one proved too strong and ate away the skin of a duke's wife."

"Oh, how horrible."

"Indeed. I was forced to flee my beautiful home for this cold, inhospitable country," he grumbled. "But fortunately I met Chandre, who recognized my genius. With her as my patroness, I was able to re-establish my atelier."

"How lucky for you." Beast. Monster.

"Never have I met one so obsessed with youth and beauty. She would trade her last coin, her last jewel for what is in these jars." He began to gather them up and put them on a tray. "She thinks to keep it all for herself, greedy witch, but she is only one woman, with one face. 'Twould be kindly of her to share this miracle with the other wrinkled crones. Do you not agree?"

"And more profitable for you."

"Ah, *cara,* you are bright, as well as beautiful. We will go far together, you and I."

Rosemary backed up a step. "You said I could go when I had made all the myrrh into cream."

"I will get more myrrh for you."

"I will write down the recipe. You will not need me."

"But I will." Eyes glittering with a lust that was more frightening than threats of harm, he reached for her.

Rosemary screamed, ducked under his hands and raced for the door. It opened just as she reached it. Her momentum carried her straight into Lady Chandre. "My lady...my lady, you must help me," she gasped, grasping a thin, velvet-clad arm.

Lady Chandre shook off Rosemary's clinging hands. "Baldassare! Whatever is going on here?"

"Nothing." He averted his head like a boy being chastised by his father.

Rosemary's spirits rose. The great man was afraid of the lady. "He kept me prisoner here."

"Did he?" Chandre looked at the count. "Is the cream done?"

"Aye. Here it is." Eager as a puppy, he held out the tray.

"Excellent. Secure the door." While her two hulking guards hurried to comply, Lady Chandre sailed into the room trailing dark green velvet and spicy perfume.

Rosemary walked in her shadow, determined that when the lady left, she would be with her. "The cream helped you, then?"

"Can you not tell?" The lady halted near the worktable, tilting her face toward the merciless candlelight.

Rosemary gasped. "'Tis a miracle."

"Aye." Lady Chandre stroked a dewy, flawless cheek. "My skin is now smoother and softer than in my youth."

"I am glad I was able to help you," Rosemary said.

"Then why have you been so slow to make the cream?" the lady snapped. "What I have is nearly gone. I must have more."

Rosemary flinched, startled as much by Chandre's ferocity as her implication. "But I finished the first batch two days—"

"And here it is." Baldassare proffered the tray.

"Is that all? This will barely last a fortnight, for my body and limbs must be as beautiful as my face."

"There should be twenty other jars," Rosemary replied.

"Twenty! Where?" Chandre whirled on the count.

"The girl is mistaken."

"I am not." Despite her fear of Baldassare, Rosemary fought back. "He is using me and cheating you. He plans to sell the rest of the cream to others. He—"

"Nay!" Chandre's breathtaking face contorted into a mask of fury and outrage. "You wretch. You ungrateful bastard."

"Wait! I can explain." Hands extended in supplication, Baldassare retreated before the stalking Chandre.

"I gave you money. I bought you this house and these miserable things." With one hand, she swept a small table clear, sending crocks and pots smashing into the wall. "I endured your lotions, though they stung and mottled my face."

"Chandre, my dearest one, 'tis just a misunderstand—"

"Shut up, you ingrate." Spittle flew from her rouged lips as she ranted on. "When you needed more exotic spices yet hesitated to buy openly lest the other apothecaries guess what you were about, did I not hire Rene to steal for you?"

"Sweet Mary," Rosemary breathed. The enormity of their crime chilled her blood. Had Chandre ordered Rene to kill? Or had that been the brigand's decision? No matter, her own position was grave, indeed. One eye on the combatants, she edged toward the door, though how she'd make it past the guards...

"Chandre," the count wheedled, back against the wall, smile oily. "Surely you do not think I would really cheat you. I thought we could make a bit of extra profit, but I can—"

"Greedy bastard!" Chandre pulled a knife from

her belt, plunged it into Baldassare's chest and twisted it.

The count's eyes widened. A hiss of sound passed his open mouth. Then his eyes closed, and his body slid to the floor.

"Men," Chandre muttered as she turned away. "They think only of themselves."

Rosemary stared at her, too shocked to move or speak.

"Where did he hide the rest of the cream?" Chandre asked.

"I do not know." Rosemary tore her gaze from the count's lifeless body and looked at the door. She had to get away.

Chandre snapped her fingers, bringing the guards to attention. "Jenkins, fetch the men we left outside and search the house. Martin, start in the count's bedchamber and bring along the jewelry I gave him. He will not be needing it."

Terrified, Rosemary edged closer to the door.

Chandre seized her arm and shoved her toward the worktable. "Find an empty chest and begin packing these jars. Put cloth around them to insure they do not break."

Not daring to argue, Rosemary seized the first likely-looking cask from a nearby pile and set it on the table. She harbored no illusions that Chandre would let her go, not obsessed as she was with her beauty. Rosemary pictured a life spent chained in some dark corner, dutifully turning myrrh into the cursed youth cream. Would that Uncle Percy had never discovered the recipe, she thought as she opened the chest.

Inside lay a single, square box. It was labeled as meticulously as the rest of Baldassare's stock. *Pipsissewa.* Pipsissewa? As Rosemary picked up the box, her mind sifted through countless herbal lessons till she recalled ground holly was the common name for this Mediterranean herb. Like most members of the holly family, this one irritated the skin.

"Do not stand there gawking," Chandre growled. "Throw out whatever is in there and see to packing my precious cream."

"As you wish, my lady." Rosemary opened the little box and threw the pipsissewa into Chandre's face.

Chandre recoiled but grabbed Rosemary's arm before she could flee. "That was a stupid thing to do," she snarled. The dark green holly leaf powder stuck to the cream on her face.

"Let me go," Rosemary cried.

"Nay, I've need of your services." Chandre swiped at her cheek, but only succeeded in smearing the goo. Her eyes narrowed maliciously. "I would have treated you decently, but now..." She winced and wiped at her cheek again. "Damn, what is this? It burns like fire. Argh! Get it off. Off, I say." She dropped Rosemary's arm and began to claw at her face with both hands.

Rosemary turned and ran. Behind her, she heard the lady scramble in pursuit. Screams of pain and livid curses followed Rosemary as she hiked her skirts and sprinted down the gloomy corridor. Dimly she recalled the route the count had taken that first night. Panic lent wings to her feet. But as fast as she ran, Chandre scrambled after her, down the hall, up a circular staircase.

Rosemary burst through the open doorway at the top of the stairs and hesitated a moment, glancing right and left. Right, she thought and plunged down the corridor. It twisted and turned, the paintings on the walls flying past in a blur, Chandre's hysterical cries echoing close behind. Too close.

Then Rosemary rounded a corner and glimpsed light at the far end of the passageway. Freedom beckoned. She put on a burst of speed, but just as it seemed she might make it, a tall, male figure appeared in the doorway.

"Get her!" Chandre shrieked.

Rosemary checked her headlong dash. Trapped. Terrified.

"Rosemary!" William's deep voice filled the hallway. And then he was there, dragging her into his arms.

"Beware!" Rosemary cried. "Chandre…behind me."

"That is Chandre?" William asked incredulously.

Rosemary turned in the haven of his embrace and looked back. Halfway down the corridor, bathed in the amber circle cast by a sconce, a woman knelt on the floor. Chandre, her gem-encrusted gown shimmering in the light, her face blistered and swollen beyond recognition.

"The poor thing," William whispered. "Did Baldassare do this to her?"

"Nay. I did." Rosemary buried her face in William's broad chest. "No matter Chandre's crimes, I am sorry."

"Hush, love. We will sort it out later." William swung her into his arms and started for the door where two men lurked. "Jasper, Arnald, see what you can do for Chandre."

"Have a care," Rosemary whispered. "Her men are above, searching through Baldassare's things for the myrrh cream."

"We'll see to it," Jasper said, drawing his sword.

Dazed, Rosemary gazed up at William's somber features as he carried her away. "You are not at sea," she murmured.

"Nay, thanks be to God." His grip on her tightening, he glanced down at her. "Jesu, what happened in there?"

"Oh, William, it was awful. You've no idea." She shuddered.

"Shh. Do not think of that now. I have you safe. Later, when you are rested, we will speak of it."

Too exhausted, too sick at heart to argue, Rosemary closed her eyes and let him carry her out into the pale light of dawn.

Chapter Eleven

Twelfth Day, 6 January

Rosemary sank gratefully into the hot water. "Ah, this feels wonderful." Sighing, she leaned her head against the wooden rim of the tub and let the heat soak into her limbs.

"Ye should still be abed," Winnie grumbled, testing the water and adding a bit more hot.

"I am not tired." It was early evening on the day following her dramatic rescue. Rosemary had slept for hours after William carried her back to his town house and gently tucked her into bed. She'd awakened a short while ago, rested, if still shaken by what had happened at Baldassare's, to find both Anna and Winnie waiting to serve her.

"Could ye eat a bit more soup?" Anna asked.

"Nay, thank you, though 'twas most delicious."

Anna beamed yet continued to hover at Rosemary's side. In contrast to her earlier coolness, she now fussed like a mother hen. "Bread then? I've kept some warm in the kitchen."

Rosemary smiled and shook her head, then asked the question that had been uppermost in her mind since awakening. "Is Lord William about?"

"Aye, he's below, seeing to things."

"Oh." When he'd brought her here very early this morn, William had turned her over to Anna's care without saying why he'd returned to London. She'd dared to hope it was because he'd changed his mind about them. What if he had not? What if he had come back for some important item, heard of her abduction and stayed only to rescue her? "What sort of things?"

Anna and Winnie looked at each other and smiled faintly, secretly. "Oh, this and that," Anna said off-handedly.

"Aye, this and that," Winnie echoed. "Yer Uncle Percy's with him, and for once his nose is not in a book. Now, we'd best get ye cleaned up before the water cools."

"What is going on?" Rosemary demanded. The query ended in a gasp and a sputter as Winnie dumped warm water over her head, and the assault on Rosemary's filthy hair began in earnest. The de-tangling, washing, rinsing and combing consumed all three of them till the water had, indeed, cooled.

"There now, let's put this on." Winnie bundled her into the bed robe that had been draped before the fire to warm.

"I'd rather dress and go downstairs." To find William.

Anna gasped. "Nay. Ye're to stay here."

"By whose orders?"

"Lord William's. He said ye were to rest till supper time."

"I will not. He does not have the ordering of me."

"But Lord William said…" Anna began.

Winnie sighed. "Does no good to argue with her when her mind's made up. We'd best nip down and tell his lordship she's being fractious." The pair of them beat a hasty retreat.

Rosemary paced and tried to brace herself for the news that William was leaving her again. But when she heard the door open, she trembled. Part of her wanted to turn, to meet this challenge as she had all others, but she couldn't bear to see in his bleak face the confirmation that there was no hope for them.

"Rosemary?" Large warm hands gripped her shoulders and squeezed gently. "Are you all right?"

Nay, she was dying inside. "Aye." Her voice broke.

"Oh, Rosemary." He spun her about and wrapped his arms around her. "Did that bastard hurt you? Anna said you were fine, but—"

"Nay." She burrowed into his embrace. "He threatened and blustered, but he did not harm me. 'Twas Chandre." Remembering, she shuddered. "To think she was capable of such…such…"

"Shh. Do not think of it." He stroked her back.

"What will become of her?"

His hands stilled. "She is dead."

"Nay." The tears she'd held in check began to fall. "I did not think the holly could kill. I only wanted to get away."

"You did not kill her." He hugged her tighter. "She had a knife hidden in her garments. While the sheriff's men searched Baldassare's house, Chandre used it to end her miserable life."

"Oh, the poor thing."

"Poor? The woman was a murderess several times over."

"She was mad, driven by an insane obsession with youth and beauty. To think I fed that craving." The tears fell faster.

"Hush, now," William said gently. "You are not to blame for her sickness. Shh, my love. I cannot bear to see you so upset."

His compassion nearly broke her heart. Truly he was the most wonderful of men, and she loved him so. Why could he not see they belonged together?

"William. Oh, William." Wrapping her arms about his neck, she stood on tiptoe and found his mouth. It slanted eagerly over hers, a moan shuddering through him as she opened to the questing edge of his tongue. His arms tightened about her; his heart pounded in concert with her own as the fire flared between them. The kiss went on and on, his hunger feeding hers.

Aye, this was what she wanted, needed, Rosemary thought, straining to get closer, brushing her aching breasts into the muscular wall of his chest, glorying as she felt the proof of his desire press hard against her belly. She was not letting him go. Not now, not ever.

"Rose!" William gasped. "Wait, we cannot—"

"Aye, we can. We must. Oh, Will," she whispered. "I feel so lost without you. Please, please do not leave me."

"I won't, but we should wait at least till I've told you—"

"Nay. I will not wait a moment longer." Emboldened by the knowledge that this was right…for both of them, Rosemary untied the belt on her robe. She felt only a little shy, waiting for him to study what she'd revealed.

His gaze remained locked on hers, free, for once, of that drawn, haunted look. "Willful minx. What am I to do with you?"

"Make love to me."

He carried her to the bed and gently laid her down. Movements quick and jerky, he stripped off his tunic and hose, giving her a brief, heady glimpse of sculpted muscles and rampant need before he stretched out and drew her into his arms.

Rosemary nestled into his embrace, welcomed his deep, hungry kiss. She was vividly aware of the clean herbal scent of his skin, the prickle of chest hairs teasing her.

"Oh, Will." Rosemary's hands tunneled into his hair to hold him close. Fire raced through her veins, and the sensual throbbing built till she could bear it no longer. "Come to me," she whispered, reaching for him.

The feel of Rose's slender fingers, urging him toward a haven he wanted more than his next breath, ripped away the last of Will's control. "I love you, Rose," he murmured, voice harsh with the effort it took to hold back, to make this moment special for her.

"And I you, Will." Her eyes filled with tears.

He knew she did not believe him, doubtless thought it was passion talking and not his heart. "Let me show you how much you mean to me." Trembling, he joined his body to hers.

As he slipped inside her, a fleeting stab of pain was banished by the sense of wonder. She wanted to tell him what he made her feel, but words were inadequate. Nor were they needed, she realized, seeing the tenderness, the joy in the handsome face poised above hers.

"Come with me, Rose," Will whispered. Filled by an utter sense of rightness, he began to move, stoking the fires that burned so brightly between them, glorying as she caught his rhythm and raced with him.

"Will! Oh, Will!" Rosemary's eyes widened as the tremors shivered through her.

Gasping, he joined her, body and soul.

Slowly, Rosemary drifted down from the heights to which he'd taken her. She became aware of Will's heart beating loud and steady beneath her ear as they lay on their sides, his arms locked around her as though he'd never let her go. Sweet Mary, she did not want him to.

"I will not leave you, sweetheart." He sighed. "Ever again. But I had hoped to be strong enough to resist you till after we were wed."

"Wed?" Rosemary gaped at him, searching his face for some clue. His eyes. Though passion was spent, they were still dark, luminous and free of ghosts. "William?"

"Aye, wed. Tomorrow or the next day. As soon as I can beg from the bishop a dispensation to waive the banns."

"What has happened? What of Ella?"

He smiled faintly. "Do you believe in miracles?"

"Aye." She was witnessing one—the change in him. "What? How?"

"I do not know the answers to those questions, but, last night, Twelfth Night, as my ship sailed down the Thames, I looked up into the sky and beheld the Christmas Star. The one the wise men followed."

"I know the story," she said, breathless with impatience.

"Well, I found *my* grace under the star's light." Hugging her close, he told her what he'd seen, or felt he'd seen. "I do not know if it was reality or imagination," he added. "But the moment her image faded from my sight, I felt such peace." He flushed. "My cheeks were wet with tears I do not recall shedding, but the peace…"

Rosemary smiled through *her* tears. "I am so glad."

"I rushed from the cabin, ordered the ship brought around and sailed quickly back to you. I arrived at the shop to find everything in confusion. Your uncle had been unable to make sense of Malcolm's ravings and didn't know where to turn. When I heard the boy call Baldassare's name, I knew where you must be. That, too, must be part of the miracle of Twelfth Night, for I barely arrived in time to save you from Chandre."

"Aye." Rosemary scarcely dared to breathe. "Are you now at peace with Ella's passing?"

"Aye. I am." He soothed the tumbled hair back from Rosemary's face. "I will always miss her, for she was my first love, my childhood friend. But now I am free of guilt and regret. Free to get on with my life. I would share that life with you, Rosemary."

"Oh, Will." A single tear, this one of happiness, slid down Rosemary's cheek.

He caught it. "None of that. This is a festive day. I've already asked your uncle's permission to court you." He grinned ruefully, looking years younger, a thousand times happier than she'd ever seen him.

A knock at the door made them both jump guiltily.

"My lord," called Walter, the steward. "Your guests are here and wondering when you and the lady will be down."

"Guests?" Rosemary whispered.

"We'll be there directly," Will answered. "But first, I am giving my wife her betrothal gift."

Will did indeed have a gift for her. A pearl necklace that had belonged to Lady Catherine Sommerville, his grandmother.

Fingering the pearls at her throat, Rosemary followed Will down the tower steps. "Your family may not be pleased to learn you plan to wed an apothecary."

He looked over his shoulder and dazzled her with a smile. "They will be thrilled. Not only because you are a beautiful person inside and out, but because now I will stay in England. Except mayhap someday I'll take you sailing with me to foreign ports. Would you like that?"

"Aye," Rosemary said promptly. "I think I would."

"And Percy, too, if he's able."

Rosemary fairly skipped to the bottom of the stairs. There she paused, sniffing the air. "Is that pine I smell?"

This time, his smile revealed a dimple in his left cheek. "Aye. And cinnamon, too, I'd wager. The servants have been busy preparing a small surprise for you. Come," he urged.

Bemused by his gay mood, Rosemary followed. In the doorway to the great hall, she stopped again, mouth agape. "Small surprise?" she said weakly.

The transformation in the hall was only slightly less spectacular than Will's own. Fir boughs, holly and ivy twined about the roof rafters. Hundreds of flambeaux flickered in wall sconces and on the tables spread with ivory cloths. If a room could be said to glow, this one did.

"Oh, Will," Rosemary murmured. "It is wonderful, but…"

"Ella bade me remember her by celebrating life, both hers and our new one together." Lifting her hands, he kissed them.

"There they are!" someone cried.

The crowd of gaily dressed people at the end of the hall turned as one, then stampeded toward them. Their shouts of congratulations and good cheer rang from the festooned rafters.

Through her joyful tears, Rosemary saw her uncle, Muriel and Herbert, Malcolm and Winnie, Edward the Spicer and a dozen other familiar faces before the tide broke over them.

"My dear girl." Uncle Percy enveloped her in a huge hug. "Is this what you want?" he whispered in her ear. "Young William seemed most certain you loved him, and vowed he'd cherish you, but if you're doing this to put a roof over our heads…"

Rosemary laughed. "I'm wedding him for the books."

"Eh? What?" Percy frowned down at her.

"I am teasing, Uncle. I love Will and he me."

"Excellent. Excellent." A crafty light entered Percy's old eyes. "Still, the books are a nice bonus. Very nice, indeed."

Rosemary smiled, then grew serious. "About the myrrh cream. I think we should tear up the recipe and make no more."

"Quite right. Too many greedy people in the world." He gave her a quick kiss. "Be happy, my dear." He hobbled off on Malcolm's arm to make way for the other well-wishers.

"Ach, ye've been like the daughter I've never had," said Winnie, clasping her close. "Be happy."

"We will," Rosemary replied. Her joy grew when she saw the way Arnald took the old woman's arm and escorted her to a table. "Is there a romance brewing there, do you think?"

"If so, you can be sure Arnald will treat her well. He's a kind and caring man for all his great size."

Before Rosemary could reply, she was enveloped by Muriel. "What a grand match you've made," her friend chirped. "Who would think he'd be so handsome when he stopped glowering. Or so wealthy." She glanced around, smiling. "'Tis miraculous."

"Indeed, it is." Rosemary grinned as she felt Will's arm tighten around her waist. Tilting her head back, she looked into his dark, shining eyes. The rest of the room with its holiday festoons and festivities faded, till it seemed they stood alone, locked in each other's arms. "A Christmas miracle."

"One that will give us joy and peace all the days of our lives," he murmured into her ear.

"And all the nights." Rose winked boldly at her husband-to-be.

"Aye, especially the nights." He kissed her tenderly, face glowing with love in the soft candlelight. "And next Christmas, we will give each other the most precious miracle of all."

"What could be more precious than our love?"

"A babe."

"Will." Rose's heart lurched, then filled. "'Twould be my dearest wish, but how can you know?"

"An angel told me."

* * * * *

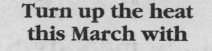
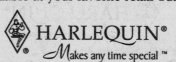